She was crying

Mitch stiffened as he tried to deflect the sound of Stephanie Shelton's anguished sobs. His stomach felt as if it were lined with hot tar. The only thing that made the situation bearable was the hope that she'd soon be reunited with her lost child.

Careful to allow her some dignity, he kept his gaze averted from her moist eyes.

"Pack a bag for you and your daughter."

"Why?" Her tone was charged with rebellion.

Then Mitch made the mistake of looking at her.

Her green-gold eyes were as dangerous as riptide and fringed with long sooty lashes. He was none too happy that he was making personal observations about the length of her eyelashes.

He was too seasoned a cop to let himself get sucked in by a pair of pleading eyes. Deliberate detachment firmed his voice.

"You're coming with me. You're both under my protection until this is over."

Dear Harlequin Intrigue Reader,

We wind up a great summer with a *bang* this month! Linda O. Johnston continues the hugely popular COLORADO CONFIDENTIAL series with *Special Agent Nanny*. Don't forget to look for the Harlequin special-release anthology next month featuring *USA TODAY* bestselling author Jasmine Cresswell, our very own Amanda Stevens and Harlequin Historicals author Debra Lee Brown. And not to worry, the series continues with two more Harlequin Intrigue titles in November and December.

Joyce Sullivan concludes her companion series THE COLLINGWOOD HEIRS with *Operation Bassinet*. Find out how this family solves a fiendish plot and finds happiness in one fell swoop. Rounding out the month are two exciting stories. Rising star Delores Fossen takes a unique perspective on the classic secret-baby plot in *Confiscated Conception*, and a very sexy *Cowboy PI* is determined to get to the bottom of one woman's mystery in an all-Western story by Jean Barrett.

Finally, in case you haven't heard, next month Harlequin Intrigue is increasing its publishing schedule to include two more fantastic romantic suspense books. That's *six* titles per month! More variety, more of your favorite authors and of course, more excitement.

It's a thrilling time for us, and we want to thank all of our loyal readers for remaining true to Harlequin Intrigue. And if you are just learning about our brand of breathtaking romantic suspense, fasten your seat belts for an edge-of-your-seat reading experience. Welcome aboard!

Sincerely,

Denise O'Sullivan
Senior Editor, Harlequin Intrigue

OPERATION BASSINET

JOYCE SULLIVAN

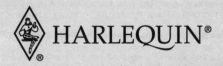

HARLEQUIN®

TORONTO • NEW YORK • LONDON
AMSTERDAM • PARIS • SYDNEY • HAMBURG
STOCKHOLM • ATHENS • TOKYO • MILAN • MADRID
PRAGUE • WARSAW • BUDAPEST • AUCKLAND

ISBN 0-373-22726-4

OPERATION BASSINET

Copyright © 2003 by Joyce David

This edition published by arrangement with Harlequin Books S.A.

® and TM are trademarks of the publisher. Trademarks indicated with ® are registered in the United States Patent and Trademark Office, the Canadian Trade Marks Office and in other countries.

Visit us at www.eHarlequin.com

Printed in U.S.A.

ABOUT THE AUTHOR

Joyce Sullivan credits her lawyer mother with instilling in her a love of reading and writing—and a fascination for solving mysteries. She has a bachelor's degree in criminal justice and worked several years as a private investigator before turning her hand to writing romantic suspense. A transplanted American, Joyce makes her home in Aylmer, Quebec, with her handsome French-Canadian husband and two children. A visit to the castles populating the Thousand Islands in the St. Lawrence Seaway gave her the inspiration for THE COLLINGWOOD HEIRS series.

Books by Joyce Sullivan

HARLEQUIN INTRIGUE
352—THE NIGHT BEFORE CHRISTMAS
436—THIS LITTLE BABY
516—TO LANEY, WITH LOVE
546—THE BABY SECRET
571—URGENT VOWS
631—IN HIS WIFE'S NAME
722—THE BUTLER'S DAUGHTER*
726—OPERATION BASSINET*

*The Collingwood Heirs

Don't miss any of our special offers. Write to us at the following address for information on our newest releases.

Harlequin Reader Service
U.S.: 3010 Walden Ave., P.O. Box 1325, Buffalo, NY 14269
Canadian: P.O. Box 609, Fort Erie, Ont. L2A 5X3

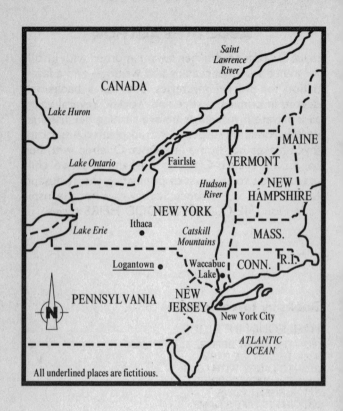

CANADA

Saint Lawrence River

Lake Huron

Lake Ontario <u>FairIsle</u> VERMONT **MAINE**

NEW HAMPSHIRE

Hudson River

NEW YORK

Lake Erie Ithaca *Catskill Mountains* MASS.

<u>Logantown</u> Waccabuc Lake CONN. R.I.

N

PENNSYLVANIA NEW JERSEY New York City

ATLANTIC OCEAN

All underlined places are fictitious.

CAST OF CHARACTERS

Ross and Lexi Collingwood—He was the Baron of Wall Street. Their precious baby daughter was kidnapped thirty months ago and never returned. One month after the Collingwoods are tragically murdered in an explosion, the Find Riana Foundation receives a ransom demand for the child.

Stef Shelton—Her world is shattered when she discovers that the daughter she has been raising is not her flesh-and-blood child.

Mitch Halloran—The Guardian hired this determined LAPD detective to bring Riana home safe and sound.

Keely Shelton—She's Riana Collingwood by birth.

Emma—Would Stef's real daughter be found alive?

Brad Shelton—Had he switched his infant daughter with Riana Collingwood?

The Guardian—Ross Collingwood had been his best friend and had entrusted him with his children's lives.

Juliana Goodhew—She was looking forward to raising Lexi's daughter as her own.

Annette York—She'd killed her sister and brother-in-law out of hatred. Was she behind Riana's kidnapping, as well?

Sable Holden—Ross Collingwood had ruthlessly taken over her family's company. To what lengths would she go to get her company back?

For my friend Jude, my emotional barometer.
And for Rickey, critique partner par excellence.

Acknowledgments

My sincere thanks to the generous people listed below
who answered my tedious questions about their lives
and their jobs for this story:

Mathematician extraordinaire Tom McCormick,
W. J. Van Dusen, Professor of Management, UBC Commerce.

Sergeant John Martinez, one of LAPD's finest.

Detective Bob Arbour, Ottawa-Carleton Regional
Police Service, and former bomb tech.

Dr. Steven W. Maclean,
who saves my wounded heroes and heroines.

Prologue

Thirty months earlier

Stef wasn't sure what woke her. Maybe the sound of the door closing in her hospital room. Or had the baby cried out? She hovered in a semialert state listening, her tired body yearning to tumble back into oblivion. She'd never been so exhausted. The last trimester of lumbering around New York City like an elephant in maternity clothes and thirty hours of labor had taken its toll, but she'd been rewarded with a beautiful baby daughter.

Tears came to her eyes. She'd seen the pride on Brad's face when he'd held Keely in his arms. Everything would get better for them now. She just knew it.

"Brad?" she whispered into the darkened room. Had her husband changed his mind about staying over with her and the baby? Her whisper was swallowed up in the silence.

Brad had spent last night in the recliner provided for new dads, but he had another job interview first thing in the morning. She'd sent him home at the end of visitor's hours with instructions to get a good night's sleep and wear the Brooks Brothers' suit with the I'm-in-charge tie.

Keely made a small sound in her bassinet like a mewling kitten. Maybe the nurse had come in to check the time of her last feeding. Stef turned on the bedside lamp and glanced at the clock. It was 2:53 a.m. With a guilty start, she realized it had been more than three hours since she'd last nursed her baby.

Keely mewled again, sounding like a ravenous kitten.

Stef felt an instantaneous tingling sensation in her breasts. "Okay, sweetie, I got the message. It's chow time. Just don't expect fast food." She pushed herself up in the hospital bed, every muscle in her body protesting. Her stomach sagged like a deflated balloon.

Getting out of bed was a Herculean effort. Maybe she should have insisted Brad stay. But he'd been so discouraged after he'd been laid off from his job as the New York City regional manager for Office Outfitters six months ago. He'd gone to countless interviews and the pressure of a first baby on the way hadn't helped. She wanted him to be at his best tomorrow. They had a daughter to support.

She shuffled to Keely's bassinet, painfully aware of the stitches where no doctor should have to put a needle, the linoleum floor cool beneath her bare feet.

Stef peered down at her daughter. A tiny miracle, even if she did look like a scrunched-up baby gorilla.

"I'm here, sweetie. Mommy's here." She picked up her daughter from the bassinet—amazed anew by the tiny infant's weight and warmth. She'd swear Keely had already gained a few ounces since birth.

Her daughter snuffled against her breast, looking for nourishment. Stef sighed with equal amounts of pleasure and discomfort as her breasts started to leak. She gingerly eased herself down into the recliner and fumbled with the buttons of her nightgown and the clasp of the nursing bra.

Keely latched on to her nipple hungrily and Stef basked in the special intimacy of the feeding bond between them. "You are my little girl, Keely Jane Shelton. I may not be the smartest or the richest or the prettiest mom, but you are my own gift from heaven and I love you with all my heart. I hope you like me and Daddy, because you're stuck with us for a long time." She gave her baby girl a teary-eyed smile. "We're a family now, little one. Forever and ever. I promise."

Chapter One

Logantown, Pennsylvania

The lost Collingwood Heir was alive and well and living beneath this roof.

Former L.A.P.D. Detective Mitch Halloran stood on the front step of the modest house, a cold spot forming in his stomach as he leaned on the doorbell.

He was dreading the task ahead of him. He had to tell this family that their daughter wasn't theirs. That two female infants had been switched at birth. Whatever pride he felt in proving himself right about the ransom note and the DNA sample that the Find Riana Foundation had received eight days ago was lost in the sickening reality that he was about to plunge this innocent family into a nightmare. With the single-minded determination he'd learned from his grandfather who'd served as a marine in the Korean War, Mitch told himself he'd make it all work out. This wouldn't be a repeat of the Lopez case. He'd do everything in his means to get them back their own daughter.

Surely it wasn't too much to ask for two miracles.

The front door opened and Mitch looked into one of the most appealing faces he'd ever seen. It belonged to the woman he'd seen with Keely four days ago when he'd conducted surveillance on the house to filch a sample of Keely's DNA.

Eyes that were green and gold reminded him of a lucky marble his real dad had given him when he was about six, and they shimmered at him, laughter in their depths. A scattering of freckles drifted across sexily curved cheekbones and dotted a nose that tilted up at the end.

"What are you selling?" she demanded, curling her hands into fists and planting them on her hips. She was wearing a blue-and-green silky blouse that seemed kind of see-through and Japanese and left no doubts that she was wearing a skimpy blue bra underneath. "I'm all yours if you're hawking chocolate bars with almonds."

"I'm sorry, ma'am, I'm not soliciting. My name is Mitch Halloran, and I'm the director of the—"

"No chocolate bars?" she interrupted him, looking genuinely disappointed.

Mitch held out his empty hands, his gut twisting at her cheery attitude. "Not a one. Sorry, ma'am."

"All right, then, what do you want? I already signed one of the petitions for the new soccer field."

Mitch sighed. She wasn't making this easy. He handed her his business card. "Mrs. Shelton, please. I'm the Director of the Find Riana Foundation. We're searching for Riana Collingwood, and I'd like to speak to you and your husband privately. It's very important."

She snatched the card from him, then held up her hand, palm out, like a traffic cop. "Stay here." To Mitch's annoyance, she slammed the door in his face.

He sighed and leaned a hip against the wrought-iron railing, wishing he hadn't left his raincoat in the car.

The chill of a November wind bathed his cheeks,

seeped into his chest. Mitch felt uncomfortably out of place on this quiet street with its middle America working-class appeal. Having grown up in a large metropolitan city, he hadn't minded the noise and the pace and the towering in-your-face size of New York City. But the tranquil motion-picture perfection of this street bothered him.

Lights blazed in living room and kitchen windows up and down the block. He could smell the scents of meals lingering invitingly in the air. Halloween had come and gone. Fake tombstones and bedraggled scarecrows populated the lush lawns and shreds of gigantic spider webs and pieces of plastic skeletons dangled from bare tree branches. It was nothing like the neighborhoods of stucco bungalows, concrete driveways and parched yards he was used to in L.A.

Halloween was one of the many holidays, along with Father's Day, Thanksgiving and Christmas that he'd grown to hate ever since Paddy, his grandfather, had died. The crime stats always went up—murders, suicides, break-ins, robberies. He'd seen people resort to desperate acts when the reality of their personal and family situations failed to live up to the impossible expectations planted in their minds by TV shows, movies and magazines.

Peace on earth. Right. Most people would settle for peace in their own home a few nights a week.

Holidays to Mitch were a brutally painful reminder that he had no family.

The door opened behind him. Mitch swung around. Stephanie Shelton had engaged the chain lock and was eyeing him up and down suspiciously, a phone plastered to her ear.

''Turn around,'' she said to him.

"What?"

She made a circling motion with her finger. "Turn around." A tiny red heart was painted on her fingernail.

"Hmm-humph? No, not Russell. I'd say more like Dennis—" she paused as Mitch glowered at her. "Nice and…um, where did you work before you came to the Foundation?" she asked sweetly.

Mitch propped a hand on the door frame. "L.A.P.D.—the Robbery Homicide Division," he replied, making a mental note to have a little chat with the hot-line phone staff.

"It's him." The door slammed in his face again. He heard the chain slip off, then the door popped open. Mitch was annoyingly aware of the outline of her bra beneath that top. Stephanie Shelton was slightly nutty and very hot. There was an intriguing line of golden flesh visible between the hem of her shirt and the black leather belt riding her hips. "Come in. The house is a mess, but that's life."

The house was not a mess. It was lively and colorful and an irritatingly normal example of how Mitch thought average nondysfunctional, middle-class families lived. He followed her through an entryway cluttered with a child-size pair of red boots, library books and Halloween decorations into a funky living room painted in dramatic colors and furnished with a beige sofa piled with pillows and two gargantuan armchairs. The armchairs covered in olive velvet made him think someone had a grandmother who'd liked Victorian furniture. In an alcove off the kitchen Mitch could see the child whose abandoned drinking cup he'd swiped the other day—dancing along with a furry critter on the TV.

"Have a seat, Mr. Halloran."

"Is your husband home, ma'am? I'd really like to speak to both of you."

Those green and gold eyes shone with dewy tears. "My husband died two years ago in a rock climbing accident."

"I'm sorry, I didn't know," Mitch said, caught off guard. The list of babies they'd been investigating had been too long to do thorough background checks on each family. They'd received confirmation from the lab about the DNA match less than two hours ago.

He took a seat on the sofa as Stephanie Shelton perched on the edge of one of those gargantuan chairs and folded her arms across her chest, bringing even more attention to the color of her bra beneath the transparent fabric of her blouse. "Why would someone from the Find Riana Foundation want to talk to me? Wasn't she the little girl of that famous couple who were killed in an explosion last month?"

"Ma'am—"

"Please, stop calling me that. Teachers and librarians swathed in polyester prints are ma'ams. My name's Stef."

Mitch started to sweat. Damn, she looked so defenseless—so your-best-buddy's-younger-sister nice. She'd already lost her husband. An image of her dancing around the garbage can when he'd staked out her house four days ago, two fingers held up in a two-point salute after she and Keely chucked a decaying jack-o'-lantern into the can, shimmered vibrantly in his conscience.

His news was going to kill her.

He cleared his throat and told himself to remain unplugged from the drama. "Stef, are you aware of the date Riana Collingwood was kidnapped?"

She frowned. "I think it was the day after my daughter was born. I remember seeing it on the news a couple of days after Keely and I were discharged and being relieved that we weren't still in the hospital. Of course, the Collingwood baby wasn't born at the same birthing center, but still, it made me nervous.'' She shuddered. ''I couldn't imagine how horrible it must be for that baby's parents to have their child taken like that. But I still don't understand why you're here. I didn't know the Collingwoods.'' Her eyes were clearly puzzled.

In the other room Mitch heard Keely singing a catchy tune about apples and bananas. He mentally cursed a blue streak as the icy hole inside him bore painfully into his soul. There was no way to put off saying the words that would change this woman's life into a living hell.

He laced his fingers together. ''Mrs. Shelton, I have evidence which leads me to believe that whoever abducted Riana Collingwood switched her with your daughter.''

Stef Shelton started to laugh. ''This is a joke, right? My brother-in-law put you up to it? He's such a *jerk*—'' The words died on her lips as her gaze met his. Mitch looked steadily back at her, trying to stay as detached as possible, while fear spontaneously combusted like twin gold flames in her eyes.

She wrapped her arms around her middle as if trying to hold herself together. ''Oh, my God! Oh, my God! What are you saying?''

Mitch felt his stomach catapult out of the wall of his torso and pass through a meat grinder as he observed her every facial reaction, her every gesture, for the tiniest hint of falseness. But there was none. His chest hurt as he sucked in air and he swallowed hard against the anger and the disgust that some lowlife scum had destroyed this lovely young woman's life.

She shook her head, her eyes pleading with him. He steeled himself against a compelling urge to reach out to her. The same type of sympathetic reaction that had had him unwisely reaching out to Theresa Lopez two years earlier when her twelve-year-old granddaughter had been kidnapped.

He'd seen his grandfather in Theresa Lopez's anxiety-lined face. Saw the thin fingers worked to the bone to support a grandchild who was her sole reason for being. He'd twisted himself inside out trying to bring Carmen home. But he'd lost precious time chasing the wrong lead. By the time he'd realized his error and directed searchers to the killer's home, Carmen was dead and her killer, the sixteen-year-old boy who did Theresa's yardwork, had hung himself.

Theresa hadn't deserved to lose her granddaughter, nor did Stef Shelton deserve what had happened to her. She probably helped old ladies across the street and baked cookies and banana bread for her church's bake sales.

"I wish to God I didn't have to tell you this, but that little girl in the other room is Riana Collingwood. DNA tests have confirmed it."

"DNA?" She glanced toward the alcove, horror streaking her beautiful face like fissures in a broken mirror. "What are you talking about? Keely's my daughter! I labored thirty hours bringing her into the world." Her angry gaze shot back to him. "I should know my own baby!"

Mitch struggled to remain detached, with his fingers glued together, so he couldn't give in to an unprofessional impulse to offer a pair of arms to hold her up.

She looked whiter than a sheet of paper and about to crumple.

''There's no mistake. Riana's family wants her back. I'm here to make sure that happens, and help you find your daughter.'' And to prove to himself that he was the kind of cop, the kind of man his grandfather had wanted him to be.

After the Lopez case, he'd transferred out of the Robbery Special Section, a bureaucratic misnomer because it handled both robbery and kidnapping investigations, into the Rape Special Section in what he saw as a strategic career move. Because of his excellent record, he was assigned high-profile rapes and serial rapist investigations and promoted to Detective II, but over time he began to perceive his transfer and his new achievements as an act of cowardice rather than a step up the departmental ladder. He'd turned his back on the children who'd needed him. He was no longer the man he'd thought he was.

The Collingwood case—or Operation Bassinet as his new employer called it—was his chance to find himself again. Failure was not an option.

Stef stared in numb disbelief at the blond Hollywood Goliath. She no longer thought that his butt was of the same superior grade as her favorite movie star's. Or that his eyes were the dark cobalt of her Mexican glassware. He was the ugliest, most horrid waste of tanned skin she'd ever seen. And she'd bet his sun-bleached-blond hair wasn't even natural.

''You're lying. Or it's a mistake…or…'' She gulped a cleansing breath, pushing her hands out as if ridding the air of toxins. She had to think clearly here, but apples and bananas were whirling in a merry-go-round pattern in her head.

The Neanderthal-brained ex-cop was more likely to see reason and come to the conclusion he'd made a mistake if she stayed calm. She pasted on the let's-be-reasonable smile she'd reserved for unruly passengers in her former days as a flight attendant. "First of all, how could you possibly have DNA evidence that says Keely isn't my daughter?"

His cobalt eyes drilled into her, dead serious. There was nothing reasonable about his tone. Each word lacked compromise and lacerated her heart. "Mrs. Shelton, the Foundation received a ransom demand eight days ago. Two items were included with the note—Riana's hospital identification bracelet and two hairs. A reputable lab conducted DNA tests which told us that while the bracelet had traces of Riana Collingwood's DNA on it, the hair came from another child. It led us to believe that there were at least two people involved in Riana's abduction and that one of them was afraid of being double-crossed so they switched Riana with another baby. Whoever sent the ransom note is obviously unaware that they have the wrong child. We checked nearby hospitals for infant girls admitted during that time and came up with a list of possible matches. I collected Keely's drinking cup from your yard the other day when you and Keely were raking leaves and cleaning up your Halloween decorations. Her DNA matched Riana Collingwood's DNA. She *is* Riana Collingwood."

The idea of this man wandering around her yard—snooping for evidence so he could rip her daughter from her life infuriated her. Her hands fisted on her hips. "You were in my yard, spying on us?"

He didn't look the least bit apologetic. "I saw no

reason to upset you unnecessarily. Keely was only one of many children we were investigating.''

Stef wanted to claw his iceberg heart out. He was demolishing her world—and her heart—with one crushing sentence after another. ''This is insane. You're *not* taking my baby from me!'' She faltered, blindsided by a memory of the second night she'd spent in the hospital with Keely.

She remembered awakening to the sound of her hospital door closing. *Oh, God!*

Full-blown panic gripped her heart. What if the person who'd entered her room hadn't been a nurse? What if the Hollywood Goliath was actually telling the truth?

''I want other tests done at a lab of my choosing,'' she snapped, clutching the arm of her chair for support.

''Of course. No one wants to make a mistake with a matter this serious.''

She hadn't expected him to agree to that demand, which convinced her this was no joke. She lurched to her feet. Her sister Lorraine worked in a law firm as a paralegal. She could help her find a lawyer. ''I'm calling a lawyer.''

He stood up, too, towering over her. For a second the serious intensity of his expression shifted to something that bordered on genuine sympathy. She had the distinct impression he was about to touch her, but then he locked his expression up tight and threw away the key.

''I'd rather you not do that,'' he said.

''Why? Because I'll discover this is some scam? I think it's time you left, Mr. Halloran.''

His jaw flexed into an intractable bulkhead, his mouth a flat line. He removed a paper from his pocket. ''Read this. It's the ransom note from the kidnappers.''

Stef heard time throb in her temples like a hammer

striking a stake as she made herself take the note from his strong brown fingers. Fingers that were strong enough to take her baby from her. But he'd have to kill her first!

She read the note, each terrifying word.

Riana Collingwood is alive. She is a bright, pretty child with her father's eyes and her mother's smile. Prepare a five million dollar cash ransom and await further instruction.

Five million dollars! Oh, God, that wasn't good. Neither was the last line.

Involve the police this time and lose her forever.

Stef started to hyperventilate.

The man who had just destroyed her life took her elbow, his hand hot as the devil's touch. "Hey, sit back down. Now bend forward and put your head between your knees, okay?

"Just breathe."

She did what he ordered, even though what she really wanted to do was to smack him.

He sat on the arm of the chair and she felt the tentative stroke of his hand on her back like a zap of electricity. "I wouldn't advise bringing a third party into this now. It could put your real child's life in danger."

She sat bolt upright, still gulping for air.

"I'm assuming that the hair samples the kidnapper sent belong to your real daughter. We'll have to do tests immediately to confirm that. Regardless, the Foundation will cooperate fully with the kidnapper's demand and pay the ransom." He rubbed a slow circle that burned into her skin and made her forget all about breathing. "There's no kind or gentle way to say this—if the kidnapper realizes he has the wrong child, he could kill your daughter."

Stef glared at him, his Hollywood-handsome face inches from hers. She'd heard all she could take. Tears welled in her eyes. God, somewhere in Mitch Halloran there had to lurk a touch of humanity. He'd tried to soothe her when she'd started to hyperventilate and he was stroking her back, infusing her with the iron-core strength of his hand.

"Please, can't you just go away? The Collingwoods are dead. Just say it's a mistake. No one will know. Mistakes happen all the time in labs, don't they?"

His cobalt eyes flickered like shadows in the night, indicating he was considering her request. Her heart filled with hope as she prayed he'd relent.

"Is that what you really want me to do, Mrs. Shelton?"

His voice dipped with scorn. "Just go away and forget about your real daughter, who doesn't have red rubber boots or a real mommy to take her trick or treating?"

Fury gripped her at his callousness. She tried to shove him off the arm of the chair. "You bastard."

To her shock, he grabbed her in an attempt to gain his balance and landed on top of her in the chair, his chest pressed against hers, his nose inches from her face. She could feel the steely hardness of his muscled body and smell the scents of citrus and sea salt on his skin.

Even his teeth were Hollywood perfect. "You're not thinking straight," he said bluntly. "I saw you in the yard with Keely. I know if you thought you had a child out there, you'd move heaven and earth to get her back.''

Stef felt hot tears slip onto her face. Her stomach knotted as she tried to imagine the face of the little girl the kidnapper had described, who'd come from her womb. Yes, in her mother's heart she desperately wanted *her* child. But all she could see was Keely's face—the beloved little girl whom she'd fed and changed, and whose voice was the sound of happiness. She elbowed Mitch in the ribs. ''Get off me!''

Oh, God, this wasn't happening!

''Are you going to take Keely from me?'' she demanded as he levered himself off her.

Stef saw the stark truth in his face before he could shutter his expression.

''That's not my job. My concern is finding out whether the child being held is your daughter and getting her back safely. I'll need a DNA sample from you. And I'll need something that might have your husband's DNA on it.''

''Like what? I have some of Brad's things stored away that I thought Keely might find comforting to have,'' she said, trying to bend her mind to comprehend the sickening thought that her flesh-and-blood child had been in the care of kidnappers for the past thirty months. Her heart jerked. Had her child been neglected? Or abused?

''Did you keep a jacket or a ball cap? Something that may have come in contact with his neck, wrist or forehead is more likely to have his DNA on it.''

''I'll see what I can find.'' She forced herself to stand and brush past his towering frame. On stiff legs, she marched to the alcove to get Keely. She wasn't leaving Mitch Halloran alone with her daughter.

Her daughter. A sob clawed up her throat. Even if another DNA test proved Keely really was the Collingwood heir, she couldn't accept for a moment that Keely wouldn't be in her life forever. As soon as this was over, she'd get a lawyer. Surely no judge in the country would take a baby away from the woman who'd raised it if the biological parents were dead?

But this isn't any baby, insinuated a doom-and-gloom voice in her mind that sounded remarkably like Mitch Halloran's blunt-edged baritone. Her sunshiney daughter who loved to dance and sing and bake cookies was the Collingwood heir—the heir to one of the largest family fortunes in the United States.

Who was she kidding?

Stef stopped in the arched doorway to the alcove, overwhelmed by the battle she was up against. Keely, the delightful center of her universe, was pretending to feed toy plastic fruits to a doll. "Eat, baby, eat," she chanted. She glanced up and saw Stef and her blue-green eyes rounded with empathy.

"Mommy—sad?"

Stef sank onto the floor and pulled Keely into her lap, committing to memory the tropical scent of her hair, the perfect peanut shape of her nose and the snug heaven-on-earth feel of her compact body. How could she bear losing this darling child? "Mommy's very sad, Kee. But when I hold you everything's better."

To Stef's dismay, Keely started to sing their "I love you" song. The tears Stef had been struggling to hold back burst out in a torrent.

She rocked Keely tightly in her arms. "I love you, too, baby. I love you, too."

SHE WAS CRYING.

Mitch stiffened as his every muscle tried to deflect

the sound of Stephanie Shelton's anguished sobs. His stomach felt as if it were coated with hot tar. The only thing that made the situation bearable was the hope that she'd soon be reunited with her own lost child.

Mitch knew what a gift a mother like her would be to that child. Everything his own mother had never been.

He'd give Stef a few more minutes, then gently prod her into action. Time wasn't on their side—there was no way of knowing when the kidnapper would again make contact with specific instructions for the ransom. For all they knew, whoever had switched Riana and Keely could have another plan in the works to switch them back.

Flexing the tight muscles in his shoulders, Mitch unclipped the cell phone from his belt and punched in The Guardian's phone number.

"The Guardian," G.D.'s militarily brusque voice said.

Mitch's lips curled in wry humor. Uncomfortable with his new boss's curt directive to address him as sir, he'd quickly dubbed The Guardian "G.D.," which stood for *goddamn*. As in goddamn he couldn't believe he'd handed in his gun and his badge because The Guardian had asked him for assistance with this case.

Mitch had wanted to be a detective since he was twelve, when he'd gone to live with his grandfather who worked as a janitor in the Parker Administration Building of the L.A.P.D.

On days when Paddy's back had pained him from his shrapnel injury—a nasty souvenir from the Korean War—Mitch would come along to pick up wastebaskets and mop the floors in the Detective Headquarters Division. He'd never thought about *not* being a police detective. He'd thought he'd probably drag his last breath on the streets of L.A.—a fitting way to go for the life he'd chosen.

Mitch angled a surreptitious glance at Stef who was guiding Keely toward the bedrooms. His heart tightened at the paleness of her face and the moist path of tears on her cheek. For the first time in two years he had no doubt whatsoever that he was right where he was supposed to be.

He could almost hear Paddy telling him to keep soldiering on. *It never gets any easier, son.*

His chest filled with an echo of longing for the gruff man who'd given him the only home he'd ever known. Who'd given him clumsily wrapped Christmas presents and had taken him to Dodger games to celebrate his birthdays where he'd slipped Mitch sips of his beer. They were not the kind of memories that made sappy movies, but they were incredibly precious to a kid starved for attention.

Mitch realized his thoughts were drifting when G.D.'s voice rumbled, "Who's calling?"

He snapped back into focus. "Operation Bassinet. It's Halloran, G.D. I just spoke to Mrs. Shelton. She's devastated, but she's on board."

Concern edged The Guardian's tone. "Is Riana okay?"

"Right as rain. We should be back in the city tonight. By the way, the husband is dead. Two years ago. In a rock climbing accident. Think there's anything fishy in that? It could be a coincidence, but whoever abducted Riana from the hospital knew how to rappel."

When Mitch had accepted the job one day after the ransom demand had been received, The Guardian had apprised him of the details of Riana's kidnapping. The suspect was a Caucasian male who'd sneaked into the maternity postpartum wing during visitor's hours using a stolen visitor's badge and a hospital identification bracelet similar to those given to the new dads. He'd hidden in an unoccupied room and zapped the nurse, who'd been returning Riana Collingwood to the nursery after a late night feeding, with a stun gun.

Within minutes the kidnapper had bound the nurse and made his escape with the baby through a hole he'd cut in the second floor window to circumvent the hospital's state-of-the-art alarm system and the high-tech baby identification bracelets equipped with receivers.

By the time the staff realized the Collingwood heir had been stolen, the kidnapper had been long gone.

"I've already assigned some men to do a background check of the family. I'll ask them to dig up what they can on the husband's death. Brad Shelton would have been in a perfect position to switch the babies. If a man walked into a hospital carrying a baby, who'd question him if he walked out carrying one?"

"We're on the same wavelength, G.D."

"Will you be able to get the husband's DNA sample?"

"I'm on it."

"Excellent. We don't want any doubts as to the identity of the child the kidnapper has. I'll be waiting for you and Mrs. Shelton at the hotel."

The Guardian disconnected the call, but not before Mitch heard the distinct cry of a baby in the background and the soothing murmur of a woman's voice.

That was odd. He hooked his cell phone back onto his belt and went to check on Stef. Had The Guardian been with another client? Or did G.D. have a personal life?

G.D. was a man cloaked in mystery and Mitch was determined to at least learn his name. A man who didn't know who he was working for was a fool of an employee.

He'd already had a buddy in L.A.P.D.'s Scientific Investigative Division lift G.D.'s fingerprints from the paper on which he'd written his ridiculously high offer to Mitch. But all he'd discovered was that The Guardian's lily-white fingerprints weren't on file. Figured.

Mitch walked down the hall and found Stef and Keely in the tiny master bedroom, which was crammed with a walnut double-bed, a matching chest of drawers and a sewing machine in a cabinet. Keely was petting scraps of orange fur on the floor near the sewing machine and calling them "kitty" while Stef rummaged through the closet.

Mitch took in the intriguing view of Stef's jeans-clad bottom as she reached for the jumble of clothes, luggage, shopping bags and shoe boxes piled up on the closet shelf. "Careful," he warned as Stef stood on her tiptoes and tugged on a shoe box.

Too late.

A landslide of shopping bags, sweaters and shoe boxes slid off the shelf in slow motion, raining down on her.

Keely giggled and clapped her hands. "Oopsie, doopsie, all fall down, Mommy!"

Stef rolled her eyes and Mitch heard the tears hovering in her voice. "It's not supposed to all fall down on Mommy, Kee. Now we have a real mess on our hands."

Shoulders hunched, Stef plucked a royal-blue ball cap

from the debris field and held it out to him, her face flooded with color that made her seem even more vulnerable. Mitch was consciously aware he was treading into no man's land, becoming too hypersensitive to her emotions. He gave himself a mental kick in the butt.

"Will this do? Brad wore it for company ball games."

Careful to allow her some dignity, he kept his gaze averted from her moist eyes and examined the inner headband of the Office Outfitter's cap. It was stained with sweat. "This'll do." He gestured at the mess on the closet floor. "Since you've already got your luggage out, pack a bag for you and your daughter."

"Why?"

Mitch made the mistake of looking at her. Her green-gold eyes were as dangerous as a riptide and fringed with long sooty lashes. He was none too happy that he was making personal observations about the length of her eyelashes. He was too seasoned a cop to let himself get sucked in by a pair of pleading eyes. The anguish in Teresa Lopez's eyes when he'd informed her that her granddaughter was dead would haunt him to his dying day.

Don't think about Carmen or Theresa, he told himself. This is another case. Another chance to save a child.

Cold detachment firmed his voice. "You're coming with me. Keely's the Collingwood heir. You're both under my protection until this is over."

THE KIDNAPPER WAS CAREFUL to arrive after dark to avoid being seen. Aunt Helen and Uncle Fred's farmhouse was set back from the road, but you couldn't be too careful.

Aunt Helen answered the door, her worn face brightening into a smile. "Well, this is nice, two visits in a month. I was just washing up the dinner dishes. Let me cut you some cake. It's chocolate with butter-pecan frosting. Emma put the pecans on all by herself."

"Then I definitely want some. Where is she?"

"Helping Fred feed the rabbits out back." Aunt Helen stopped in the dingy hallway papered with faded blue windmills and folded her gnarled fingers in prayer, her voice a fervent whisper. "Have you heard from him?"

"Sorry, but I got an e-mail from Emma's mother's sister. She was looking for her sister and didn't know about Emma."

"Did she offer to take her?"

"I didn't ask in so many words, but I told her about Emma and offered to send a picture. I'm hoping once she sees her she'll be open to the idea of looking after her."

"That would be wonderful. I can't understand how adults can just abandon their children and their responsibilities. Fred and I love her dearly but we won't be able to take care of her forever. Fred's getting more and more forgetful. Yesterday he forgot he'd turned the kettle on and nearly started a fire."

The kidnapper made sympathetic noises. What Aunt Helen didn't know wouldn't hurt her. Killing her son had been an unpleasant, but necessary precaution. And frankly, the world was better off without that shiftless SOB. "I'm sure he will turn up eventually. You know I'll do whatever I can to help with Emma's expenses. I'm just sorry I can't come by more often."

Aunt Helen shook her head. "We know you're busy." She made shooing motions toward the kitchen.

"Now come sit down and tell me what's going on in your life."

The kidnapper winced, the question striking too close to home. Everything would work out according to plan as long as The Guardian cooperated with the ransom demand. "Didn't you say something about cake?"

Aunt Helen cut a thick wedge of cake and served it on a chipped china plate.

The fork rattled as boots clomped up the back steps and the rear kitchen door burst open.

Emma, barely as tall as Uncle Fred's knee, entered first in a navy-blue jacket, her blue eyes glowing beneath a dark fringe of bangs and her cheeks like polished apples. "Gamma, we're ba-ack."

"So you are, little duck. Take off your jacket and your boots," Aunt Helen said with a smile, rising to help her. "And come say hello to your daddy's cousin."

"Quack-quack," Emma sang back vociferously.

"That means hello," Uncle Fred interpreted, shrugging out of his red-and-black plaid wool jacket and hanging it on a wooden peg near the door. The retired electrician looked thinner than ever, his pants held around his waist with a belt cinched small as a dog's collar. Even his handshake felt feeble.

They sat around the table and talked while Aunt Helen fixed tea and Emma drew pictures on construction paper with stubby crayons.

When it was Emma's bedtime, the kidnapper offered to read her a story. It was simple enough to snap a picture of her in her pajamas holding the front page of today's edition of the *New York Times*.

Soon, the picture would come in very handy.

Chapter Two

Stef held Keely in her arms and stared mutinously at Mitch Halloran over the roof of the black luxury sedan as he stowed their luggage in the trunk. She was not ready for this. Night surrounded them with cold velvet. The stars were crystal-clear overhead.

Stef couldn't bring herself to touch the door handle. It had been hard enough to pack clothes and toys for Keely and to allow Mitch to collect a DNA sample from their mouths with a swab. She did not want to get into this car and drive toward an uncertain future, which might not include the precious baby she held in her arms.

She couldn't do it.

She had to do it. Another *child* needed her.

Mitch closed the trunk and stared back at her, not saying a word, but his Goliath expression said plenty.

She hated him, she really did. Hated how he loomed over the car—a golden malevolent griffin with sun-bleached hair. Hated how she noticed how endlessly broad his shoulders were and how she could feel his eyes silently reminding her that her flesh-and-blood child was spending yet another day without her real mommy.

That was the worst part of it. Nausea and anger churned in her at the heart-wrenching thought that she'd only known her real baby for a day. What if her real daughter was dead? Or would be killed once the ransom was paid. What if she never *saw* her again?

"Mommy?" Keely's voice sounded pitifully small and tired in the darkness. "I don't like that man. He makes you sad. I want my snuggie and my beddy-bye time."

"Kee, that was rude. Mr. Halloran is a detective, which is kind of like a police officer, and he needs Mommy's help. So we're going to go with him and help him, okay? It'll be fun. An adventure."

Keely didn't look convinced. Her brow wrinkled like a plump raisin. "No."

Stef saw the white flash of Mitch Halloran's patient smile in the darkness as he walked to the driver's side door. He obviously knew better than to clash wills with an obstinate two-and-a-half-year-old. She smoothed the hair back from Keely's forehead and kissed her frown away, her throat tightening with suppressed emotion. "Sometimes, Kee, we have to do things even when we don't want to do them." God, what an understatement! "I have snuggie and I'll tuck it around you and we'll have our beddy-bye time in the car."

As she spoke, Stef opened the rear door of the car. The door handle felt cold in her grasp. "Okay, baby gorilla, into your car seat. I'll sit right beside you."

To her relief, Keely obeyed, though she moved at an excruciating turtle's pace. Stef fastened her daughter into the car seat and covered her with her snuggie, the crocheted rainbow-pastel blanket that had been a gift from Brad's former boss. Then she handed Keely her cup of milk with the leak-proof lid.

Stef was uncomfortably aware of Mitch Halloran's unrelenting size filling the car, his scent commingling with the scents of leather and the sweet baby smell of Keely's blanket. She couldn't remember the last time she'd been so aware of a man's presence. It had probably been her wedding day when she'd walked down the aisle and seen Brad waiting for her at the front of the church.

Brad. He'd been handsome, engaging and unreliable. Funny how she'd fooled herself into thinking he'd always be there for her. The fact that he was estranged from his parents, who hadn't been invited to their wedding, should have been her first clue that family wasn't at the top of Brad's priority list. She wouldn't be going through this nightmare if he'd stayed overnight in the hospital with them. But he'd had that job interview the next morning, which he'd blown anyway by arriving late.

Guilt struck her. It wasn't Brad's fault that someone had stolen their baby.

Mitch looped an arm across the back of the front passenger seat, his face a study of intense sharp angles as he backed the car out of the driveway—away from the home she'd bought with the money from Brad's life insurance policy. At least he'd been responsible enough to buy life insurance when Stef had discovered she was pregnant.

Angry tears blurred her vision. She licked her dry lips as Mitch put the car in drive and her house receded from view. Next time she came home, would Keely be with her?

She straightened, lightly stroking Keely's hair. She had to think positively. As soon as her real daughter was safely returned, she'd hire a lawyer and fight for custody of Keely, even if she had to sell her house and everything she owned to pay the legal fees.

Were there even any Collingwood family members who'd fight for custody of Keely? The Collingwood murders had been all over the news—speculation running rampant on the talk shows over who would get the money because there were no other living relatives except Lexi's greedy sister, Annette York. Annette was probably going to get the death penalty for killing her sister and brother-in-law.

Stef cleared her throat and glared at the back of Mitch's head. "Where are we going?" she asked.

His face was reflected in the rearview mirror. He drove the way the cops on those reality TV shows drove, both hands on the wheel, his body language vigilant as if he expected trouble to come leaping out of the bushes.

Oh, God. Did he?

Visions of car-jackings raced through her mind. She suddenly realized that if Keely really *was* the lost Collingwood heir, she'd stand to inherit a fortune, which was why she'd been kidnapped in the first place. Her inheritance would make her vulnerable all of her life.

"We're going to New York City," Mitch said, his baritone bursting Stef's panicky realization that he hadn't exaggerated when he'd said Keely needed protection. "The Foundation has offices there. My boss has reserved a suite at a hotel. He'll meet us there."

"Who's your boss? Is he related to the Collingwoods?"

"He calls himself The Guardian."

Stef wasn't sure she'd heard correctly. "Excuse me?"

"He's a private security consultant who keeps his

identity under wraps to protect his clientele. Ross Collingwood hired him after Riana was kidnapped. He was the one who nailed Annette York for killing Ross and Lexi Collingwood.'' Mitch's voice held deference and respect. ''When I was with the L.A.P.D., I heard stories about him from officers who'd assisted him with celebrity stalking cases.''

Stef didn't care who The Guardian was or what he'd done. She was prepared to dislike him on sight. As far as she was concerned, The Guardian was just a man who wanted to take Keely away from her.

''Are there other family members? I've only heard about the sister—she doesn't sound like someone I want to meet.''

''That information is being kept under wraps.''

Stef rolled her eyes. From the tone of Mitch's voice, she wasn't going to get any information out of him about the Collingwoods. Maybe she'd have better luck with his boss.

Keely popped the cup out of her mouth and twined her tiny fingers in Stef's hair. ''Mommy, beddy-bye story?''

''Sure, baby.'' Stef curled an arm across her daughter's body as if shielding her from Mitch's real-life tales of pseudonymous detectives, celebrity stalkers and murderers.

''Once upon a time, there was a little girl named Keely, who lived in a cozy blue house on Maple Lane. One fall day Keely and her mommy were outside raking leaves when they heard a bell-like voice say, 'Ouch!' Keely looked down into the grass and found a tiny fairy who was just big enough to fit in her hand. The fairy was crying. The rake had ripped one of her beautiful wings and now she couldn't fly home.''

She made a scooping motion with her hand and held it up to her daughter's face. "Keely took the fairy home and made a soft bed for her with her snuggie. And her mommy put a special bandage on the fairy's wing. The next morning when the fairy woke up, her wing was all better and she could fly home. To thank Keely, the fairy promised to grant her one special wish. And what did Keely wish for?"

Kee popped the cup out of her mouth again and yawned sleepily. "A daddy."

Stef gaped at her in surprise. Where the heck had that answer come from? Keely had never said anything like that before. But then, she'd never been whisked away from her bed at night by her mommy and a towering stranger, whom she perceived as making her mommy sad. Keely was just a baby. Too young to understand that her daddy had died and gone to heaven. But instinctively old enough to articulate that she wanted a daddy to protect her and her mommy from Mitch.

Stef's heart broke. Keely didn't need a daddy. She *had* a mommy who loved her more than life itself and surely a judge would recognize that and rule in Keely's best interests even if Stef wasn't Keely's biological mother. No matter how big of a fortune was involved.

Yeah, and Stef had bought into the fairy tale that she and Brad would live happily ever after, too.

"Oh, Kee," she whispered, pressing her mouth against her daughter's silky head and fighting to keep her tears from clogging her throat and upsetting Keely even more. "That's a lovely wish. Now close your eyes and go to sleep just like the fairy."

Softly, very softly, Stef sang her daughter the "I love you" song they'd invented and glared at the sleek golden outline of Mitch Halloran's head.

MITCH SWORE under his breath as he attempted to tune out the love and desperation in Stef's voice as she sang to Keely.

He'd witnessed some horrible things in his career—butchered bodies, neglected and abused children, junkies so strung out they'd take a life for a couple of bucks to buy their next fix. Now he could add this poignant moment to that list of worst evers.

All he could do was hold fiercely to the fragile cord of hope that somehow Stef Shelton would get her real daughter back alive. Or this would destroy her.

Just as another girl's death had destroyed another heartbroken woman who had depended on him. Theresa Lopez had died of a stroke eight months after Carmen's death.

Decisions usually came easy to Mitch. He didn't waste time agonizing over what to do. He made a decision and went with it until the circumstances changed and he had to make another decision. Paddy had taught him that valuable lesson after Mitch had been dumped on his doorstep because his mother's boyfriend didn't like having a teenage boy with an attitude hanging around. The visit with his grandfather was supposed to be for a few days. But those few days had stretched into a month, then a couple of months.

After watching Mitch check the window every time a car pulled in the drive, Paddy had told him he had to quit worrying about when and if his mother was coming back—events he couldn't control—and to make a decision to soldier on and focus on things he *could* control such as making friends, getting good grades and figuring out what his mission in life was. Most importantly, deciding what kind of man he wanted to be.

Mitch had used Paddy's advice to control his destiny

ever since—cracking the books to get the grades he needed to get a degree in criminal justice, busting his ass in the police academy and distinguishing himself as a detective.

He stole another look at Stef in the rearview mirror. Her left arm was curled protectively around the top of the car seat, her head pillowed on her shoulder. He steeled his emotions to the heartbreaking story of love and fear her body language projected.

"Is she asleep?" he asked tentatively, trying to establish a rapport with her. Whether she liked it or not, he was in this with her.

Her tone was charged with rebellion. "Yes, finally."

Oh, boy.

He kept his tone even. "I know this is rough, but I need to ask you some questions."

"Such as?"

"Do you remember anything unusual happening in the hospital after Keely's birth? Did you see anyone suspicious near your child? Maybe a nurse or a hospital worker?"

"Why would I tell you anything that would help you succeed in your ridiculous claim that Keely isn't my child?"

"Because, ma'am, deep down you know my claim is not ridiculous and beneath the anger and the fear you're feeling, you want to do everything you can to get your daughter back home to you safely."

She snorted. "If you knew anything about my feelings, Mr. Halloran, you'd stop calling me 'ma'am.' Or maybe you don't want to do that because you sleep better at night by treating people as if they're just another nameless face."

He felt a strong poke in his shoulder. It took every

ounce of his self-control to remain relaxed and to not tense up. He assumed it was her finger and not a gun, but who knew to what extremes a distraught parent might go under the threat of having to give up their child?

"You take a good look at my face, Halloran," she continued bitterly. "My name is Stef Shelton. This is *my life* we're talking about. *My family.* So don't you talk to me like I'm some nameless, faceless person."

Her words hit Mitch like a match to a fuse. He jerked the car over to the side of the road, switched on the overhead light and turned to face her.

There was no gun. Just one very defiant woman, who was in real danger of losing her family. His stomach catapulted again.

He pointed two fingers at his eyes, his voice just as hard as hers had been. "Stef, look at me. Right here. I can't afford to be emotional or I'd spend half my waking hours guzzling beer and the other half puking my guts out over the stuff I see day in, day out. I am thinking about *your life. Your family. Your daughter.* I want to know who took her, and I want to get her back for you alive. Now answer my goddamn question." The hardness in his voice turned to a plea. "Please."

He saw the defiance leak out of her, saw her eyes turn to liquid gold in her pale face as they filled with new tears. His chest grew unbearably tight. She *was* a nice woman. And hot enough that he'd take a second interested glance if she weren't intimately connected with the case. Stef Shelton loved Keely the way mothers were supposed to love their children. She'd never dump her child with a relative and disappear for years. Mitch didn't even know whether his mother was alive or dead.

He hadn't seen his own dad except for that one time when he was six years old.

"I know this doesn't seem fair, but we have to move beyond that and make smart decisions." He snapped his mouth shut before he added the sorry platitude that life was rarely fair. He knew damn well that there was a chance that Stef Shelton's real daughter could be buried in a shallow grave that would never be found.

But he wasn't going to consider that possibility until he had strong evidence to suggest it was the case. He reached into the back and touched her knee, breaking the fundamental rule of successfully sustaining detachment, the line he never should have crossed with Carmen's grandmother: don't touch, don't feel.

The moment he felt the wiry strands of Teresa's gray hair against his cheek as she'd hugged him desperately, he'd lost his perspective. But he needed Stef's cooperation. He had no badge that he could wave to induce her to talk.

She felt brittle and delicate as if sheer force of will was holding her together. "Trust me," he said. "I only want to help."

She took a shaky breath, her eyes still fixed on his. He could see the decision-making process going on in her head. Do I hate this bastard? Or do I trust him to help me?

Trust won out.

Mitch had the uncanny sensation he were staring down a gold-paved tunnel into her soul as she wet her lips and finally confided, "I woke up around 3:00 a.m. The sound of the door woke me. I thought it was the nurse or my husband coming to check on us because he'd decided not to stay overnight in the hospital with us. Dads can do that, you know."

And she blamed her husband for not being there. He could tell by the defensive shift in her body language and the rigid tilt of her chin. But then, she was probably still angry with her husband for dying. Mitch was familiar with that kind of anger. Paddy was the one person he'd counted on being there for him. Always.

"Did you see the person? Could you tell if it was a male or female? Did you notice anything they were wearing?"

"No, sorry." She sounded sincere.

"Did you notice anything unusual about Keely at all? Her hair? Her weight? The ID bracelets?"

She frowned, thinking back. "Nothing significant. It was two and a half years ago. To be honest, I don't think Brad or I looked that closely at the ID bracelets. Having a baby is a pretty exhausting experience."

"I'll bet. I don't have any kids, but I suspect they call it labor for a reason." He squeezed her knee, intending to leave things on a friendly note and to get the sedan back on the road, but she stopped him, catching his hand with hers. Mitch's heart kicked up a beat at the hesitant, light-as-a-feather touch of her fingers.

"Mitch...?"

He nodded encouragingly. It was the first time she'd used his name. But it also triggered a tremor of unease on the back of his neck at the level of intimacy it created.

"The ransom note you showed me—it said the little girl had her father's eyes and her mother's smile. W-what color were Ross Collingwood's eyes?"

He held her gaze, smiled gently, relieved to see that she was rallying and wasn't going to stay in denial about her biological daughter's fate. He imagined Stef Shelton had strengths she hadn't tapped yet. "They were blue. And the hairs that accompanied the note were dark brown.''

''Brad had blue eyes,'' she said wistfully, releasing his hand.

Mitch searched her determined, tear-streaked face and Keely's slumbering form for a second longer, then turned out the overhead light and pulled back onto the road.

Her lost daughter was becoming real to her.

HUNTER AND JULIANA SINCLAIR waited anxiously in the penthouse suite of the New York Clairmont Hotel for Riana's arrival. Unbelievably, incredibly, after thirty long months, Ross and Lexi's daughter was safe in Mitch Halloran's custody and on her way home to them.

But what should have been a joyous event was overshadowed by the grim knowledge that another child's life was perilously at risk. Poor Stephanie Shelton, the woman who'd unknowingly been caring for Riana, had just learned that the child she'd raised was not her own.

Juliana empathized with what Stephanie must be thinking and feeling. When Ross and Lexi Collingwood were murdered in an explosion six weeks ago, The Guardian had expected her to give up the Collingwoods' five-month-old son, Cort, whom she'd been raising in secret to keep him safe from harm. Ross and Lexi had appointed The Guardian as the legal guardian of their children, Riana and Cort. Even though Juliana had been raised in the Collingwood household, it spoke to The Guardian's intense security that she hadn't known that Ross and Hunter were best friends or that Hunter was Cort's godfather.

Regardless, she had not been willing to give up Cort without a fight. To protect her precious charge until he was old enough to claim his inheritance, she had married Hunter Sinclair, aka The Guardian. They were raising Cort as a Sinclair, their own son, giving him all the love that Ross and Lexi would have given him.

She rested her head on her husband's solid shoulder, her heart bearing equal burdens of elation and anxiety. In the short time since their marriage she knew Hunter so well she could practically hear the gears turning in his pragmatic mind, assessing the extraordinary situation for legalities and lawsuits and risk management options.

He'd been overcome with emotion when he'd taken the call from Mitch Halloran earlier this evening. He'd excused himself from the dining room when the call came, then returned a few minutes later and silently held out his hand to her, blinking back tears.

She'd walked out to the greenhouse with him where he'd told her the news. They'd wept together at the miracle, mourning the fact that Ross and Lexi weren't alive to welcome their lost little girl home themselves.

Hunter had promised her that he'd do everything possible to ensure the safe return of Stephanie Shelton's real daughter. Then he'd put on his Guardian hat and told her in his endearingly arrogant way that they were going to act with the utmost caution until they knew who was behind Riana's kidnapping. Riana's return could be a trap.

The timing of this ransom demand so shortly after Annette's arrest for the Collingwood murders *was* awfully suspicious. Annette and her lawyers were claiming she was innocent—that she'd been framed for the bombing and murders by someone higher up in the Collingwood Corporation.

The new ransom demand could be an attempt to make

it appear as though another party was behind both the murders and Riana's kidnapping. Annette had already proven herself a master of plotting and deception. They still couldn't fathom why Annette hadn't revealed Cort's existence or Hunter's identity as The Guardian to the press. Either she didn't want to share the media spotlight or she planned to use the information as a trump card during her trial.

"I'm coming with you tonight," Juliana had insisted.

He'd kissed her forehead, gently, tenderly, in that protective way that told her he was afraid.

"I'm not sure that's wise at this point."

She'd smoothed her palms over his chest, emotion choking her voice. Beneath his ever-present shield of caution and restraint, her husband deeply valued his family. "She's Cort's sister. Our daughter. I want to see her."

"I want to see her, too. But I don't want to put you at risk if it's a trap." His azure eyes clouded. "I came too close to losing you last month. And Cort needs you. You're safer here. Del and Lars aren't going to let a fly land on this island without their scrutiny and permission."

Juliana wasn't taking no for an answer. Lexi's daughter, *their* daughter, needed her. "I'll be fine. I'll be with you. I'll stay away from rivers and other bodies of water," she added, referring to the terrifying night when she'd jumped into the St. Lawrence River to avoid being shot by Annette after Lars and Del had been seriously injured by her hired assassin. "I promise."

Hunter sighed. "It constantly amazes me how frequently I give in to your unreasonable demands. You may come, but Cort stays at FairIsle with your father and Prudy. And, you'll accompany me as the Collingwoods' butler's daughter, not as my wife. Leave your wedding rings here. I have no intention of revealing that I'm Riana's legal guardian until we know what's really going on. I still haven't told Mitch about Cort or our marriage.''

Juliana had smiled and slid her finger inside the collar of his black sweater. He was the sexiest, most suspicious man she'd ever met and she loved Hunter with her whole heart and soul. Their marriage may have been brought about by the tragic deaths of Ross and Lexi Collingwood, but there was nothing artificial or contrived about their feelings for one another now.

''Does that mean we can't make love to celebrate Riana's return while we're in New York?'' She rose on tiptoes to nibble his ear. It was his Achilles' heel, guaranteed to instantly divert his thoughts from logic to lovemaking. It brought the desired wolfish grin to his face.

His hand had slipped under her skirt, warm and proprietary. ''How about a pre-celebration now?''

Juliana jumped as the ringing of the phone in the penthouse suite yanked her into the present. Hunter took the call. ''That was the front desk. They've arrived.''

Juliana smoothed the black pantsuit she'd changed into for the helicopter trip to New York and tucked her long blond hair behind her ears. She was so nervous. What if Riana was afraid of them? Didn't like them? She shot a quick glance at her husband.

He had his imperturbable Guardian face on again. They'd agreed earlier that she would make the introductions. It would be less threatening.

''Riana's going to be so confused,'' she said. ''She's not old enough to understand any of this.''

His eyes warmed lovingly. ''We'll make it work.''

"But what if—"

He laid a finger over his lips and motioned for her to greet their guests as the private elevator that served the penthouse suite arrived. The doors slid open.

With her heart in her throat, Juliana smiled at the gorgeous blond man who must be the hot-shot L.A. detective and the defiant dark-haired woman carrying a sleeping toddler. The toddler was wrapped in a blanket that Juliana could only describe as a dream coat because of its beautiful colors.

Riana.

The delicate nest of Riana's dark curls brought a fluid rush of warmth coursing through Juliana. She could almost feel Lexi's smiling presence in the room with them.

Juliana stepped forward, aching to touch those beautiful curls, but sensing that such a gesture would be ill-advised. "How do you do, Mrs. Shelton? I'm Juliana Goodhew. My family has worked for the Collingwoods for many years." She gestured at Hunter. "And this is The Guardian, the Collingwoods' chief security consultant."

Hunter nodded. "Mrs. Shelton."

This was so awkward. Juliana felt a warning chill pass over her spine as the tension mounted. Stephanie Shelton looked scared to death and she noticed that Mitch Halloran moved slightly behind the young woman as if providing her with emotional and moral support.

Juliana's heart went out to Stephanie. This situation was going to be difficult on them all. "You've had a long drive and must be exhausted. Perhaps you'd like to get Riana settled first, then we can sit down and talk privately."

Stephanie Shelton didn't budge. Her green eyes glittered with the ferocity of a lioness protecting her cub. "Her name is Keely. Even if the DNA tests prove she's Riana, I'm not giving her up without a fight. You can relay that message to her family on my behalf."

Oh, dear. Juliana shot Hunter a look of dismay.

Hunter stepped forward. "Be that as it may, Mrs. Shelton," he said courteously, "we still need your cooperation. If you're the parent of the child the kidnapper is holding, then only you can make certain decisions about the ransom demand and how you wish to proceed. I suggest we leave the legal battles for the lawyers. Have you provided Mitch with some DNA samples? It takes three to four days to get DNA test results back from the lab, and we may hear from the kidnapper again before then. I have a courier standing by in the lobby."

"This should do it." Mitch Halloran passed Hunter two DNA test kits, then partially slid a royal-blue baseball cap from a paper bag. Office Outfitters was embroidered in red above the bill of the cap. "This was his ball cap."

A guarded stillness came over Hunter. "Was your husband associated with Office Outfitters, Mrs. Shelton?"

"He worked for them for seven years until he was laid off when it was taken over by some big corporation." She faltered, fear illuminating her eyes like flashbulbs.

"Taken over by whom?" Hunter prodded gently.

Stephanie Shelton took a hesitant step backward and bumped into Mitch Halloran's muscled bulk. The detective's hands shot out to steady her. With nowhere to go, Stephanie clutched Riana more securely to her breast and admitted baldly, "The Collingwood Corporation."

Chapter Three

Stef guessed what they were all thinking—that Brad was involved in Riana Collingwood's kidnapping and had switched the infants. "Brad wouldn't put his own baby in that kind of danger," she insisted.

Oh, God, didn't any of these people believe her?

"What makes you so certain?" Mitch Halloran asked.

She whirled around and saw the skepticism radiating from his hard features. How could she have found his hands so supportive on her shoulders a few seconds ago?

She struggled to stay calm and to keep her voice from waking Keely. "Because I *loved* him. He was my husband! He was upset after he was laid off. He had trouble finding another job, but I can't see him plotting a kidnapping as revenge against the Collingwoods. He didn't have a vindictive bone in his body." He'd just given up on finding a job when it got too hard, just as he'd given up on his relationship with his ailing parents. Stef didn't even know where they lived anymore. She'd sent a letter to an address she'd found after Brad had died, but she'd never received a response.

Sympathy lit Mitch's eyes, stoking her anger. She didn't want his sympathy or his pity.

"Your faith in your husband is admirable, but your real daughter's life is at stake. We have to examine every possibility with or without your assistance."

Stef grit her teeth. She hated it when he talked like that. He sounded so infuriatingly reasonable, but she knew he'd already decided Brad was involved and was champing at the bit to prove it. Keely stirred in Stef's arms, grumpy as a bear cub without a pot of honey. Stef wanted to bolt for the door, to escape Mitch Halloran and his insinuations, but she could hear a little voice— a child's voice—inside her calling out to her for help.

Oh, God, Brad couldn't be involved, could he?

Juliana Goodhew stepped between Stef and Mitch like a referee about to break up a brawl. "Let's not continue this in front of Keely. Please, Mr. Halloran, surely your questions can wait a few minutes while Mrs. Shelton sees to her daughter. Follow me, Mrs. Shelton."

Stef gladly accompanied Juliana into the other room. But her underlying disquiet grew when she saw that the hotel room had been stocked for Keely's arrival with toys, picture books and child-friendly snacks. There was even a child's trundle bed shaped like a ladybug for her to sleep in. While she honestly believed that Juliana and the Collingwood family had only had Keely's comfort in mind, Stef was consciously aware that the toys had probably come from a toy store whose merchandise was more pricey than she could afford.

She told herself that the toys were only things. A mother's love was not so easily replaced.

But still…what if Keely fell in love with the ladybug bed and didn't want to leave it? She suddenly couldn't bring herself to put Keely down on that bed.

Tears swam in her eyes. When she looked across the room at Juliana, she saw she was crying, too.

Juliana wrung her hands, looking as awkward and uncertain as Stef felt. Sincerity shone in the dampness of her warm brown eyes. "This is so awful. I see the same fear in you that I saw in Lexi after Riana's abduction. She tried to be so brave. So strong. You have no reason to trust me, Mrs. Shelton, but you can. Lexi would have wanted that. She was a children's social worker before she married Ross. If she were alive, she'd be putting Keely's needs before her own right now. And she'd do whatever she could to help you get your baby back."

"I only have your word on that," Stef said stiffly.

Color infused Juliana's cheeks. "You're in good hands with The Guardian and Mr. Halloran. I wouldn't be alive today if it weren't for The Guardian. He saved me from Ross and Lexi's killer. I don't know Mitch Halloran all that well, but if The Guardian hired him, you can be sure he's the best there is."

Stef had no doubt that Mitch Halloran knew exactly what he was doing. He was ripping her life apart one foundation at a time. First, questioning her child's identity. And now, casting doubt on her husband's integrity.

She eyed Juliana warily. "Does Riana have family who want her back?"

Juliana nodded, tears glimmering bright in her eyes again. "Yes. Very much."

It was not the answer Stef was hoping for. "Who?" she demanded. "Mitch won't tell me who they are."

"I'm afraid I can't either for security reasons. The Guardian will introduce you to the family when he determines it's safe to do so."

Despite her frustration with the answer, Stef felt herself thawing toward Juliana, viewing her as less of a threat. "Thank you for the honest answer. We'll get along better if you call me Stef."

Juliana's shoulders dropped their tautness. "Can I give you a hand helping you settle your daughter, Stef?"

Your daughter. Stef felt a knot of gratitude tighten in her throat at Juliana's sensitivity. "I don't want to wake her up too much. But it would be a big help if you could get her pajamas from her bag."

"Consider it done."

Stef sat on the foot of the ladybug trundle bed and eased off Keely's shoes and jacket. Her worry that Juliana's presence might be obtrusive was unfounded. She handed her the pajamas, then turned down the sheets of Keely's bed and dimmed the lights before she left the room.

Keely whined and demanded to go home. Stef soothed her with soft words as she removed her sweatpants and top and slipped on her pajamas. Then coaxed her under the covers.

"Look at this special bed, Kee. It's a beautiful mama ladybug. There's even baby ladybugs on the sheets," Stef whispered, tucking her daughter into bed. "I told you this trip would be special."

Keely gave her a groggy combative look, her tiny chin stubborn and determined. "Fly away *home,* Mommy."

"Fly away to sleep, Kee." Stef kissed her daughter's brow, breathing in the fruity scent of her hair and the milky sweetness of her skin. Keely rolled onto her side, clutching her snuggie to her body before Stef had even begun the first bars of their "I love you" song.

Stef's gaze lighted on the shimmering pastel colors

of her daughter's blanket. Sable Holden, the former owner of Office Outfitters, had personally sent the gift after Keely was born—a good six months after Brad had been laid off.

In the shadowy stillness of the room, fear gripped Stef's heart. She'd defended her husband against the blunt accusations in Mitch Halloran's eyes. She'd insisted Brad would never be involved with something that could place his own child's life at risk.

But what if she was wrong?

SMOOTH MITCH, real smooth.

Way to earn her confidence by jumping all over her dead husband and getting her back up.

Mitch felt like a jerk as Stef followed Juliana from the suite's sitting room, her back as rigid as steel-reinforced concrete and her arms clutching Keely.

Worry rocked through him. How much could Stef take? If her husband was involved in the kidnapping, she'd lose more than Keely. She'd feel humiliated and betrayed by the man she'd loved and lose her fundamental beliefs about her husband and her marriage. And she'd blame herself for not knowing, not realizing, what Brad had done.

He swore silently, telling himself that thoughts like that were none of his concern. He couldn't not investigate a viable lead because it would destroy Stef. Mitch's job was to get to the truth.

Mitch prowled the perimeter of the sitting room. The Guardian had given him copies of the files pertaining to the Collingwood murders, but he hadn't finished reading them yet. "So, what's the scoop on this Office Outfitters, G.D.? Just how hostile was the takeover?"

"Let's just say that Sable Holden didn't concede defeat quietly or graciously. She'd revamped her grand-father's office supply chain from the name to the way the product was sold to the customers. She was one of the first to capitalize on the concept of warehouse shopping. Several hundred employees were let go when the Collingwood Corporation took over and restructured—Brad Shelton, among them. Sable wrangled a seat on the Collingwood Corporation's board of directors as a condition of the takeover. She is one smart lady.''

"When did this takeover happen?"

"Just before Ross and Lexi's wedding. Sable was invited to the wedding as a matter of etiquette. Lexi was five months pregnant with Riana at the time, and Sable made a smart-aleck remark to her at the reception about the child's paternity.''

"Sounds like there was some bitterness between Sable and Ross Collingwood.''

"Lexi's sister, Annette, told me Sable had a love-hate relationship with Ross. She hated that he'd outwitted her, but she was hot for him. It didn't matter that he was married." G.D.'s mouth twisted wryly. "Of course, we can't assume anything Annette York said is truthful. But Juliana witnessed a few public exchanges between Ross and Sable and she concurs with Annette.''

Mitch shoved his fists into his pockets. "Think there was any hanky-panky going on?"

"No." The Guardian's response was unequivocal.

Mitch shot him a questioning glance. "Why so sure?"

"Because Ross was deeply in love with his wife."

"You really believe that—that couples are still faithful to each other in this day and age? The statistics suggest otherwise, my friend. Ross had power, money and a good-looking head shot. You just said Sable was hot for him. He must have been some chick magnet.''

G.D. raised a skeptical brow. ''You've never been in love, have you?''

Surprised at the question, Mitch shrugged. No, he'd never been in love. Outside of the department he didn't have much of a life. No steady girlfriend. He'd done his fair share of lusting, but it had always worn off. The women he'd dated always thought it would be great to hook up with a cop until he disappeared for days on end on an investigation or said he didn't want to talk about what it felt like to see the empty display cabinets of a jewelry store splattered with the store owner's brains.

Frankly, that suited him just fine. He was only interested in catching the bad guys.

He'd seen a few good marriages among the officers he'd worked with over the years. Mostly he saw a lot of guys who stopped telling their wives what the job was really like because they didn't want their families to worry about them.

But The Guardian seemed dead certain that Ross Collingwood hadn't cheated on his wife. Mitch circled the room, wondering if G.D. had ever been in love. His boss wasn't sporting a wedding band.

''As I see it, we got two possibilities, G.D. Brad Shelton staged the kidnapping on his own or Sable Holden recruited him to do the dirty work. Shelton had means and opportunity. We know he had some climbing experience and Stef—I mean, Mrs. Shelton, told me her husband was home alone the night Riana was kidnapped.'' He paused significantly. ''She also remembers someone entering her hospital room around 3:00 a.m. She thought it might have been a nurse or her husband, but she isn't sure. She called out but nobody answered.''

G.D. leaned forward, his fingers tapping pensively on the arm of the sofa. "It could have been her husband switching the babies. We can show Shelton's picture to the nurse who was assaulted during Riana's kidnapping. She might recognize him even though it's been over two years. But we can't discount Sable Holden's possible involvement. After the Collingwoods' funeral service, Juliana caught Sable wandering around alone upstairs in the Collingwoods' home—even though the area was clearly cordoned off. Sable claimed she was looking for a powder room. She was questioned and searched to see if she'd tucked any souvenirs in her purse, but the police didn't find anything.''

Mitch halted cold in his tracks. "Maybe they were looking for the wrong thing. What if Sable was after samples of Ross's and Lexi's DNA? She could have swiped used tissues from a coat pocket or hairs from a brush.''

G.D. didn't look convinced. "If she'd been successful, she'd know the child she has isn't Riana,'' he pointed out.

Damn, G.D. was right. "But what if Juliana intercepted her before she could find what she was after? Sable would have had no choice but to assume she had the right child.''

G.D. nodded, his ice-blue eyes sharp as lasers. "I'll buy that.''

Mitch snapped his fingers. "And wasn't there something in the files you gave me about Sable trying to hire the Collingwoods' chef to cater a private function? If memory serves, you thought she was trying to establish an in with someone in the Collingwood household staff.''

G.D.'s mouth curled up slightly at the corners. ''Your memory serves you well, Mitch.''

Mitch shrugged. ''It's hard to forget a loony chef who turns down a client because she doesn't like her aura. But let's backtrack a sec. What if your initial instincts were right and Sable *was* trying to get an in with the household? You really think she was planning to return the child?''

''Hard to say. Her goal may simply have been to make Ross suffer the same losses she suffered when the Collingwood Corporation took over her company. But then again, she may have been waiting until the timing was right to wrest back control of her company. The ransom amount jumped from two million in the first demand to five million in this demand. Maybe she's planning to use the five million dollars to help her achieve that.''

Mitch's interest was whetted. This was a lead worth pursuing. ''I need to meet this woman.''

The Guardian steepled his index fingers and smiled indulgently. ''You will. Tomorrow. Mrs. Shelton needs to drop by Sable's office unexpectedly. You'll be a friend of the family accompanying her. After your visit, you'll convince Mrs. Shelton to let you search her home for any evidence that would link Brad with the kidnapping. And while you're at it, dig up a picture of him. I'll assign some men to investigate the cause of Brad's death. It may not have been an accident.''

Mitch's lips pressed into a taut line. Convincing Stef Shelton to cooperate at all was going to be a tall order. ''Can we get a list of the staff working in both hospital nurseries the night the babies were switched? I don't want to overlook the possibility that someone on either hospital staff may have been involved.''

"Good point. I'll get you the list."

"I still think you should notify the FBI agent assigned to Riana's case of this latest ransom demand. The FBI has considerable resources."

The Guardian's tone was unyielding. "I'm following the kidnapper's demands to the letter this time. That's why you're here. You have the police experience without currently being a police officer."

Mitch let his posture silently inform G.D. that he was making a bad decision. "Anything else, boss?"

G.D. drilled him with his trademark dry-ice stare, but Mitch refused to be intimidated. "Keely will *not* be leaving the hotel. She'll stay with Juliana where she can be kept secure under the constant surveillance of a security team."

Mitch swore under his breath and resumed his pacing, picturing how Stef would react to that dictate. "I'm sure that will go over big with Mrs. Shelton."

"She doesn't have to like it. She just has to live with it. And, Mitch, I would never presume to tell a seasoned investigator how to do his job. But you might charm more information out of Mrs. Shelton if you were slightly less aggressive. You're not in L.A. anymore."

Mitch managed to keep his jaw from sagging like a door kicked off its hinges. "What, I'm not charming?"

G.D. laughed. "You call me G.D. and given your colorful vocabulary, I suspect it's not an abbreviation for The Guardian."

WHILE STEF WAS LOATH to leave Keely sleeping in the ladybug bed, she did. Questions were beginning to form in her heart as well as a need to prove her husband's innocence. She returned to the suite's luxurious sitting room as a butler pushed in a serving cart laden with sandwiches, fruit and soft drinks.

The sight of the butler gave Stef another case of the willies. Keely didn't need a butler or an army of servants looking after her, she needed her mommy.

The Guardian sat on one end of the plush sofa, his air of unquestionable authority both calming and intimidating. Juliana occupied the opposite corner of the sofa, her hands folded in her lap and her polished brown eyes darting anxiously between The Guardian and Mitch Halloran.

Mitch Halloran, on the other hand, prowled the room, munching on a sandwich he'd plucked from the cart. He reminded Stef of the TV detectives who ate donuts and drank coffee while attending a murder scene. But then she remembered what Mitch had told her about remaining detached from his work to prevent himself from drowning in alcohol or puking his guts out and she decided that it was okay that he was so overwhelmingly intense. So forceful.

He was wrong about Brad. But she wanted her baby back.

Mitch checked his stride as her gaze collided with his cobalt eyes, his expression forcibly softening around the edges like an ice sculpture melting in the glare of the sun. Stef was instantly on the defensive.

"How's Keely doing?" he asked.

Stef bit back the urge to say that her little girl wanted to go home, knowing that appeal would fall on deaf ears in this audience. "She's sleeping," she said tightly.

He tugged at his tie as if it were strangling his thick tanned throat. "Good. Sometimes it's hard for kids to settle down in strange places. I had trouble with that when I was a kid."

She shot him an abrasive glance that seemed to roll off his sleek perfection like a bead of oil on water. Mitch possessed more brash self-confidence than she'd ever encountered in a real-life man. And while his confidence was as irritating as his unabashed handsomeness, she realized to her dismay that she *was* listening to him, depending on him to deliver on the promises he'd uttered, even when a part of her was desperately afraid he'd fail her just as Brad had failed her so many times before.

He jerked a thumb at the serving cart. "Are you hungry? Would you like something to eat before we get started? A cup of coffee? The sandwiches are pretty good."

She twisted her fingers together, trying to read the thoughts behind the earnest appeal of his expression.

"Is this your 'good cop' routine? Offer me food and coffee so I'll confess that my husband was involved in a kidnapping scheme? I don't think so."

She experienced a bittersweet feeling of satisfaction as Mitch's jaw clenched and he transmitted a barely constrained message of pure frustration to The Guardian.

Juliana cleared her throat as if to intervene, but The Guardian silenced her with a lift of his hand.

Mitch sighed. "F.Y.I., I am a good cop. Or I *was* a good cop. Now I'm a damned good investigator who recognizes that people who are tired and hungry don't make good interview subjects because they aren't thinking clearly. You've had a shock today. You need to eat to keep up your strength."

Stef didn't know whether to burst into tears or to

scream in frustration. She marched to the cart and helped herself to two tuna sandwiches and a can of diet soda. Then she plopped down in an armchair across from the sofa, her green-gold eyes glittering and vulnerable. "Satisfied?"

Mitch felt the place in his chest where his heart should be crumble. He smiled at her in an effort to be charming, but he felt like gnashing his teeth in despair. He had a nasty intuitive feeling that he would never be satisfied when it came to this case. He might find Stef's real daughter, but her life would still be in emotional turmoil over Keely. There was no happy solution.

He dug into his questions. Charming might work for The Guardian, but it wasn't working for him. "How long did your husband work for Office Outfitters?"

"About seven years. It was his second job out of college. He was an assistant manager at one of the stores and worked his way up. He liked the team atmosphere—each store was a team and his job as regional manager was to keep the teams in his region happy and working well together."

"So he was loyal to the company?"

Stef lifted her chin and Mitch could feel her cold anger pulsating toward him in a wave. "Yes. Very. I don't think that's a crime."

Mitch ignored the gibe. "How well did he know his boss, Sable Holden?"

"They were on good terms. Brad respected her for turning the company around and he worked hard to live up to her expectations. She was a tough boss, but in a big sister kind of way. She wanted everyone to feel like the company was their extended family and that she cared about each and every one of them. She even called Brad from time to time after he was laid off to see if he'd had any luck finding a job.'' She paused and nibbled a corner of one of her sandwiches. Mitch sensed a *but* lurking in her.

"Say what you're thinking,'' he ordered.

Stef set the sandwich on the plate and stared at it, a frown creasing her brow. "I thought it was nice of her to call Brad. She was obviously shaken about the take-over and felt guilty that so many of her employees were fired. But knowing what I know now, is it possible that she had an ulterior motive for staying in touch with Brad? She knew when Keely was due—Brad was a typ-ical new dad, bragging to anyone who'd listen that he was going to be a father and that we were going to have a girl. Sable sent us a baby gift a few days after we came home from the hospital, so Brad must have called her when Keely was born.''

Mitch felt an adrenaline bomb ignite in his gut, along with a healthy dose of admiration for Stef. She might be grasping at straws trying to pin the kidnapping on Sable alone, but at least she was thinking. Cooperating.

He sat in the armchair next to hers, close enough that he could see the spatter of freckles across her upturned nose. Had her husband ever appreciated what an in-credible wife he'd had? "Did Brad find another job?''

Stef shook her head, her dark hair swinging in a glossy curtain around her pale face. "He tried, but he couldn't find something he felt passionate about.''

In Mitch's humble opinion, providing for your wife and child was a passionate enough motivation to find a job. Any job. But quite possibly Brad hadn't been job hunting as seriously as he'd claimed because he and Sable had come to an agreement about the split of the ransom. Maybe they'd even had a falling out that had resulted in that first ransom attempt being aborted.

He leaned over and touched her arm, feeling a corresponding tightness in his chest at the soft vulnerability of her skin. A wary prickle skated across the back of his neck warning him that he was allowing himself to get physically close to her again. "This will probably sound insensitive, but I'd like to know more about how your husband died because it could be important."

Her slender throat worked as she swallowed hard. "Rock climbing was one of his hobbies. He took it up after Office Outfitters sponsored a rock-climbing day to reward employees for good performance evaluations. Brad was one of the recipients. He got hooked and he kept it up to reduce stress. He went to the Giant's Kneecaps by himself to spend the afternoon—it's a popular place for climbers. But he was the only one there at the time. The police explained that he must have lost his hold and fallen. His head hit the rocks. They said he died instantly."

He gentled his tone, detecting the unbridled fear and the confusion his last question had created in her. "When did this happen?"

"Two months after Keely was born."

"Was there an autopsy?"

She took an uneven breath. "Yes. It ruled his death accidental. Why? What are you implying?"

Mitch met her gaze unflinchingly. "Let's look at the facts as we know them. Whoever snatched Riana exited the hospital from a second-floor window and rappelled to the ground. Then Riana was somehow switched with your daughter. A ransom demand is received by the Collingwoods, but it's aborted. Two months later your husband dies in a climbing accident under suspicious circumstances with no witnesses. You tell me how that adds up to you."

She jerked her arm free of his touch, the gold flecks in her eyes firing sparks. "You know, I'm really starting to hate you. You think Brad switched our daughter with Riana, then committed suicide because he couldn't live with himself?"

Across the room Mitch heard Juliana's soft gasp. He half expected The Guardian to intercede with a few charming three-syllable words. But he didn't.

Mitch hated what he was doing, too, but he had to keep pushing her. The kidnapper could make contact again at any time. At least he'd gotten Stef to voice her worst possible fears. She'd known her husband better than anyone.

"Suicide is one possible explanation," he admitted. "Or maybe someone helped him fall."

Chapter Four

"Peekaboo!" The kidnapper awoke to a boisterous shout and the insistent tugging of tiny fingers on the blankets.

"Emma? What are you doing up at this hour?" the kidnapper mumbled sleepily. Good grief, it wasn't even dawn yet. Through a half-raised eyelid the kidnapper noticed the little girl was wearing a crown on her head and a chunky bead necklace over her nightgown. On the edge of the bed was a small pile of picture books.

"Read me a story?"

The kidnapper groaned. How had she gotten in here without Uncle Fred or Aunt Alice noticing? The kid was worth billions of dollars and she was running around loose. "Go back to bed, Emma. It's too early for stories."

Emma behaved as if she didn't understand English.

The kidnapper tried to ignore her and drift back to sleep. But Emma climbed onto the bed chattering gibberish about stories and horsies. Before the kidnapper was fully cognizant of what was happening, she'd looped her necklace around the bedpost and was riding astride the kidnapper's hip, giggling, "Giddy up!"

A split second later the necklace broke and beads scattered onto the pine floorboards in all directions.

Wailing, Emma jumped off the bed onto the floor with a thunk that made the old floorboards shake and the beads rattle. ''Mine! No!'' She crouched, trying to gather the beads in her tiny hands.

Stifling an urge to yell, the kidnapper threw back the covers and turned on the bedside lamp. Shouting wouldn't make Emma's screeching stop. This brat had been one complication after another since day one. Life would have been much simpler, and much different, if the first ransom attempt hadn't been aborted.

The kidnapper thought back to the day of the Collingwoods' funeral. There had been too many wasted frustrating days spent agonizing over what could have been. What could still be—despite everything—thanks to a generous infusion of Ross Collingwood's money.

The plan was coming together, each part carefully examined for flaws and fitted into the master plan. The kidnapper knew The Guardian would follow the ransom instructions to the letter. He wouldn't involve the police or risk Riana's life. Not after the last time.

The kidnapper shushed Riana. ''Don't cry, Emma. I'll help you pick up the beads. I'm sure Gamma can put them back on the string and make your necklace good as new.''

Big crocodile tears stretched down Emma's cheeks as she lifted her face trustingly toward the kidnapper. Her lower lip jutted out like a river bank, stopping the flow of moisture. ''There's a good girl.''

Together they crawled across the floor gathering the beads into a cheap plastic beer mug that had held pens on the desk.

Emma tried to squeeze her fingers underneath the

curved front of the dresser. "There's some under there!" she cried, sniffling. "I can't reach."

"Don't cry. I'll move the dresser. Stay back."

The kidnapper hefted the ugly maple dresser to one side. As Emma pounced on the stray beads like a kitten pursuing a shadow the kidnapper noticed the jagged line of a saw mark in a plank where the dresser used to stand. The plank was about six inches wide and twenty inches long and there wasn't one nail in it. If someone had lifted the plank to repair a pipe or wiring in the space between the floor joists, he'd done a sloppy job.

The kidnapper knew Uncle Fred, a professional electrician, hadn't cut that floorboard. Uncle Fred and Aunt Alice's son had done it. And he'd probably had something to hide.

The kidnapper took Emma by the hand. "Come on, Emma. You want to watch cartoons?"

Emma hopped like a bunny. "No cartoons. I want Little Mermaid!"

"Okay, but you have to be real quiet so you don't wake Gamma and Pappy."

After settling Emma in front of the TV with some juice and a handful of cereal, the kidnapper returned upstairs and used a dinner knife to lift the plank.

A shoe box was concealed in the space under the floor.

The kidnapper removed the lid of the box. Damn! Leave it to that stupid SOB to leave evidence lying around.

The box contained a handgun, ammunition, a stun gun, several types of hospital identification bracelets and a birth announcement torn from a newspaper with the names circled. "Bradley and Stephanie Shelton of

Queens, New York, are thrilled to announce the birth of their first child, a daughter, Keely Jane Shelton.''

The kidnapper noticed the date of the child's birth and the name of the hospital and smelled a double cross.

The child downstairs was not Riana Collingwood.

HAD BRAD been murdered?

Stef recoiled from Mitch in horror, wanting to hit his sensual mouth and break a few of his very perfect teeth. She'd vowed to love, honor and cherish Brad, not suspect him of being a criminal.

Stef squeezed her fingers into tight fists assailed by soul-crushing doubts about the man she'd loved. Had Brad even had an interview the morning after Keely and Riana had been switched? Or was it a story to cover his tracks? Maybe all the job interviews he'd supposedly gone to were fictitious.

She couldn't even believe she was entertaining the idea that her husband had been involved in Riana Collingwood's kidnapping. But to not do so might put her baby's life at risk, might delay finding her.

"Why would someone want to kill Brad?" she choked.

Mitch's cobalt gaze didn't waver from her face. "Because he had a falling out with whoever he was working with. It's the most logical reason. He'd switched the babies, but his accomplice obviously didn't know that. There was one ransom attempt three days after the abduction, but it was aborted. The falling out could have occurred then. There might have been an argument over when to initiate a second demand and what to do with the child. Or the falling out could have happened later when Brad began to get anxious with the unanticipated delay."

"It was a high-profile crime," The Guardian elaborated. "There was a lot of pressure on the police to apprehend the abductors. A decision may have been made to lie low for a few weeks until the pressure cooled. Your husband may have been trying to learn where his daughter was being held, which roused his accomplice's suspicions. It's very important, Mrs. Shelton, that we keep an open mind and consider every possibility, no matter how terribly painful those possibilities may be."

"I assure you my mind is wide open," Stef said, digging in her heels and glancing from Mitch to The Guardian. They were like night and day, in manner and looks. The Guardian was dark and coolly controlled. Mitch was blond and explosively intense. "I'm just wondering why you aren't considering the possibility that Sable switched the babies without Brad's knowledge? Do you know something I don't?"

Mitch cleared his throat. "Trust us, Sable is high on the suspect list. And now that we know Brad learned to climb through a company-sponsored program, we'll nose around and find out how knowledgeable Sable is about the sport. But Riana's kidnapper was definitely male—brown hair, medium height, medium build. The nurse got a glimpse of him before he zapped her with a stun gun."

Nausea swirled in Stef's stomach. The description fit Brad. He hadn't been an in-your-face kind of guy. She couldn't imagine him striking a woman. Using a stun gun suited his passive-aggressive nature.

"I see," she said. Was she imagining it or were Mitch's eyes softening, offering her encouragement? She felt the fight ebbing out of her, reality sinking in.

"What was Brad's frame of mind after you brought

Keely home from the hospital? Did he behave like one would expect a new dad to behave? Did he seem stressed?''

She licked her dry lips, experiencing a jab of pain as she remembered the look on Brad's face when the doctor had announced that they had a baby daughter. Had there been something significant in his reaction?

''Brad was disappointed that Keely wasn't a boy, even though we'd had an ultrasound and knew we were having a girl. The first week or so he was really nervous about holding her—especially bathing her or changing her diapers. I thought he was finally feeling the responsibility of being a parent, but we didn't talk about it. I mean, he was unemployed and he needed to find a job to support his family. Talking about it would have only put more pressure on him. But you only have to look at a picture of him holding her to see how much he loved Keely.''

She couldn't tell what kind of impression her answer made on Mitch. His cobalt eyes shielded his thoughts. But she found strength and comfort from the squared width of his shoulders and the determination etched in his jaw. He was going to bring her baby home no matter what, wasn't he?

''Was he depressed? Showing signs of not sleeping, not eating, not bothering to get dressed?''

''A little,'' she admitted reluctantly. ''I went back to work when Keely was five weeks old and Brad was home taking care of Keely in a little two-bedroom co-op. But I think new mothers experience that—the day goes by and you're still in your pajamas because the baby is fussy. Brad found the isolation hard to deal with.'' She didn't mention that she'd found it difficult to return home to find her husband anxious to escape their baby when she would give anything to be the one staying home caring for Keely. "I tried to give him lots of free time when I was home. He'd play pickup basketball or meet a buddy for a beer. Sometimes he'd go biking or rock climbing."

"How were things at home the days before the accident?"

Guilt swirled in Stef's belly. Having a new baby was overwhelming. Could she have done more to help Brad cope with the pressure? She'd been exhausted, too, trying to nurse Keely around her flight schedule. "Keely had had a cold and was up a couple of nights in a row. Brad was edgy and had cabin fever. He was waiting for me at the door when I got home. He wanted to go rock climbing so I shooed him out the door and asked him to buy diapers on the way home."

Mitch nodded as if he were memorizing all her answers, taking them apart and analyzing them. "Here's another one of those tough questions. Take a breath before answering if you need to, okay? Did he say anything to you or kiss you goodbye in a way that might suggest he knew he wasn't coming home?"

Tears scalded Stef's eyes. She gulped twice before replying. "No. He didn't do either of those things. Or leave a note. He just took off. That's why I don't think he committed suicide. The police didn't seem to think so, either, because they asked me some questions like that."

Juliana had materialized at Stef's side with a box of tissues. Her brown eyes were warm and compassionate and she deflected Mitch's frown for interrupting his interrogation with a try-and-stop-me look. Stef was really beginning to like her, especially when Juliana proceeded to sit on the coffee table, visibly aligning herself with Stef in a show of emotional support.

Mitch flicked his gaze uncertainly from Juliana to Stef, and back to The Guardian. Stef almost laughed when The Guardian shrugged his shoulders as if he wished Mitch luck for pitting himself against two females.

The ex-detective focused again on Stef. "Did Brad have life insurance?"

"Yes. One of the guys he plays basketball with sold him a two-hundred-and-fifty-thousand-dollar policy as soon as Brad told him we were expecting."

Stef stilled a twinge that that purchase had been a little out of character for Brad. But it wasn't a huge sum of money. A house cost more than two hundred thousand dollars these days.

"I'll need the date the policy was purchased."

She wrapped her arms around herself, feeling cold and tired. "Of course. I can give it to you."

Something warm patted her knee. Mitch's hand. The heat from it traveled up to her core, warming her from the inside out. "I think you've had enough for tonight. Get some rest for tomorrow. We've got a lot to do."

"Such as?"

"Visiting Sable. I hope you're a good actress."

Stef smiled thinly. "I think I can rise to the occasion." All that experience of telling passengers the beige lump on their meal tray was chicken ought to count for something. "I'll say just about anything to save my baby."

ANNETTE YORK had plenty of time in prison to think about her defense. And plenty of time to think about Darren.

After everything she'd gone through, she was *not* going to be executed for Ross's and Lexi's murders. Not when she'd been so close to having everything that had belonged to Lexi. The prosecution had very little corroborative evidence—she'd been too smart to leave a trail.

And the butler's daughter would be foolish to take the stand to testify against her, especially when Annette's lawyer could force her to reveal the reason for her marriage to Hunter Sinclair—and Cort's true identity. Oh, yes, the media would have a field day with that information!

Goody Two-shoes Juliana wouldn't put a helpless little baby in danger. Cort might be abducted like his older sister had been.

What Annette needed was a messenger she could trust to deliver a warning to Juliana. Who she needed was Darren.

She'd trusted him more than she'd ever trusted another man in her life. He'd loved her, thought she was beautiful and had begged her to be his wife.

Sometimes in those transitional moments just before she fell asleep or just as she was waking up, she thought of him. Remembered how soft the brush of his beard was against her fingers. Against her breasts. Remembered the warm fervent kisses they'd shared and the way his hazel eyes had lit up when he entered a room and spotted her.

That she'd missed the most.

She closed her eyes to blot out the pain of seeing Darren at the funeral. She'd hurt him again when she'd brushed him off. She knew he didn't understand why she couldn't marry him. But she couldn't hurt him by listing all the reasons he couldn't be her husband. None of which had mattered to her until Lexi had come home pregnant and engaged to a billionaire. And Darren, a college mathematician, had suddenly ceased to measure up to Annette's mother's high standards.

Annette sighed and brushed at a tear gathering in her eyelashes. Her parents were dead now, as were Ross and Lexi. With Cort still alive, she wouldn't get the Collingwood fortune, but an acquittal would leave her free to reap a satisfactory amount of attention off this tragedy. Convince the world that she'd been a victim, too. Her lawyer had already received five offers for movie deals.

And there was always Darren.

He'd never belonged to Lexi.

And somehow the old dream of being his wife, having his children—children whom she'd love equally with all her heart, seemed the one true course of action. She'd hoped he might visit her in prison, but he hadn't.

She'd get her lawyer to arrange an interview with that journalist from the *New York Times*. She knew just how to summon Darren to her aid.

STEF SURPRISED MITCH by coming up with an impressive cover story. He never would have thought of it himself, but it fit Stef Shelton and it sounded genuine.

An air of nervousness hovered in Stef's overbright smile as the elevator rose at warp speed to the seventeenth floor of the Collingwood Corporation's offices in the heart of the financial district. Her black leather coat open, Stef looked gorgeous and sassy in a short turquoise sweater dress with a soft cowl neck and black leather boots that laced up to her calves. A black leather belt was slung provocatively across her hips and caught the eye of every hot-blooded male they passed, including Mitch's. He had to look hard beneath the makeup and the color brushed on to her cheeks to see the freckles that sometimes made her look as though she were still a vulnerable teenager.

A slender brunette wearing a caramel wool pantsuit and a jewelry store heist around her neck, waited for them at the reception desk. They'd had to call up to Sable's office from the lobby and were each given a visitor's pass. The Guardian had increased security measures in the building since the explosion that had killed the Collingwoods.

Sable greeted Stef with the effusive smile of a talk show host and gave her an air kiss. Mitch instantly pegged her for a cobra. Sleek, spitting and dangerous.

Stef flushed becomingly. "Thank you for seeing me on such short notice." Mitch thought a man could spend a lifetime watching the color spill over her cheeks like the first blush of the sun touching the sky, before he caught himself and obliterated the thought.

"I really should have called sooner," Stef said, sweetly apologetic.

Sable waved a manicured hand studded with enough diamonds to cut a plate-glass window. "Nonsense, I'm happy to see you. Though I'm afraid it'll be a brief visit. I have a meeting in twenty minutes." She turned unusual silvery eyes on Mitch. "Who's your handsome escort?"

Mitch felt as if he'd been laid out spread-eagle on the carpet with metal stakes driven through his hands and feet.

"This is Evan Mitchell. He's a biographer."

Sable's plucked brows rose. "Really? How interesting."

Stef didn't miss a beat. She glanced uncertainly at

Mitch. "Well, I hope you still feel that way when I tell you the reason for my visit."

Sable gave a throaty laugh. "Now I'm definitely intrigued. Come into my office. How's Keely? Do you have pictures?"

Mitch ceased worrying about Stef's ability to pull this off when she produced a cache of pictures from her purse. She didn't have to act to be a proud, adoring mom. "What kind of mother would I be if I didn't have pictures? She was so cute in her Halloween costume this year. I sewed it for her. She was an orange-striped tabby. She's so cute."

"I'll bet."

Stef dealt Sable a small stack of photos as if they were playing cards.

Sable slowly sifted through the pictures as they traveled down a hallway appointed with a series of watercolor landscapes of the New York City skyline. "O-oh, she's adorable. I'll bet she keeps you busy."

Mitch thought he detected a note of envy in Sable's voice. But maybe, Sable, like him, recognized a mother who truly loved being a mother. God, had his mother ever carried his picture in her wallet? Or had she thrown his school pictures away like she'd thrown him away? His jaw clenched with iron-hard determination to rescue Stef's little girl. Give her a mommy who'd appreciate every wonder of her budding life. Every child deserved that.

Sable gestured toward a door. "Here's my office. Please, sit. Can I offer you some coffee?"

"No, thank you. We're fine," Stef assured her as they each took a seat in the brocade-covered chairs clustered around Sable's ornately carved desk. Mitch suspected the gold leaf on the desk was as genuine as the gold chains around her neck. "Now, before I begin, I just want to say that I know you're busy and I'll completely understand if you say no to my request."

A guarded smile hovered on Sable's lips. "So noted. Spell it out for me."

"It's an idea that I had for Keely so she'd know her dad, know who he was." Stef began haltingly. "I wanted to give her a book about Brad's life. A biography, actually. And I've asked Evan to write it."

Sable eased back in her chair and Mitch felt her eyes slide over his torso as if she were slathering oil on him. He gave her an encouraging smile.

The cobra had the audacity to touch the tip of her tongue to her upper lip. "What a thoughtful idea, Stephanie. But I'm still unclear as to how I can help."

"I was hoping you'd be willing to write something about Brad—stories, anecdotes. Or allow Evan to interview you if you'd prefer to do it that way. It would only have to be a few pages. Brad enjoyed his work at Office Outfitters so much—it was a big part of his life. I thought you would know his history with the company better than anyone."

A shadow of pain—or regret—flickered through Sable's silvery eyes. "Brad was a good man—irreplaceable as far as I was concerned, but that's water under the bridge now. Of course I'll be happy to contribute something—for Keely."

Stef's smile was irresistible. "That would be wonderful, Sable! Oh, and I was also hoping that you might be able to give me the names of other people Brad worked with. Maybe some of them would be willing to contribute a story, as well."

"Hmm." Sable paused, considering. "Your request should really be made through Simon Findlay. He's the

Director of Human Resources and Corporate Relations. But he's only going to quote you some rules and say no.'' She pulled a face. ''Mixing personal pursuits with work is an alien concept around here, but things are lightening up a bit now that Kendrick Dwyer is our new CEO. There are rumors circulating at the espresso machine that he gave David Younge, the guy who replaced Ken as Chief Financial Officer, a month's personal leave to be with his family. So maybe there's some humanity yet to be had in this company.''

Mitch felt Sable's gaze drift back to him. ''How about we do this, Evan? I'll give you a few names as long as you promise to talk to the employees during their breaks and don't make a pest of yourself. I'll have my secretary prepare a list and fax or e-mail it to you by the end of the day. And maybe we can meet for drinks and I'll share what I can about Brad. Writing is not one of my strengths.''

Mitch had a feeling one of her strengths was sharing body parts. He pulled a business card from his pocket, complete with a cover address, phone number and e-mail address provided by The Guardian's amazing resources. He turned on the wattage, feeling as if he were in a pickup bar. ''How about I call you later and we'll arrange a convenient time?''

Sable took the card with a female purr. ''I'll look forward to it.''

Stef rose from her chair. ''We should really be going. Thank you, Sable. From me and Keely. You know she loves that blanket you sent. It's her special blanket.''

''I'm glad.''

Stef turned wide green-gold eyes on Mitch. ''Evan, would you mind waiting outside in the hall? I just wanted to share one private thing with Sable.''

Mitch didn't like this unscheduled change in plans, but he had no choice but to acquiesce. "Sure, no problem. Nice meeting you, Sable. I look forward to our interview."

He ducked out into the hall and paced a path in the carpet. What the hell was Stef up to?

STEF'S HEART beat double time as the door closed behind Mitch, granting her a few moment's privacy with Sable. He was probably going to be furious with her for this, but she didn't care. Brad was her husband. She had every right to ask questions and to find out the truth.

"He's a catch. Hunky *and* cerebral. Are you and Evan involved?" Sable asked, leaning back in her chair.

Stef blinked, taken aback. It was bad enough she was attracted to Mitch. Sleeping with him was out of the question. He was making it his personal obsession to destroy her life. "Definitely not. It's too soon, anyway."

"Not that I'm not happy about your answer," Sable said slyly, "but it's been well over two years since Brad died."

"Actually, that was what I wanted to talk to you about privately, Sable. Brad's death."

Stef felt perspiration dot her brow. Was it her imagination or did Sable look slightly on edge? But it was too late to be a coward about this. She had to find out if Brad had been involved in what happened to their baby. "I was wondering when you saw Brad last and what he was like."

Sable tilted her head to one side and frowned. "I can't remember the precise date. We had a beer somewhere and he showed me pictures of Keely's birth. I was concerned he hadn't found another job yet and I was trying to encourage him. I gave him glowing references.''

''I know. You were very supportive. It's just…'' Stef paused, struggling to find the right words.

Sable touched Stef's arm. ''Talk to me. It's just what?''

''The police think his death was an accident, but I can't help wondering if Brad killed himself.'' Scalding emotion tightened Stef's throat and brought a hot rush of tears to her eyes. ''Did Brad seem depressed to you?''

''I think discouraged would be more accurate. Did you find a note or anything that would suggest he would do something like that?''

Stef wondered if Sable was a little too interested in her answer. She jammed her hands into the pockets of her coat. ''No, nothing. But I can't help thinking that he may not have been seriously looking for work and was spending a lot of time wallowing in self-pity about the takeover.''

''He wasn't the only one, Stef,'' Sable said. ''But climbing is a high-risk activity. Maybe Brad was too distracted by his problems to be climbing that day.''

''You really think that's all it was?''

The chains around Sable's neck rattled as she enveloped Stef in a hug clouded with perfume. ''I'm sure that's all it was. Brad had a lot to live for.''

STEF UNDERESTIMATED Mitch's wrath when she joined him in the hallway. A white-toothed grin plastered on his handsome face, he hooked his hand beneath her elbow and propelled her to the bank of elevators. But she could feel the intensity inside him waiting to explode.

The explosion came as he whisked her inside an

empty elevator car and hit the button for the lobby. He backed her up against the side wall and planted his hands on either side of her face. Anger ignited his cobalt eyes as his towering strength loomed over her. "What the hell was that stunt you just pulled? Do you *want* to lose your daughter?"

Stef flinched, her stomach lurching as the elevator began its rapid descent. "No! I just—"

"You just what?" he breathed in a dangerous tone that scraped over her emotions like a plane, leaving her raw and bleeding. "What did you say to her?"

"I told her I was worried that Brad killed himself."

Mitch swore. "What did she say?"

Stef's shoulders arced into a taut bow and her arms trembled at her sides as she recounted the conversation.

She could see Mitch thinking, his eyes flashing, his head nodding as he absorbed and processed every word. "Okay, this could be salvageable. I'd be a lot happier if you hadn't mentioned you were questioning Brad's death. If Sable's involved, it could make her suspicious of our visit today. But from what you told me, she may think she convinced you that Brad's fall was accidental."

Tears of helplessness overwhelmed Stef. "I'm sorry! I thought Brad might have been hiding his feelings from me and that he may have confided in Sable. It's driving me crazy wondering whether he was involved in this and if he took his own life. *I loved him. He was my husband.*"

"I know." To her surprise, Mitch lowered his forehead until it touched hers like a hot brand. His voice broke, the sound fracturing her heart. She felt the drive in him pulse from his body to hers. Her bones sagged as she felt his own fight to maintain control, to be in charge. "I know this is driving you crazy. But, Stef, let me make the decisions here." Agony ravaged his voice as the elevator continued to drop downward. "You don't want to know what it feels like to have a child's death on your conscience."

Chapter Five

She shoved her palms against his chest as if demanding he release her. He could feel her hate, her anger directed at him for saying those terrible, callous words. "How could you say such a horrible thing to me?'

"Because it's the truth, and I want you to remember that before you decide to do anything else on your own," he said bluntly, dropping his arms and stepping back as the elevator touched down in the lobby with a faint jerking motion. In the split second before the elevator doors slid open he was sucked into the maelstrom of emotions swirling in Stef's beautiful face. Fear immobilized him. Tangible, my-emotions-are-spinning-away-from-me fear that had no place in an investigation. He couldn't afford to lose his detachment on this case.

Couldn't afford to even let himself think about how it might feel to have a woman like Stef Shelton in his life. The kind of woman who could tell a child a story at the drop of a hat, who sewed Halloween costumes and who stood by the man she'd loved and married. And who looked incredibly sexy in short skirts and black lace-up leather boots. He couldn't afford to let himself wonder what it might be like to comfort her.

He didn't want another child's death on his conscience.

Stef stormed past him out of the elevator, leaving him feeling lost and alone with the lingering scent of her hair. He caught up with her in the lobby, careful not to touch her as they exited onto the street. He hailed a taxi, rattling off an address to the driver. A chopper was standing by to take them back to Logantown. Stef had agreed to let him search through her husband's belongings, which she'd stored away for Keely.

She caught him looking at her and jabbed an elbow into his ribs. "I won't do it again. I promise," she said.

Mitch grunted and ran a hand over his face. He hadn't slept much in the past week. "I know you won't. You're a smart lady."

He saw her swallow hard and the heart painted on her fingernail disappear into her clenched fist. He tore his gaze away from her fragile, hunched form, to look at the sea of cabs hemming them in on the crowded avenue.

"Mitch?"

He risked glancing back at her. Her eyes were huge and reflected something he didn't want to see—a combination of pity, compassion and fear. As if he were not quite human. Damn. "Yeah?"

"Do you have something like that on your conscience?"

Mitch felt something inside him tilt off center as a rush of regret hit him like a locomotive at full throttle. He'd never told anyone how he felt about Carmen Lopez's death. As far as the department was concerned, he'd done a good job on the case. He'd figured out who'd taken her and the family had recovered a body. Case closed. The chances of recovering a kidnap victim alive were slim. But Mitch always wanted more. Against all odds, he often succeeded.

He debated telling her the truth, wondering if, as the women he dated, she'd retreat as soon as he gave her a straight answer. He sighed. He wanted her to retreat, grant him distance, didn't he? "I've been a cop for a long time. There are a lot of cases I wish could have ended differently."

Moisture shone in her eyes. She lightly stroked his arm. "I'm sorry. I wish I'd never met you, but I do trust you. I don't know why you became a cop but I'm glad you're here…because I'm so scared."

The wavering in her voice nearly undid him. Mitch wanted to thread his fingers through her silky hair and pull her head to rest against him. He flexed his fingers, his mind battling his emotions with *stay detached* orders.

His cell phone rang. Mitch eased his arm from beneath her stirring touch and flicked the cell phone on, thanking his lucky stars for the interruption. "Halloran, here."

Keely's voice, tiny and demanding, came over the line. "I want my mommy."

Mitch felt a tight smile work his lips. Like mother, like daughter. They both despised him. "Sure thing, Keely. She's right here."

He handed Stef the phone. "It's for you."

Stef shot him a worried glance and snatched the phone from his hand. "Kee, is that you, baby?"

Mitch tried to turn deaf ears to Stef's conversation as she reassured her daughter that they'd be back soon and asked questions about a tea party Keely was having with Juliana. Even when she was frightened to death and was faced with losing the child she'd raised, Stef made the world of being a mommy sound extraordinarily wonderful. ''You're eating pink cakes and jelly beans? Oh, Kee, that's so unfair! Mommy's getting very hungry just thinking about pink cakes and jelly beans.'' Stef's voice grew strangled. ''I'm glad you think Juliana's nice, Kee. Have fun! Mommy loves you a whole bunch. Save one of those pink cakes for me and a green jelly bean.'' She rolled her eyes at Mitch. ''And maybe a black jelly bean for Mitch.''

She turned her shoulder to him and dropped her voice. ''I *know* the black ones are yucky, but we don't have to tell *him* that.''

Mitch smothered a grin. He happened to like black jelly beans. Stef disconnected the call and handed the phone back to him. ''How about that?'' she said, her voice still strangely tight. ''My daughter's wearing a real princess dress and enjoying a tea party with pink cakes and jelly beans without me.''

Mitch didn't hesitate to pull her into his arms when her shoulders crumpled and she started to cry. She felt so fragile he was worried he'd crush her if he held her too tightly. He smoothed a trembling hand through her silky dark hair and promised himself he'd do anything, absolutely anything, to bring her back her real daughter.

He didn't think he could bear it if he didn't.

SABLE TAPPED her pen on her desk, her thoughts dwelling on Brad Shelton's death. Seeing his widow today had been a shock. When Stephanie had asked her how Brad had seemed before his death, Sable had been afraid that she might know something. Might suspect that her meetings with Brad had been something other than helping him find new employment.

Sable took a sheet of engraved stationery from her

desk drawer and wrote a short list of names. It was the least she could do. She'd always believed in rewarding loyalty. And Brad had been loyal, if not patient.

Not that Sable blamed him.

She'd been impatient to humble Ross Collingwood, too, to ruin his life as he'd ruined hers. Even though Ross and his oh-so-sweet wife were dead, Sable was still impatient to regain complete control of the company that she'd created with her blood, sweat and ambition.

Sable reread the list. She'd have her secretary provide the store contact numbers and fax it to that to-die-for writer, Evan Mitchell. Now there was a man, like Ross, who'd be a challenge worthy of her.

Sable had never walked away from a challenge. She had to know if Brad had left behind any evidence that was fueling Stephanie's fears.

ALTHOUGH THE SHELTONS had moved, it didn't take the kidnapper long to locate their new address in Logantown, Pennsylvania, on the Internet. The cute message from "Stef and Keely" on the answering machine confirmed it.

After lurking in the shrubbery outside the modest house for more than an hour, the kidnapper was convinced that no one was home. Maybe the kid went to day care.

It was child's play to gain access to the house. The kidnapper found a key tucked in the decorative birdhouse nailed to the wall of the garage.

Silence greeted the opening of the front door. So much the better that there were no dogs or other four-legged creatures to get in the way. The kidnapper threw the dead bolt back into place.

Handgun at the ready and heart thundering at the possible risk of discovery, the kidnapper moved through the house, learning the layout of the rooms and planning the best route to get inside late tonight to snatch the child.

On the mantel in the living room, the kidnapper discovered a cluster of photos. Saw a laughing, dark-haired child taking her first steps, blowing out a candle on her first birthday cake and filling a bucket with sand on a beach. Keely. Riana.

The kidnapper swiped the beach photo.

The little girl's bedroom was located beside the master bedroom. The kidnapper paused inside the door of the pastel-striped room and noted the proximity of the sliding-aluminum window to the twin bed piled with kitten-theme pillows. The kidnapper unlocked the window, then lowered the pink Roman blind a few inches to cover the latch.

Now all that was needed was a DNA sample. The kidnapper went into the bathroom and took one of Keely's hair elastics that had several strands of Keely's hair knotted around it.

The kidnapper had pocketed the elastic and was about to leave when the sound of a key being inserted into the front door lock snickered through the house.

A palm damp with sweat gripped the handgun more tightly. The kidnapper hid in the bathtub behind the folds of a Paris in Springtime shower curtain. Maybe an opportunity to snatch Keely had just presented itself.

HER DAUGHTER was playing princess and having a tea party in a swank hotel and Stef was coming home without her to search for evidence that her husband had been a criminal. Stef knew she was hanging on by a thread with a little help from Mitch.

She took a deep breath as she entered her home, remembering the salty citrus scent of Mitch's skin when he'd held her in the taxi earlier. He was wrenching Keely from her life but she'd found unexpected comfort and strength in his arms. How incongruent was that?

An image of Keely decked out in a princess dress rooted in Stef's mind as she stood in the entryway and saw her home through fresh eyes. Saw the plump cushions, the books and the splashes of color that she loved. Her home was comfortable, but nothing compared to what the Collingwood riches could provide. Her chest grew unbearably tight. She couldn't let thoughts like this overtake her!

She felt the warm squeeze of Mitch's fingers on her shoulder. "You still with me, Stef?" he asked.

She squared her shoulders and opened her eyes, her breath catching in her throat when she saw the cobalt of Mitch's eyes reflect concern. He was so handsome, his skin a rich mocha against the crisp blue collar of his shirt, which still bore the stains of her tears. She knew every muscle beneath his navy suit jacket was rock-solid.

"Yes, I'm with you."

"Good girl."

"Sexist pig."

Mitch laughed, his mouth easing into a grin that she found incredibly irresistible. "That's more like it, spitfire. Stay tough. Where are these boxes of yours?"

"In the cellar." Stef set her purse on the hall table amid a decorative arrangement of fall leaves, then removed her jacket and hung it near the door. "I kept his laptop, too. But that's in the TV alcove. I know there are a lot of Office Outfitters files still on the hard drive. I never got around to deleting them.''

"Let's start with the boxes in the cellar,'' Mitch suggested, hanging his blazer beside her coat. "We can take the laptop back to New York with us.''

Stef warily eyed the gun tucked into the holster on his right hip. Please God, she didn't want anybody to get hurt. She just wanted her baby back.

Mitch touched the gun. "Got a problem with my friend?''

"Not as long as you play with him by yourself,'' Stef said, giving the gun a wide berth as she headed for the alcove to grab the computer bag and the laptop.

"You're not the first woman who's said that to me.''

"Really?'' she called back over her shoulder. She couldn't imagine many women being happy to have a loaded gun in their homes. "I'll bet you even have a name for him.''

"Sure, it's Scout. Which way is the cellar?''

Stef reached for the laptop and prayed it wouldn't prove the worst fear in her heart. "Ask Scout.''

NEW YORK?

Gun still drawn, the kidnapper huddled in the bathtub until the second set of footsteps had descended the cellar stairs. Keely wasn't with them. They said they were going back to New York. Was Keely in New York, as well? Where?

The kidnapper slowly crept out of the bathroom and down the hall toward the front door. The cellar entrance was in the kitchen at the rear of the house.

Stephanie's purse on the hall table gave the kidnapper pause. As did the coats hanging on the rack by the door. The kidnapper searched the pockets of the jackets first.

In the breast pocket of the navy blazer the kidnapper found a plastic hotel key card—for the Clairmont Hotel.

The name seemed vaguely familiar, but the kidnapper couldn't place it.

The kidnapper reached for the purse on the table. Key cards were usually provided to guests inside a paper sleeve marked with the room number. As the kidnapper groped through the contents of the black leather purse, a tube of lipstick clattered to the parquet floor.

The kidnapper winced. Had the sound been loud enough to be heard downstairs?

Not willing to take a chance on being caught, the kidnapper propped the bag on the table so it looked as if it had fallen on its side, then quickly eased the front door open and left the house.

Armed with a key card and a picture of Keely, how hard could it be to find one little girl in a hotel?

"DID YOU HEAR SOMETHING?" Mitch froze, his head cocked to one side as his ears strained to identify the sound he'd just heard.

"I—"

He silenced Stef by laying a finger over her lips.

The floorboards overhead creaked. Was that a footstep? It was different from the first sound.

"Stay here. I'm going up," he mouthed to Stef.

Pulling the Smith & Wesson Chief's Special from his holster, he moved up the basement stairs, keeping to the outer edge of the treads.

Stef had left the door open into the kitchen. Mitch paused at the top for a half beat, listening, then, with his back to the door frame, he moved in a slow semicircle into the kitchen at a crouch, arms extended ready to fire, his eyes scanning the room.

Moving with the silent grace of a predator, he stole across the kitchen and peered around the corner into the hall. A tube of lipstick lay on the parquet floor as if it had fallen from Stef's purse on the table above. Was that what he'd heard? Unwilling to take a chance on being wrong, Mitch stealthily moved through the house to sweep each room for intruders....

Stef was going crazy waiting for Mitch to come back. An eerie silence stretched over the house like the drawn-out squeak of a hinge. The thought of Mitch being armed and confronting an intruder was almost as frightening as the thought of someone breaking into her home. What if she and Keely had been home alone this morning?

Her knees wobbled. What if the intruder was armed? Mitch was alone upstairs. Shouldn't he have backup?

Stef looked for a weapon. Brad's softball bat projected from a box. She eased it free and crept toward the stairs. She could call the police from the kitchen.

She'd made it halfway up the stairs, moving as carefully as Mitch had, when his frame suddenly filled the doorway. Stef had never thought she could be so glad to see him. His gun was back in the holster.

"False alarm," he told her, nonchalant. "Your purse tipped over on the table and something fell onto the floor. I checked the house and there's nobody lurking in the closets or under the beds. But I locked a few windows just for kicks." He paused as she lowered the bat and sagged against the hand railing. "What were you planning to do with that bat?"

"I was going to protect you," Stef said stiffly.

She clenched her teeth as Mitch's rich laughter echoed down the stairwell. "With that little bat?"

He jogged down the stairs and snagged the bat from

her fingers. Although laughter lit his face, his eyes were dark and solemn. "I appreciate the thought, truly I do. But seriously, I could have seen the mean end of that bat before I saw you. Keely would give me a handful of black jelly beans if I hurt her mommy."

Stef found herself laughing. He was incorrigible and cocky and totally capable of protecting himself and her, and Keely. She hadn't felt this safe since her father had carried her to the hospital after she'd fallen off her bike and broken her ankle. "So you don't think I'm ready for the police academy, huh?"

He lightly traced the curve of her cheek, the pad of his thumb warm and calloused against her skin, and Stef felt her pulse race to meet his touch.

"Don't sell yourself short." His mouth slid into an appealing grin, part devil, part seducer. "You'd be great in undercover assignments. No one could look at your face and not think you were on the up and up. That was an ingenious cover story you laid on Sable this morning."

Stef felt a glow light within her. Okay, she had done one or two things right to help find her daughter. And she'd never countermand another of Mitch's orders.

She tucked her hair behind her ears and scooted past him down the stairs. "There are a couple of boxes near the workbench that we haven't checked yet. I gave away Brad's clothes but I kept a lot of his personal things. He was estranged from his parents. I thought if they ever made contact I could share some things with them, too."

She threaded her way around Keely's old crib and her highchair, aware of Mitch following close behind. The cellar's low pipe-lined ceiling made him seem larger than life. Goose bumps prickled her arms as she pointed at two sealed cartons. "These had Brad's brief-case, tools and unidentified male stuff in them."

Mitch's eyebrows rose as he lifted one of the boxes onto the workbench. "'Unidentified male stuff'?"

"You know, boy toys. Gadgets that look like tools but you can't figure out what they could possibly fix. Brad got a lot of promo gifts from suppliers."

Mitch opened the carton with a box cutter. Stef pulled an object out of the box. "Like this, what is it?"

He laughed. "It stamps your initials on golf balls."

"If you say so. How about I just remove the known objects and let you deal with the rest?"

"Works for me."

They worked in silence for a few minutes. Stef won-dered what was going through Mitch's mind as he sifted through her husband's belongings. Did he see a man who'd loved his family? Who'd clung to a job he'd lost because it was part of his identity and he didn't know who he was without it? Mitch paid particular attention to Brad's portable CD player and played the CD. "That's one of Brad's motivational sales tapes," she explained when a slick male voice expounded on brand and company image.

His concentration intense, Mitch sifted through the other CDs in a plastic case, then set them aside. Han-dling Brad's things reminded Stef of happier times when she and Brad had lived in New York City. The people, the divergent cultures and the ever-changing face of the city had been an exciting switch from the small town near Philadelphia where she'd grown up and where her parents still lived when they weren't explor-ing the country in their camper.

Her memories were brought to a painful halt when Mitch pulled Brad's briefcase from the bottom of the box. Stef had bought it to celebrate his promotion to regional sales manager four years ago. Shortly after Brad had gotten the job, they'd decided to start a family. Or was she the one who'd decided? Stef pressed her hand to her mouth. Ever since Mitch had arrived on her doorstep she'd been questioning her marriage. Questioning her love for her husband.

Her heart clenched as Mitch's strong brown fingers released the twin locks on the retro metal case. She must have made a small sound, because Mitch looked at her intently, the kindness in his eyes belying the hard set of his jaw. "I'll need photos of Brad and the date he bought his insurance policy. It would save time if you took care of that while I finish up here. I know you're anxious to get back to Keely."

"I'd rather stay," she insisted, battling the weakness in her knees that Mitch's consideration of her feelings evoked. He was searching her husband's belongings for proof that Brad was a kidnapper.

"You sure? They aren't handing out any prizes for bravery today."

They weren't handing out awards to cowards, either. She wanted her baby back. It was the only thing she had to live for if Keely was taken from her. "Darn, I thought today was my lucky day."

Her gaze fell to the interior of her husband's briefcase. Whatever Brad kept in there had always been a mystery to her. She'd never been a prying wife. She pointed at what looked like a compact TV remote control. "Now why would a man have a TV remote in his briefcase?"

Mitch frowned as he picked it up. "It's not a remote control. It's a tape recorder." He pressed a button.

Sable Holden's voice suddenly purred into the basement, laced with seductive overtones, "Ross, you came. I was afraid that annoying secretary of yours wasn't going to cooperate. You're a hard man to find." She paused for a sexually charged beat. *"Very hard."*

A male voice, feral with a warning note in its tone replied, "I didn't come for lunch, Sable."

Was that Ross Collingwood?

Heat climbed in Stef's face. Judging from the clinking of cutlery in the background, the recording had been made in a restaurant and she could picture Sable sliding a hand beneath a pristine linen tablecloth to gauge the hardness of a certain part of Ross Collingwood's anatomy.

Nausea stirred in the back of her throat at the thought that Brad must have been nearby, recording the conversation. She gripped the edge of the worktable as Sable's laughter spilled into the gloom of the basement.

"What a delicious choice of words, Ross. I can see we're of the same mind. I've reserved a room *upstairs.*"

"Sable, I'm married. I *love* my wife."

"Yes, and how long has it been since you slept with her? A man like you has physical needs and desires, and so do I."

Ross cursed sharply and the tape went eerily silent.

Stef started to shake as she met Mitch's stony gaze. What had Brad planned to do with that tape?

Chapter Six

Mitch saw the significance of the tape recording explode in Stef's eyes.

"I thought we weren't going to find anything," she said in a small voice.

Mitch found himself coming dangerously close to losing the control he'd been holding in check since he'd held her in his arms in the taxi earlier this morning. No, who was he kidding? Since he'd met her last night.

This woman got under his skin in a thousand ways he couldn't resist. He liked that her house wasn't magazine perfect because she was too busy spending time being Keely's mommy. He liked that she fought him every step of the way because he was threatening the one thing she held most dear. Despite the fact that she hated him, she'd even been willing to put herself at risk to protect him a few minutes ago. It humbled him to think she believed he needed protecting.

He did. *From her.*

Even though his mind warned him to step back and detach before it was too late, Mitch deliberately snared Stef's chin in his hand, forcing her to look at him. Desire, fear and an emotion that left his stomach doing somersaults jolted through him as he drowned in her pain, tried to absorb it, shoulder it and make it his own. Her skin was so incredibly soft, incredibly tempting, he wanted to touch his lips to it to see if it tasted as divine as it felt beneath his fingertips.

He wanted to kiss her. Needed to kiss her in a way he'd never needed to kiss another woman. It had nothing to do with finding her child.

It had to do with finding himself.

Sweat chilled his skin. Somewhere in the logical half of his brain he knew kissing Stef would be a mistake and might have disastrous consequences, but the decision was made somewhere deep inside him and was stronger than his willpower. He couldn't fight it any longer.

He meant for it to be gentle. Comforting. But the instant he tasted the sweetness of her mouth, he was beyond controlling it. The kiss happened. Wild. Deep. Searching. Escalating from, *This isn't a good idea* to *I want you* in three seconds flat.

Incredibly she kissed him back, her softness moving against him, her fingers digging into his shoulders. Mitch growled low in his throat, kneading her buttocks with his fingers, falling victim to the intoxicating scent of her hair, to the honeyed taste of her on his tongue and the pressure of her fingers urging him closer. Sensations rampaged through him in vibrant images, igniting him, tormenting him, soothing him. He couldn't get enough.

Her softness seduced him, robbed him of coherent thought. He was barely cognizant of his hands pushing up under her sweater—exposing a ripe golden breast in a delicate wrapping of pale blue lace. The tip luscious and swollen pink.

He took it into his mouth, lace and all, his body thickening and hardening with a desire so strong he felt empowered rather than shaken by it. Stef's skin was silken to his touch. She moved beneath his seeking fingers like a cat begging to be stroked. He thrust a hand under her skirt and encountered her thigh and more lace.

She whimpered impatiently, grinding her body against his. He felt a soul-deep need to touch her. To be joined with this amazing woman. To feel her strength and spirit coursing through him. And to be buoyed by her joyful enthusiasm for life.

Her panties were damp. For him.

Mitch nearly came unglued. She wanted him, too. She felt what he was feeling.

The wonder of it burned through him and settled firmly in his heart like a keystone. He laved her other breast through its protective layer of lace and slid a finger into her damp cleft. Into her core.

She gripped his shoulders and shuddered around his finger. Instantly. She was so tight.

''That's it, baby, that's it. Let it go,'' he whispered hoarsely, stroking her, encouraging her.

She bucked against him, and Mitch played her, suckling her breast until she cried out his name, then pulling away and plunging his tongue into her mouth the way he wanted to plunge into her and be healed. The fierceness of it frightened him. She frightened him, because she felt so dammed perfect and unattainable.

It should be wrong.

He knew it, but he couldn't bring himself to stop. Holding her, touching her, was like breathing. He couldn't hold his breath long enough to stop.

Her fingers tugged impatiently at the clasp of his belt, then gripped him through the fabric of his trousers. His blood thundered through his veins as he pulsed against her palm. This was crazy, this was madness. He couldn't wait to be inside her.

Her fingers fumbled with his zipper. "I need you, Mitch. Promise me you'll find my baby."

Mitch's body turned ice cold, his fingers froze in their desperate race to tear a condom from the depths of his wallet. A deep rumbling of protest rose from his soul.

She was desperate. She was afraid and vulnerable. There was so much he could give her. So much he wanted to give her, but that was the one thing he couldn't promise. Not now. Not ever. He couldn't make love to her with a promise like that on his conscience.

The detachment he'd struggled to find earlier dropped back into place like a glass shield, separating him from her.

With an effort, he forgot about the condom and caught Stef's hands in his, her wrists as fragile as thin ice. "I can't promise you that. I wish I could, but I can't lie to you about something as important as that."

Her beautiful eyes widened with understanding and she slumped against him like a rag doll. Her tears dampened his shirt as he cradled her against his chest and let her cry. His body still throbbing painfully, Mitch stroked her hair and pressed kisses against her temple and imagined what his grandfather would think to see him now. His pants were undone and he was comforting a victim's mother. The captain would have his badge if he were still a detective.

The Guardian would have his ass.

He was jeopardizing the investigation. Possibly the safe return of Stef's real daughter.

Yet he still couldn't let her go. Instinct and pigheaded stubbornness kept his arms locked securely around her. He needed Stef's cooperation to save her daughter.

Needed her complete trust. The tape they'd just found was suspicious. If they kept digging they might discover who was holding her biological child hostage and why the two little girls had been switched.

"I know you're scared," he whispered. "But you're not alone, okay? I'm here with you for the whole nine yards. You're going to get tired of looking at my ugly mug. You'll have my whole wardrobe memorized." Mitch hoped that wouldn't be because she was removing his wardrobe one piece at a time from his person.

He really didn't. His body still throbbed. She smelled like flowers and vanilla and cookies from the oven— and sex.

Focus. His legs still trembling with the need coursing through his body, his mind replayed the tape they'd just heard. What the hell had Brad Shelton been up to? Mitch needed to check the tape for other conversations. He had to finish searching the briefcase.

He still didn't move. His legs trembled.

Stef inhaled a long, ragged breath and tilted her face up to his, her body subtly inching away from him. He felt the sharp pang of physical loss as he loosened his hold on her. He could still smell her hair. Still smell her musky vanilla scent on his fingers.

He told himself she didn't really want him. She was angry at her husband. Hurt. Destroyed. She'd needed a release, a way to vent her fears. Someone like her wouldn't normally undress someone like him. He'd bet Brad was probably her first or second lover.

"I'm sorry, Mitch. I shouldn't have done that or—" she paused, her tear-streaked face turning scarlet. "Or ripped your clothes off." She retreated another step and ran her fingers through her hair. "I'm going crazy. I don't know what I'm doing."

Mitch felt the heat of his own embarrassment flash through him. He eased his zipper over his still-engorged member. "I know. That's why I'm trying really hard to convince myself that I wasn't going to let us have sex."

Through the spiraling anger and disappointment that the tape they'd just found might implicate Brad in Riana Collingwood's abduction, Stef's womb registered the impact of Mitch's words. She shoved the thought away, not able to deal with the guilt of how much she'd wanted him. Wanted his strength, wanted his confidence. Wanted so much to put her blind faith in him—even though he was ripping her precious little girl from her life. Somehow she believed he could guide her through this nightmare. That nothing he said or did would be a lie.

She could count on Mitch to be brutally honest with her. She tugged on the hem of her sweater, trying to ignore that she could still feel the damp heated imprint of his mouth on her bra. "What do you think the tape means? Do you think Brad was blackmailing Sable or Ross Collingwood?"

"It's hard to say. The tape ends abruptly. Let's see if there's anything else on it."

He used a gold pen from Brad's briefcase to press the play button. "We'll have it dusted for fingerprints," he told her when she asked why he was using the pen. "It's a long shot, but we might find someone else's fingerprints on it—like Sable's. We've got her fingerprints on file." Silence spun on the tape. Mitch played with the fast forward button, but there was nothing else.

Disappointment, like bile, rose in her throat as they looked through the file folders in the briefcase. One of them held copies of Brad's résumé and his list of references. She felt a hysterical urge to tear them into pieces. "You know, I'm beginning to wonder if he ever actually used them. He never mentioned the name of the companies the job interviews were with. He told me an employment agency was setting up the interviews for him."

She sighed and scraped her hair back from her face. "I'm not sure if I mentioned this, but the reason Brad didn't stay with us in the hospital that night was because he supposedly had a job interview the next morning." Her shoulders stiffened with rage. "He told me he didn't get the job because he was late. He overslept. I'm not sure he even had a job interview now."

Mitch's gaze centered on her, dark and intense. The gold pen was balanced perfectly on the tip of his tanned index finger like a scale of justice weighing in a verdict. "No, you didn't mention that. What time did he show up at the hospital?"

"He didn't. My parents brought me and Keely home. Brad arrived home around one o'clock and he had beer on his breath. I was too tired to say anything and my parents were staying with us."

Mitch toyed with the pen as if he were trying to take it apart. "Did he have a favorite watering hole?"

Stef frowned. "Sure. He'd meet a few friends from time to time at this place called Herman's in Queens."

"Which friends?"

Stef came up with a half dozen names. "He played basketball with them." Goose bumps prickled over her arms as she remembered a name Brad had mentioned a couple of times in the last few months before his death. "And there was someone named Tony. I don't know his last name, but he played basketball, too."

"Did you ever meet this Tony?"

Stef shook her head.

"Did he come to Brad's funeral?"

"I'm not sure. There were a lot of people I didn't know. I have the guest book from the funeral service upstairs. He may have signed it."

Mitch's mouth tugged up in an approving grin and her breath hitched involuntarily. Her body tingled with remembered awareness of where he'd touched her. How he'd kissed her. How close she'd come to forgetting who he was.

"I'd like to see the guest book. It'll give us a list of Brad's friends. Now, answer me a question." He waved the pen under her nose. "Where did Brad get this?"

"I don't know. Why?"

"Because it's not a pen. It's a video camera." Horror inched over her skin as he indicated a small hole on the side of the pen. "This is the lens. You clip the pen on a shirt pocket and no one knows you're recording. This might tell us the rest of the story that wasn't on that tape."

Stef gulped and hugged herself. Even though she was still resistant to the idea that Brad had switched their daughter with Riana Collingwood, a ray of hope pierced the bleak despair in her heart. "Or it might show us my real daughter and where she's being held."

IT TOOK ANOTHER two hours to finish searching Brad's belongings. Stef hoped they would find the special cable Mitch explained was needed to plug the pen into a VCR to view whatever was recorded on it, but she realized she must have thrown it out during the move to Logantown. While Mitch called The Guardian and gave him a rundown of what they'd found, Stef slapped ham and cheese onto slices of wheat bread and grabbed two sodas from the refrigerator. The food was Mitch's idea.

She didn't think she'd be able to swallow a bite, but she knew Mitch would make her eat. Oh, God, what were they going to find on that videotape?

Mitch came into the kitchen, filling the cheerful yellow room with his bulk. He'd put his blazer back on and the navy wool fabric enhanced the startling deep blue of his eyes. ''The Guardian's tech team is standing by to analyze what we found. They'll have a cable ready and waiting.''

Stef sagged against the counter. The other day her biggest problem had been whether or not she could put off buying new tires for her car until after Christmas. ''Good.''

Mitch squeezed her shoulder and Stef felt her body respond to the strength and the support telegraphed in his fingers. ''I told the helicopter pilot we were on our way.''

Stef handed him a sandwich wrapped in a napkin. ''Then you'd better eat fast.''

He took the sandwich. ''I know you must be feeling really anxious. But just remember that if we find something that links your husband to Riana's kidnapping, the decisions your husband made are no reflection on you.''

Stef's nerves snapped like a flag whipping in a brisk wind. She knew he expected to find something incriminating on the video camera. ''How can you say that? Brad was my husband.'' She narrowed her gaze on him. ''I'll bet you've never been married, have you?''

His gaze centered on her in its full intensity as if pushing a door open into her emotions. ''No.''

''Well, have you ever really loved someone who was a part of you?''

His jaw tightened reflexively and his eyes shuttered like blinds being drawn. ''I can't say that I have,'' he said bluntly, biting into the sandwich. His jaw worked and Stef followed the movement of his Adam's apple as he swallowed. "Not too many women want to share their lives with someone who deals with the stuff I do."

Her heart twinged. She had a feeling there was more to the story, some hurt he was burying beneath his tough cop facade. Perhaps the same driving hurt that had motivated him to become a cop, but she didn't pry.

It was hard enough trying to forget that she'd wanted him to make love to her. She didn't want to be detoured by the possibility that Mitch wasn't just a brash and incredibly handsome detective. But a man who'd lived his own amount of pain, and perhaps had dreams of his own that hadn't turned out as he'd planned. That maybe he needed comfort and solace, too.

No, she absolutely did not want to think about that. Not when the physical release Mitch had given her still lingered like a balm in her veins.

She put the mustard and mayonnaise back in the refrigerator. "Brad and I made a baby together. He was part of me," she explained, glancing at Mitch. He'd just about finished his sandwich. She should have made him two. "I can't just disassociate myself from him, no matter what he may or *may not* have done."

Mitch skewered her with a do-you-really-believe-what-you're-saying? look. "Just remember it's not your fault. Now eat. I just heard the taxi pull up in your driveway. I'll get the boxes. You lock up."

"Wait!" Stef ripped the sandwich in two and gave him the larger half. "I'll eat half if you eat the other half."

He switched halves so she had the larger piece. "Deal."

Stef took a large bite as she followed him out of the

kitchen. Somehow, she was going to find her biological child. And she was going to find a way to keep Keely, too.

THE GUARDIAN and a team of technicians awaited their arrival in a sleek modern conference room equipped with a wall of equipment that made the cockpit of an Airbus 320 look like a child's toy. Stef's nails dug into her palms as she was shown to a chair at The Guardian's right.

"Did you hear from the kidnapper again?" she asked him.

"Not yet, Mrs. Shelton. But the ransom is prepared and we're ready to cooperate. I suspect that the extraordinary delay is designed to increase our anxiety."

Stef exhaled unsteadily. "It's working." She kept her eyes glued on Mitch and The Guardian as they divvied up the contents of the boxes to the men and women in black suits seated around the huge glossy table.

A bronzed man with shoulders like a professional wrestler and three dimples that formed a triangle in his right cheek introduced himself as he took the empty seat next to her and asked if he could take her fingerprints. "I'll use them to eliminate your prints from any of the objects we'll be dusting," he explained courteously, laying out a white card, an ink pad and alcohol wipes. "It won't take long."

Stef willingly offered her hands as she eavesdropped on The Guardian. He'd given Brad's pictures to a hook-nosed balding man named Edwards with instructions to show them to the nurse who'd been assaulted by Riana's kidnapper.

One tech with dreadlocks departed with Brad's laptop, while an ice-blond woman with Nordic features took custody of the tape recorder Stef had thought was a remote control.

The basketball trophies Brad had won in high school, several disks from his laptop and Brad's briefcase were given to the fingerprint expert beside her. "Pass the disks to Foster to examine after you check them for prints," Mitch told him. "There might be something worthwhile on them."

"You can count on it, Halloran." The expert winked at Stef as he started fingerprinting her other hand. "Bossy son of a gun, isn't he?"

"I heard that Wendell."

Wendell ignored Mitch. "You gotta forgive him. He comes from California. There, they do things sloppy. Just look at the Nicole Simpson case. Here, we do things right." He gave Stef a star-dimpled smile as he handed her an alcohol wipe to remove the ink smears from her fingers.

Her gaze centered on Mitch as she cleaned her fingers. His cobalt eyes were dark as a tech with a brush cut and narrow black eyeglasses hooked the miniature video camera up to a VCR.

Ants crawled in Stef's stomach. Would whatever was on that tape prove that her husband hadn't been involved in the kidnapping? Or would it give them a clue to their baby girl's fate?

She said a silent prayer asking for strength as an image filled the huge TV screen. The image shook as if the camera was being jostled and she heard her husband say under his breath, "Here goes nothing."

Stef pressed her hand to her mouth to block the conflicting emotions rushing to her throat. It had been so long since she'd heard Brad's voice. She hated that the good memories she had of their life together were now tainted by a cloud of suspicion. A green door with a Customer Hours sign appeared on the screen. The door was shoved inward and images of a dimly lit room with tables and chairs emerged. A bar.

Herman's. Stef was sure of it. She recognized the captain's chairs drawn up to the tables.

Brad walked to the booths at the back of the bar.

Suddenly the blurry form of a person sitting at one of the booths came into focus.

Stef gasped. It was Sable!

Sable was wearing casual clothes—a tank top with a thin gold chain around her neck. A beer was on the table in front of her. Stef told herself that there was nothing wrong with her husband meeting his former boss in a bar. Brad had told her about it. But still…why would Brad record the meeting on film?

Sable's smile widened as Brad swung into the booth. "How's the proud father?"

"Proud. Exhausted. I never knew babies peed so much or slept so little."

"I've heard that. I hope you brought pictures."

"Damn straight. I brought a cigar, too."

Okay, this wasn't so bad, Stef thought as Brad presented Sable with one of the special cigars he'd bought in anticipation of his child's birth. Maybe Brad was making a little impromptu film for Keely to show her how happy he was to be her daddy.

The camera jerked as Brad removed a packet of photos from a pocket and narrated them for Sable.

Stef looked at Mitch uncertainly as Brad described the agonizing hours of labor Stef had endured before their baby daughter was brought into the world. How could he possibly think Brad had switched his daughter with another baby?

"Look at all that dark hair!" Sable cooed. "May I keep this photo? A lot of people will be thrilled to see it."

"Sure."

The video camera captured Sable slipping the photo into her purse. Stef was more convinced than ever that Brad had nothing to do with Riana Collingwood's kidnapping. Sable must have been using Brad.

A cocktail waitress took Brad's order. After the waitress left, the conversation changed abruptly.

Sable leaned across the table, the valley of her breasts visible. "So, Brad, when will it be ready?"

Stef squirmed. When would *what* be ready?

"Soon. I can only work on it when the baby is napping and Stef isn't home. The baby doesn't sleep too much."

"Can't you hire a baby-sitter?"

"One of the neighbors would notice and tell Stef. Give me another week. I want my job back as much as you want your company back."

"Does your wife suspect anything?"

Suspect what? Stef wanted to scream. Anger rioted through her bloodstream at the thought that Brad had been hiding something from her. She felt naive, like a wife who'd suddenly discovered that her husband was seeing another woman. Her fingernails dug half moons into her cheek. What were Sable and Brad talking about? Were they having an affair?

"Relax, she's doesn't suspect a thing," Brad replied.

That clinched it. Stef was convinced that Brad had been sleeping with that bitch. And to think she'd stupidly shrugged off Brad's declining interest in sex to her pregnancy and his unemployment status. Suddenly, Brad's dismissal from the company after the takeover took on a whole new light. Stef kept her gaze rigidly fixed on the screen even though she wanted to sink into her chair in humiliation. At least all the other techs had left the room before the show had begun.

But she was very much aware that Mitch was listening to every word. Judging Brad. Judging her.

"Okay," Sable said. "A week, no longer. Ross is distraught over Riana's kidnapping. He's vulnerable."

Great, Stef thought dully. They weren't having an affair, after all. But they were definitely involved in the kidnapping. Small comfort.

Tears ran silently down her face as Brad said, "What if he thinks you're involved in the kidnapping?"

Oh, Brad, what did you do?

"Let me handle Ross Collingwood. You do your part and you'll be rewarded, which reminds me." She opened her leather handbag and handed him several hundred dollar bills. "This ought to keep you in formula and diapers for a while."

Stef's world disintegrated and her heart withered to dust as Brad's fingers closed over the money. Mitch, damn him, was right about Brad!

Stef blinked, realizing Sable was rising from the booth and leaving.

"Call me when it's ready, Bradley," she heard Sable say.

When *what* was ready? Stef itched to leap into the TV screen and grab Sable by her gold necklace and throttle the truth out of her. She pressed her hands to her cheeks, realizing the enormity of the risk she'd taken by asking Sable about Brad's death.

Had Sable killed Brad because she was afraid he would link her to Riana Collingwood's abduction?

"Pause it," Mitch ordered.

The tech complied.

Tears ran silently down her cheeks as she willed herself the courage to ask the question that hovered in the air among them. Her throat felt raw, abraded. To her surprise, she felt Mitch's hand on her shoulder. Sensed the strength and the power of his body behind her. She told herself she could endure the shame of knowing Brad had been involved in something so horrendous. She had to—for her real daughter's sake.

She tilted her head back to look Mitch in the eye. The nonjudgmental compassion and the support she found in his gaze made the pain and disappointment of Brad's betrayal somehow easier to bear. She took a deep breath, feeling his strong fingers squeezing her shoulder comfortingly. "What do you think Brad was preparing for Sable?"

Mitch shook his head. "I'm not sure. It could have been related to the tape we found of Sable and Ross."

"You mean Sable was using Brad to record the affair she was having with Ross Collingwood? Why would she do that? And why would Brad help her?"

"To get her company back. Ross was a married man. Just as Sable said a few minutes ago—Ross was vulnerable. He and his wife were grief-stricken over their daughter's kidnapping. If his wife received evidence that he was having an affair it might destroy his marriage and destroy both him and his wife emotionally. That could be exactly what Sable wanted."

The Guardian cleared his throat. Stef felt a tremor of apprehension as his brows pulled together into a formidable line. "Mitch played the tape recording over the phone for me. I wrote down what was said word for word. I investigated Riana's abduction and I reported to Mr. Collingwood at least once a day during the first two months of her disappearance. I knew his character. I don't believe for a minute that he succumbed to Sable Holden's charms, but I believe Sable wanted it to appear that way.''

"So why did Brad wear a hidden camera to this meeting with Sable? And why did he say 'Here goes nothing' before he went into the meeting?'' Mitch asked, his mouth twisting into a puzzled line.

"Maybe he was testing the camera because it was the little something Sable asked him to prepare. Maybe she wanted his help in getting something on videotape.'' The Guardian waved a hand at the video tech. ''Let's see what else the camera picked up.''

The tech pressed the play button. The tape spun forward, capturing Brad's fingers clenched around a sweating bottle of beer on the table.

A man's voice, rough around the edges, let out a low catcall. ''Now that's what I call a woman who's lookin' for a real man. You gettin' any of that action, Bradley?''

The camera jerked a little to the right as Brad turned around. Stef saw a faded pair of jeans with a tear in the pocket and the hem of a white T-shirt in the lower right corner of the TV screen.

''Yeah, right. You off tonight?''

''Sure am.'' A hand liberally sprinkled with dark hair placed a bottle of beer on the edge of the table. Stef could just make out the man's watch. ''Haven't seen you around much, buddy. That baby keepin' you busy?''

''Something like that.''

''You still playing Mr. Mom?''

Aggression crept into Brad's voice. ''You got a problem with that, Tony?''

"No, sir. Not me. I was just wonderin' what your schedule was like and if you were serious about us going climbing one of these days?"

Climbing? Stef shot Mitch a wary wide-eyed glance as Brad took a long swallow of beer. Brad had only gone climbing two or three times since Keely's birth.

"Sure, I'll take you out. My wife's working the New York to Chicago route next week, I should have an afternoon free. I'll give you a call."

"Cool, man."

The blood siphoned from her face at Brad's mention of the New York to Chicago route. She felt numb as the man walked off. A few seconds later the tape ended.

She looked to Mitch for help, confusion and anxiety coursing through her. She was no longer certain whether Sable had killed Brad.

"You okay, Stef?" Mitch asked, his fingers lightly brushing the hair at her temple. It was an intimate gesture. One that suggested caring and understanding.

She shook her head, fresh tears blurring her vision. She remembered Brad's impatience to take off for the Giant's Kneecaps as soon as she'd walked in the door that day—as if someone were waiting for him. "I started working the New York to Chicago route the week Brad died—I was replacing another flight attendant who'd just gone on maternity leave. Do you think this Tony was with Brad the day of the accident?"

Chapter Seven

Mitch's heart knotted at the pallor of Stef's face. Her freckles stood out on her cheeks like cinnamon on milk. She'd been through a hell of a lot. And that little conversation on the videotape between Sable and Brad suggested that things were going to get rougher still. He took a step toward her. As he did, Stef tucked her silky dark hair behind her ears and tilted her chin at a determined angle. She might be pale, but a survivor's spirit shone in her green-gold eyes. He had to admire her stamina. She'd been through so much.

"Brad's little show took place at Herman's—the bar I told you about in Queens," she said, reaching toward the center of the conference table to grab the guest book from Brad's funeral. Mitch was uncomfortably aware of the way the soft knit of her blue sweater molded to her firm breasts with every movement. She glanced at The Guardian. "We brought this because Mitch wanted a list of Brad's friends. There were a lot of people at the funeral I didn't know. Maybe Tony was there."

As Stef opened the guest book, The Guardian asked the video tech to rewind the tape.

Mitch saw something whiz by on the screen that caught his attention. "Whoa, freeze it on the watch," he said. He rose and approached the TV screen, pointing at the face of the watch. "It's 9:37 p.m. And the date on the calendar feature is July tenth."

Stef's small pain-laced voice penetrated his soul like a needle. "Brad died July seventeenth, one week later."

It took everything Mitch had in him to distance himself from the desire to hold her, to comfort her. He had to remind himself that she was a victim's mother and that he was going to blow this case if he didn't shape up and maintain his objectivity. He'd lost his detachment and part of himself when the Lopez case had ended so tragically. He didn't think he could bear to lose the part of himself that felt such a strong affinity for Stef if this case had a tragic end.

G.D. caught his eye and lifted a brow as if he was picking up on the vibes of Mitch's emotional skirmish. Mitch shrugged his shoulders and paced the length of the conference room, forcing himself to concentrate. From what they'd seen on the tape, either Sable or Tony could have met Brad to go climbing. But something on the tape bothered him. What was it?

G.D. slid a blue folder across the glossy surface of the black conference table toward Mitch. "These are copies of the police report and the autopsy report from the accident. You might see something I missed."

Mitch palmed the folder, perusing it as The Guardian continued. "According to the police report, Brad was found just after five by a couple walking their dog. The medical examiner estimated he'd been dead a couple of hours and that he was approximately two-thirds of the way up the face when he fell. He was climbing without proper safety gear. The parking lot was gravel. No tire tracks. No witnesses came forward who saw him there.

There's no way to tell if Brad arrived alone or met someone.''

Mitch spared a glance in Stef's direction and he felt his stomach catapult out of his body again. He'd come precariously close to having sex with her today and his body still hummed with tension. Her jaw was hinged tight, as if that were the only thing holding her together. ''You sure you're okay with us talking about this in front of you?''

Her gaze burrowed into him, right into the place that wanted to believe she held the key to happiness. To simple joys. He'd bet holidays in her family were really something special. A nice dinner. Hand-made decorations. People laughing and teasing. He'd bet there were never any drunken brawls. No cans of chili or stew heated over a burner in a cheap motel. ''I want to know everything.''

She was a tigress.

Mitch dragged his attention back to the autopsy report. ''He hadn't been drinking. There was no alcohol in his system. Tony could have met Brad at the Giant's Kneecaps, then got scared and ran after Brad fell. The fall could have been a simple accident. Or it could have been more sinister if Brad met Sable that day. He could have handed over whatever he was supposed to do for her and Sable could have decided to cover her tracks.''

G.D. leaned back in his black leather chair. ''If we find Tony, we may find more answers. I'm still working on acquiring a list of the attendees from the rock climbing course that Brad attended courtesy of Office Outfitters. It'll be interesting to see if Sable's name is on the list.''

Stef closed the guest book with a frustrated sigh. ''Well, there are no Tonys, in any form, in here.''

Mitch shoved his fingers through his hair, trying to keep his concentration on the papers in front of him and not on the fragility of Stef's slender shoulders or the discouragement stamped on her pale face. "If he's a regular at Herman's, the bartender may know him. I'll drop by Herman's after I have drinks with Sable tonight. Did Sable send a fax with a list of people I can interview at Office Outfitters, G.D.? There might be a Tony on that list."

G.D. arched a brow. "I believe it's in your file."

Mitch swore silently under his breath, feeling like a rookie cop again as he found the sheet of names beneath the autopsy report. The fear that he was going to screw up this case sent a bead of sweat trickling down his spine. This was how he'd screwed up the Lopez case—he'd let himself get too involved in Theresa Lopez's situation. Her pain. Her fears that she'd never see her granddaughter alive again.

He'd seen his grandfather and himself in their lives.

And he saw in Stef and Keely something beautiful and magical that had always been beyond his reach. He wanted to preserve and protect their special world as he'd wanted to preserve and protect Theresa and Carmen Lopez.

The clock was ticking. The kidnapper could make contact at any moment with the instructions for the ransom drop. The odds of recovering Stef's daughter would be improved if he could figure out who the kidnapper was and where the child was being held before that happened.

Mitch studied the list of names Sable had sent until the heat of his stare practically burned a hole in the paper. "There's no one named Tony or Anthony on this list, either. But then it's unlikely that Tony worked for

Office Outfitters—otherwise he would have recognized Sable as the founder of the company.''

The Guardian's dry-ice gaze settled on Mitch with an intensity that made Mitch's skin itch. He noticed there was one last item in the file that G.D. had given him— a bound document. ''What's this?''

''A copy of Sable Holden's day planner—the year Riana Collingwood was born. In case you were wondering where she was on certain key dates.''

Mitch grinned. G.D. ran a sweet operation the likes of which Mitch had never seen. He could get used to information appearing at his fingertips as if by wizardry. He flipped to July seventeenth, the day Brad died. ''What do you know? Sable had a manicure at two o'clock, but she crossed out the appointment. Guess she had other plans.''

Stef realized this was how Mitch thought best, on his feet, prowling, his energy as intense as it had been today when he'd touched her. Kissed her. Lit her on fire.

She blushed at the memory—and felt the gentle contractions of a craving that still lingered deep within her. Followed by shaming guilt. At least Mitch had the decency to stop that kiss from becoming something more. If he'd left it up to her, could she have stopped?

She looked at the man who had walked into her life and destroyed everything she held dear. Her biological daughter was being held hostage by a kidnapper and Mitch was the only person she trusted to help her. She had to believe he could perform miracles.

Her shoulders drooped. She was tired and she needed to see Keely, to hold her. Memorize every perfect detail about her.

Mitch seemed to notice her exhaustion without her saying anything. ''You look like you're about to drop.

Give me a minute to call Sable and set up a meeting
and I'll take you back to the hotel.''

She smiled at him gratefully. "All right. But hurry.
Keely's not used to me being away from her this long.''

The Guardian rose from his chair, silent and swift as
a hawk. "You can make your call from my office,
Mitch. Then I'd appreciate a private word with you. I'll
see that a security team escorts Mrs. Shelton to the hotel
so we don't delay her unnecessarily.''

Mitch winked at Stef. "Tell Keely I'm really looking
forward to that black jelly bean.''

Stef's heart tweaked at a mental image of the day
Keely had spent—a princess presiding over a tea party.
Far too many hours had passed since she'd hugged her
darling girl.

HUNTER SINCLAIR PAUSED in the hall outside the conference room and took a shuddering breath into the tight
recess of his chest. The tension in the conference room
had been thick with emotional undertones. Hunter had
sensed immediately that something had changed between Stephanie Shelton and Mitch Halloran. Stephanie
Shelton had looked less like she wanted to skewer
Mitch and roast him over a roaring fire, and Mitch had
seemed wary and protective of her. Less brusque.

Stephanie Shelton needed a protector. Her words still
echoed in Hunter's tormented thoughts. *Keely's not
used to being away from me this long.*

He had joined Juliana and Keely at the hotel for
lunch, presumably to check on the security arrangements for Keely's safety, but he'd been drawn there by
his heart's desire to become acquainted with Ross's
daughter. The little minx had Lexi's dark beauty and
Ross's stubborn determination. And she was bright for

a two-and-a-half-year-old, her sentences more complex than his nephews had uttered at the same age.

While she'd daintily dipped nuggets of chicken into honey sauce, Keely had regaled Hunter with a story her mommy had told her about a fairy with a torn wing. When Keely had finished, she'd imperiously demanded that Hunter tell her a story in return.

Juliana had laughed at her husband's blustering attempt to comply, her mahogany eyes glowing as he'd told Keely about a castle that was crumbling into disrepair until a beautiful princess came to the castle and made it beautiful again, planting beautiful flowers in the greenhouse and making the lonely prince who lived in the castle happier than he'd ever been.

Juliana had promised Keely that someday she would invite her to see the castle and the greenhouse.

"Can my mommy come, too?" Keely had asked innocently.

Juliana had searched Hunter's face for a long moment before she'd smiled and replied, "You may pick out a special room in the castle just for your mommy. And one for you, too. There are lots of bedrooms in the castle."

And Hunter prayed there would be need of a bedroom for Stephanie Shelton's real daughter. That he and Stephanie Shelton could come to a quiet arrangement that would keep Riana's name out of the headlines and a legal battle out of the courts. Hunter had no intention of losing Riana. He'd made a promise to Ross and Lexi. He'd failed them thirty months ago when Riana was kidnapped and again when Annette had succeeded in killing them. He would not fail them now.

He took another breath past the suffocating disquiet that had gripped him since he'd received the new ransom demand from the kidnapper nine days ago. Why hadn't the kidnapper made contact with the delivery instructions?

Hunter made arrangements for a security team to see Mrs. Shelton back to the hotel, then returned to his office. The paneled cherry door was open. Mitch must have completed his phone call because he was standing near the window, absentmindedly rubbing the back of his neck. Something about his solitary stance reminded Hunter of himself.

He cleared his throat to announce his arrival. "Did you reach Sable?"

Mitch swiveled on his heels, his brow furrowed. "Got her secretary instead. I'm meeting Sable at seven in Greenwich Village."

Hunter closed his office door and leaned against it. "Excellent. Why the frown?"

Mitch paced restlessly in front of the window. "I don't know—something doesn't feel right about what we saw on that tape. Jeez, I need a run. I'm not used to going so long without one."

Hunter narrowed his gaze on Mitch and voiced the doubts tormenting him. "It's been nine days and no further word from the kidnapper. That's more than enough time to run DNA tests and make arrangements with the bank for the ransom. What do you think it means?"

Mitch stopped pacing, his stark gaze colliding with Hunter's. "Just what you told Stef—the kidnapper's being careful and wants you sweating blood. Or," he paused, his face contorting, "the kidnapper has no further use for the child now that Ross and Lexi Collingwood are dead and has killed her and dumped her body. The letter the Foundation received with the bracelet and the hair could be the kidnapper's way of ensuring that the child's body will be positively identified once it's found. He wants this to be over with. Maybe wants to take pleasure in the world knowing that the Collingwood heir is dead. You might prepare your employer for that possibility.''

Hunter's mouth pressed into a grim line at the horror Mitch described. Nothing in the world could compensate Stephanie Shelton for the loss of her biological child. ''My employer is well aware of the risks involved,'' he admitted with a leaden heart. ''Annette would want the child dead because it was her sister's. And so would Sable. In Sable's mind, Ross destroyed her family by wresting her company from her. I've had operatives digging into Annette's life since her arrest, hoping to discover that she owned property where a child could be held hostage. But nothing has turned up. I'll assign someone to do a property search for Sable. Maybe we'll come up with something.''

Mitch snapped his fingers. ''What about Annette's ex-fiancé, Darren Black? Does he own any property?''

''We checked it out after the explosion that killed the Collingwoods. He owns a four-bedroom house in Ithaca near Cornell University where he works. Nobody lives with him. And the only recent contact he's had with Annette was at her sister and brother-in-law's funeral— and she gave him the brush-off.''

''Still, try the name Annette Black. If Annette broke off her engagement to Darren because he didn't measure up to her sister's fiancé, symbolically it would make sense for her to rent or buy property using the last name that should have been hers.''

''Consider it done.''

Mitch grinned. ''I'm going to have to start calling

you the wizard. Now what do you say we watch that videotape again? You can help me write a list of questions that Evan Mitchell can ask Sable Holden about Brad Shelton.''

Hunter felt the coolness of the brass knob beneath his fingertips. ''How about you finesse your way into finding out if she was sleeping with Brad?''

Mitch shot Hunter a thunderous glare. ''Yeah, and while I'm at it, I'll just pound the last nail into Stef's coffin. It's going to kill her if she finds out her child is dead.'' His eyes grew haunted. Hunter thought soon he was going to make a point of asking Mitch why he specialized in these types of cases.

He clapped Mitch on the shoulder. They'd watch that tape as many times as necessary, analyze it frame by frame. ''God willing, Mitch, it won't come to that.''

''MOMMY!''

Keely traipsed toward Stef in a beautiful pink-and-white satin gown, her dark curls bouncing beneath a jeweled tiara, her cheeks rosy and a cupcake with a green jelly bean on top carefully balanced between her chubby hands.

''Kee!'' Stef scooped her up and kissed her rosy cheeks. Tears sprang in her eyes at the knowledge that her little girl was a princess with a future grander than she could ever imagine. ''I missed you, baby girl.''

Juliana gave Stef a wave and a smile, then discreetly disappeared. Stef breathed in the scent of Keely's hair. The scent of Nirvana.

Keely squirmed in her arms. ''Missed you, too, Mommy. Here's your cupcake!''

Stef took a bite right from the center, capturing the

jelly bean and getting pink frosting on her nose. "I was so hungry. I was dreaming of that cupcake."

Keely giggled. "You need a napkin!"

"No, I don't! I'm not finished yet." Stef took another bite, nearly choking on the sweetness. Oh, God, it felt good to have some silliness with Keely in the midst of this chaos. Life always made perfect sense when she had Keely in her arms. "Have you had dinner yet?"

Keely's curls bounced as she shook her head no.

"How about we eat and let Mommy rest for a bit, then we can go for a swim in the pool? Hotels always have a pool."

"Yippee!"

Stef took another bite of the cupcake, lemon cake crumbs dribbling down her sweater. Mitch was having drinks with Sable tonight.

She looked at the child in her arms, the child she had raised from birth, believing this was the child of her womb.

But there was another child out there. The real child of her body. Stef wasn't willing to give up either of them. How would she ever live through this nightmare?

Her body recalled the strength with which Mitch had held her today, the intensity with which he'd kissed her, seeking her every surrender. His caresses stole through her limbs like a solemn promise that would never be broken. He was different from any man she'd ever known. Intense, fierce and so protective he made her feel that she could lean on him when she didn't have the strength to hang on by herself. She would trust her life to him. And the lives of both her daughters.

She prayed with every fiber of her being that he would find out where that bitch was holding her baby.

THE KIDNAPPER SPOTTED them in the lobby. Riana Collingwood and Stephanie Shelton parting ways with the Madonna-like blonde—the butler's daughter—who'd stood beside Annette throughout the Collingwoods' funeral service.

Wary of being seen by Juliana Goodhew, the kidnapper hid behind a potted palm and considered the options and probabilities of a successful escape with the child. An abduction in the middle of a hotel lobby would be foolhardy. There was armed security near the revolving glass doors. A diversion would be necessary.

The butler's daughter headed toward the concierge's desk, the lights from the lobby's chandelier gleaming off her blond hair. Holding Riana by the hand, Stephanie Shelton entered the hotel's swank restaurant.

The kidnapper waited until Juliana Goodhew had finished her business at the concierge's desk before threading through the guests in theater clothes crowding the lobby. Thanks to the child's high-pitched announcement that she had to go potty, it was relatively easy to pinpoint their table and to secure a nearby table.

The kidnapper ordered soup and salad.

Heads turned as Stephanie Shelton returned to the table, little Riana singing a song about a deep blue sea. As Riana climbed into the booster seat she said in an imperious tone worthy of her lineage, "We're going swimming after dinner, right, Mommy?"

"After Mommy rests after dinner, sweets."

"After after?" Keely sang.

"Yes, sweets, I promise."

The kidnapper smiled. The pool. Say goodbye to Mommy, brat.

"BABY WHALES GO SPLASH, splash, splash," Keely shrieked gleefully, the yellow floaties circling her arms resembling angel wings as she splashed in the shallow end of the pool.

Stef laughed and splashed back, savoring the joy that rippled the pond of her heart. Her decision to take Keely down to the pool had met with opposition from The Guardian's security team, but Juliana had consulted The Guardian by phone and a compromise had been reached. One guard was stationed in a lounge chair in the patio area. Another guard monitored the key-card-operated door to the pool area and the change rooms. Stef chased away the sobering knowledge that for the rest of their lives she would have to be vigilant of Keely's safety.

They were in a pool with several other guests. What could happen?

"EVAN, HOW NICE TO SEE you again so soon," Sable purred, her body arching as if she were about to wrap herself around his legs when Mitch joined her in an intimate corner of a jazz bar. Her breasts spilled like plump pillows from the neckline of her black cocktail dress. Her silvery eyes glittered as she took a sip from a martini.

Mitch ordered her another martini, a Johnny Black straight up for himself and a plate of appetizers, then put the small notebook he and The Guardian had prepared for the interview on the table. Despite the fact that he and G.D. had scrutinized the videotape several times, he still couldn't pinpoint what it was about it that bothered him.

"I know you're a busy lady, Sable. Thanks for agreeing to help out with this project."

Sable toyed with the olive in her drink. "How could

Get FREE BOOKS and a FREE GIFT when you play the...

LAS VEGAS
GAME

Just scratch off the gold box with a coin. Then check below to see the gifts you get!

YES! I have scratched off the gold Box. Please send me my **2 FREE BOOKS** and **gift for which I qualify**. I understand that I am under no obligation to purchase any books as explained on the back of this card.

381 HDL DUYN   **181 HDL DUY4**

FIRST NAME	LAST NAME

ADDRESS

APT.#	CITY

STATE/PROV.	ZIP/POSTAL CODE

(H-I-03/03)

7	7	7	Worth TWO FREE BOOKS plus a BONUS Mystery Gift!
🍒	🍒	🍒	Worth TWO FREE BOOKS!
🔔	🔔	♣	TRY AGAIN!

I resist Keely? It's a terrible shame that adorable little girl is growing up without a father.''

Mitch wholeheartedly agreed. "You sound like a woman who'd love children of her own."

"I would. Someday—when I have all the right things to offer them."

"What would those things be?"

Mitch almost regretted the question when Sable's carnal gaze stripped him bare. "A father, for starters."

He wasn't biting. After the taste of bliss he'd had with Stef today he couldn't even imagine indulging in casual sex. But he could imagine making love to Stef. She was more appealing than any woman he'd ever met. She had strength and spirit and an enthusiasm for life.

He quickly extinguished the thought of peeling off the lace bra and panties he'd become acquainted with earlier today, and gave Sable a speculative grin. "What else? A summer place in the Berkshires or a winter place in Miami? Maybe a house on Long Island?"

Sable laughed as the waiter brought them their order. "If you must know, my family has a place in the Catskills. I wouldn't part with it for all the gold in the world. I was speaking more about getting back control of Office Outfitters. It was entrusted to me, and I failed to live up to the work ethic my grandfather taught me. I was too greedy. Too ambitious." A shadow crossed her silvery eyes. "When my sister and I were younger, my grandfather would pay us to sweep the floor in the store. When business was slow, he'd coach us in the inventory in case a customer ever asked us a question. He was convinced that customers were impatient by nature and might only have the patience to ask once before trying another store. He was happy with his business.

He knew his employees. Valued them. Treated them like family.''

''The same way you treated Brad like family?''

Sable nodded, tears shining unexpectedly in her eyes. ''There was something about Brad that I identified with right away. He was the kind of person my grandfather would have hired. He loved his job and his enthusiasm showed in everything he did. Unfortunately, his loyalty to me made him one of the first to be axed by Ross's cost-cutters.''

Mitch helped himself to a zucchini stick from the tray of appetizers. ''Tell me more about Brad.''

He jotted down notes as Sable described some of Brad's on-the-job experiences. Her face transformed as she spoke nostalgically, making her appear younger. Nicer.

''Stef mentioned that you kept in touch with Brad after he was let go.''

Sable dipped a cheese stick into the spicy tomato sauce. ''Yes, I was worried about him. I knew he'd have difficulty finding another job. Office Outfitters had become his family—he told me once he was an only child and he wasn't close to his parents. It's not that easy to sever those kinds of connections. So that's what I want you to tell Keely in your book—that her daddy was incredibly loyal and his loyalty will never be forgotten.''

Mitch underscored the word loyalty on his notepad and stared at Sable thoughtfully. There was an unmistakable ring of sincerity in her words. Despite her overt sensuality, on a gut level he didn't think she would sleep with an employee. Especially not someone she considered family. But she might have turned to Brad—

counted on his loyalty—to help her get back the company she'd lost.

"When was the last time you saw Brad?"

Sable lowered her gaze and took another sip of her drink. "Didn't Stef tell you?"

Mitch encouraged her with a coaxing smile. "Humor me, I'm a writer. I'd rather hear it in your own words. Wasn't it the week Brad died? You met for drinks?" He let his gaze drift casually down to the pillows of Sable's breasts. But all he could think of were Stef's golden breasts and pale blue lace. Even now he could imagine Stef cuddling with Keely in the hotel, creating their own magical world with love and stories and jelly beans. For the first time in his life Mitch yearned to have a woman create a magical world just for him. A home.

Not just any woman. Stef.

But he and Stef would never have a prayer. Even if he managed to bring home her real daughter safe and sound, she had no chance of retaining custody of Keely. Not with the Collingwood wealth backing the legal guardian her parents had appointed. Keely's loss would be an insurmountable barrier between them. If he hadn't figured out the baby switch, she'd still be Keely's real mommy.

Tension skittered through him as an air of watchfulness couched Sable's expression. "I think Stef must have misunderstood. We met for drinks, but it wasn't the week Brad died. It was two or three weeks before that."

Now Mitch knew she was lying outright. Tony's watch had marked the date and the time of Sable's last known encounter with Brad.

"What bar was that?"

"Does it matter?" Sable hedged, running a finger along the rim of the glass of her second martini.

"Writers like details. It's what makes a personal story like this seem real. And it will make Brad come alive in Keely's eyes."

"I wish I could remember. It was somewhere out in Queens. We each had a beer."

"Did Brad say anything at that last meeting that you think should be included in your piece?"

"Yes, he showed me pictures of Keely's birth. And he said being a father was the most incredible thing that had ever happened to him."

Mitch made a pretense of writing that down. Beneath the table, Sable's hand crept over his thigh. Mitch didn't move a muscle. "How did you find out Brad had died?"

Sable's fingers beat a hasty retreat from his thigh. "I got a call at home from Pasquale Pedroncelli—a manager at one of the stores Brad had supervised. It was about eight o'clock. I'd just had a bath. I was shocked. Brad was a good climber. Stef hinted that Brad may have committed suicide, but I don't think that was the case. Brad might have been discouraged, but he knew he had a great future ahead of him with Stef and Keely."

Mitch dodged Sable's hands and her questions about Evan Mitchell's personal life for another half hour to maintain his cover, then caught a taxi to Herman's on Junction Boulevard in Queens.

The bar looked just as dim and drab in person as it had on videotape, except tonight a drunk couple in matching jeans and muscle shirts were belting out an Elvis song on the karaoke machine. Mitch sidled up to the bar and placed a one-hundred-dollar bill beneath an empty beer glass. "There's plenty more where this came from for a little information."

"You a cop or something?"

"Or something. Does it matter for a hundred bucks?"

The bartender—a beefy guy with a tattoo of an eagle on his neck—shook his head. "You want something to drink?"

Mitch ordered a beer and helped himself to a handful of peanuts from a bowl on the water-smeared bar. "You remember a guy named Brad Shelton? He used to live around here a couple years ago. He was a regular."

"Sure, I remember Brad. But you're wasting your money, tough guy. He's dead. Took a fall off a cliff. It wasn't pretty apparently. Closed casket if you know what I mean."

"Yeah, I know about that. I'm trying to track down some of his friends—guys he shot some hoops with."

"A couple of those guys still hang out around here." The bartender eyed the hundred-dollar bill. "That real?"

"As real as they come. I want names."

"Pete O'Shay, Mike Lipetzky. They play ball at the rec center Thursday nights and drop by for a drink on the way home—usually around nine-thirty."

Mitch set a second hundred-dollar bill on top of the first one. "Anyone named Tony?"

"There was a guy—I never knew his last name. I haven't seen him since Brad died."

"What'd he look like?"

"Dark hair, wiry. He had a tattoo on the back of his shoulder—red lips. He told me it gave women ideas of where he wanted them to put their lips. He was a funny guy."

"How tall?"

"He wasn't that big. He was probably the wing or the point guard on the team."

Medium height, Mitch translated. "You know what he does for a living? Where he works?"

"Sorry."

Mitch believed him. He put a third hundred-dollar bill on the bar. Sweat beaded on the bartender's broad forehead. "Brad ever meet a woman here?"

"Maybe a couple of times while I was here, but I try to keep my nose out of that kind of business. I don't ask questions, nobody gets hurt."

"Was she blond? Brunette?"

"Brunette. The kind of dame who can make a man real nervous. Demanding, if you know what I mean."

Mitch knew. The woman was definitely Sable. Not Stef. "You notice any hanky-panky going on between them? Hand holding? Exchanges of bodily fluids?"

"I might have seen some money change hands. But she was paying *him,* not the other way around."

Mitch was relieved. He didn't want to walk around with the knowledge that Sable and Brad had been swapping spit in public. The prospect that Brad might have cheated on Stef made him want to hit something.

He hailed a taxi to take him back to the Clairmont Hotel, pondering the information that the bartender had seen Brad and Sable together at least twice and money had changed hands. Had Brad ever delivered what he'd been preparing for her?

Mitch sighed, images of Stef and Keely and black jelly beans infiltrating his thoughts. Absently he reached for the hotel key card in his breast pocket. It was just after 8:30 p.m. Would Keely already be in bed? How much should he tell Stef of what Sable had said?

The key card wasn't in the breast pocket of his suit.

Frowning, Mitch tried another pocket. Where the hell was it? Had Sable helped herself to the card when they were in the bar? Had that little hand trick on his thigh been a distraction? Or had someone been in Stef's house earlier? A chill seized his heart. Maybe Stef's purse hadn't fallen over on its own.

Mitch wasn't taking any chances. He called G.D. He wouldn't feel better until he was sure Stef and Keely were safe.

THE GUESTS IN THE POOL had thinned out. Stef finally succeeded in coaxing Keely out of the water with promises of a story for her beddy time. She wrapped a thick white towel around her daughter's body, smiling as Keely scuttled like a crab to the ladies' change room. Stef heard a shower running. A warm shower sounded wonderful. She should have asked the towel boy for extra towels.

"I gotta go potty, Mommy," Keely announced, her voice booming off the Art Deco tile walls of the locker room.

The shower would have to wait a few minutes. "Okay, sweets, the rest rooms are this way."

Stef let Keely pick a stall and entered after her daughter, latching the door behind them.

She heard the door of the stall beside them swing open.

She'd just helped Keely onto the toilet seat when a massive stinging sensation jolted through her right leg as if she'd been bitten by something. Her brain felt strangely murky and she was having trouble standing. Stef grabbed on to the walls of the stall and looked down in dismay, trying to identify what was going wrong.

An arm snaking from beneath the stall next door was pressing a black object to her calf. She tried to move her leg to avoid the object, escape the pain, but her body seemed paralyzed.

Stef's thoughts were disjointed. The pain wouldn't stop. She tried to reach for Keely, to protect her as her knees buckled and she fell forward. Her head struck the tile wall and everything went black.

Keely giggled as her Mommy sank to the floor. Usually Mommy fell in leaves. Not in the bathroom. "Ha, ha, Mommy."

She waited for Mommy to get up. It was taking a long time. Keely finished tinkling.

She shook Mommy's head, her giggles turning to a whimper when she saw the red sticky blood on her fingers. "Mommy? I need toilet paper."

"Keely?" a voice crooned like a troll beneath a bridge. "Your Mommy's hurt. Can you unlock the door so I can help her?"

Keely didn't like that voice. "No."

"Hurry, your Mommy needs a doctor."

Keely recoiled in fear as the troll's big scary hand reached for her leg.

Chapter Eight

Mitch's breath turned to frost in his lungs when he saw the ambulance pulled up at the entrance to the Clairmont Hotel. Swearing under his breath, he thrust some bills at the taxi driver and bolted out of the cab.

The pool.

G.D. had said Stef and Keely had gone to the pool.

Mitch sprinted across the lobby to the elevators and jabbed at the up button until the doors opened. He'd never forgive himself if something had happened to either one of them. Carmen Lopez's murder and her grandmother's stress-related death were already more than he could bear.

He'd only met Stef yesterday, but she'd impacted his heart. She lit up every room, every inch of space around her. She awakened hopes inside him that Mitch would just as soon stay discarded and buried, but he wasn't holding it against her. He'd never known anyone so alive, so vital.

He couldn't bear the thought she, or Keely, would be silenced. He wouldn't be able to bear the resulting silence in his own world.

"Come on, come on," he urged as the elevator finally lifted upward. Dread curdled in his belly when the elevator came to a halt on the pool level. Mitch heard screams as the door slid open. A child's screams.

Keely's screams.

He raced down the hallway toward the line of uniformed security officers blocking the access to the pool area. "Get the hell out of my way. I work for The Guardian," he said. "Where's your head of security?"

"He's in the ladies' room. Through there," a black female guard told him, letting him pass.

Mitch didn't know what the hell to expect as he entered the ladies' change room. Keely's hysterical screams made his blood run cold. A couple of EMTs and several men were crowded around a bathroom stall.

"I'm Mitch Halloran, I work with The Guardian. Which one of you is the head of security?" he demanded over the sounds of Keely's screams. "What's going on?"

An Asian man with salt-and-pepper hair turned to him, giving Mitch a terror-inducing glimpse of two golden female feet with heart-dotted toenails lying deathly still on the tile floor. "We're not sure. The little girl won't let us near. But we got a pulse at the victim's ankle."

Thank God.

Mitch had no idea how a toddler could hold so many adults at bay. "Step aside," he ordered the two EMTs who were trying to coax Keely out of the stall. Mitch had seen hundreds of traumatized children in his career. But nothing in his lifetime had prepared him for the sheer terror he saw in Keely's red, tear-stained face. She'd wedged herself between the toilet and Stef's body and was holding on to the straps of Stef's bathing suit for dear life. There was blood on her hands and on Stef's face and chest.

Mitch couldn't distance himself from the horrendous pain that seared his heart. Had Stef been shot?

He hunkered down and held out a hand to Keely, her distraught cries tearing through him like daggers. "Keely, it's Mitch," he said very firmly so that she would hear him. "I'm here, kiddo. You're safe. Tell me what happened."

Keely gasped in midsob. Her eyes opened and he saw the guarded uncertainty stamped in her expression when she recognized him. But she didn't let go of her mother. Mitch understood her desperate panic. When his mother had abandoned him at his grandfather's he'd clung to her the same way Keely was clinging to Stef. He still remembered her red-painted nails peeling his fingers from her skirt.

He talked to Keely the way his grandfather had talked to him. Quietly. With compassion. He kept his hand steadily held out to her even though she regarded it with distrust. Inside, he knew she needed someone to reach out to her.

"Tell me what happened, Keely. Are you hurt? You have blood on your hands. Is Mommy hurt?"

Keely's blue-green eyes were round with terror. "There was a troll. It hurt Mommy. Did you scare the troll away?"

A troll? Had someone attacked them?

"Yes, he's gone now, Kee," Mitch assured her. "You're both safe, but Mommy needs a bandage for her owie—just like you do when you're hurt." Behind him he heard the head of security organizing a search. He plucked Keely off Stef's chest, amazed when she came without complaint.

Her arms and legs twined trustingly around his neck and waist like vines. As much as he wanted to touch

Stef, to reassure himself she was okay, Mitch focused his attention on the tiny child he held in his arms. The hummingbird pace of Keely's heartbeat commingled with the frantic pace of his own as he rose and backed out of the stall, letting the EMTs in to examine Stef. Keely was so small. Still just a baby, really. And yet such a force to be reckoned with. All personality—like her mother.

And just as impossible to resist.

What would her life be like a month from now? A year from now? Would she be embroiled in a custody battle, pining to remain with her mommy?

Would Stef have lost Keely and lost her will to live? Or would she have her real daughter to help ease her through the pain of having to give up Keely?

He smoothed his fingers over Keely's damp hair, attempting to reassure her as she burrowed her head under his chin. She was still trembling and her lips were blue. Her bathing suit wasn't on her properly. The female EMT handed him a towel to wrap around her little body and checked her over to make sure she didn't have any injuries. Keely screeched at the EMT's efforts until Mitch convinced her that the nice lady only wanted to help her.

"She's not hurt. The blood's from her mother's cut," the EMT assured him.

Mitch exhaled in relief. That was one worry removed from his mind. But he couldn't take his eyes off Stef. His stomach felt as if it were being stitched by a needle and thread. Who had attacked her and Keely? Did someone know Keely was the Collingwood heir? Or was it an unrelated attack?

The Guardian hurried into the change room, Juliana clutching his arm. "Mitch, what's happened?"

"Oh, my God," Juliana said, her face turning white as she took in the sight of Keely in Mitch's arms, the blood stains on Mitch's shirt and the EMTs kneeling over Stef's prostrate body. "Stef. Is she—?"

"Her vitals are good," one of the EMTs said. "She's really groggy. She says she can't move. She might have hurt her neck when she fell. There's some kind of burn on the back of her right calf."

Burn?

From what? A stun gun? The shock from a stun gun could have caused her fall.

Mitch was half out of his mind with worry. How hard had she struck her head? The EMTs immobilized Stef's neck with a C-spine collar, then began the slow process of straightening her body so she could be log-rolled and a backboard placed against her neck and spine. Mitch had never felt so helpless in his life. Stef needed his support, his reassurance, but Keely needed him, too. He had no doubt that Stef would want him taking care of her little girl.

Be strong, spitfire. Be strong.

He spoke to The Guardian in a low tone. "Keely says a troll attacked them and he went away."

G.D.'s brows rose. He told the security director he wanted to question the security team who'd been protecting Stef and Keely. Mitch had a feeling heads would roll.

"Keely, baby," Stef murmured.

The sound of her voice uplifted Mitch's spirits like a glimpse of a rainbow.

Juliana went immediately to Stef's side and squeezed her hand. "Keely's fine. She'll be with me—us," she amended, glancing at G.D. for confirmation. There was something in the silent message that transpired between them that flagged Mitch's attention. "Don't worry about a thing," Juliana soothed Stef. "You just get better."

The Guardian patted Keely's leg. "You okay, princess?"

Keely nodded and popped her thumb into her mouth, her head braced on Mitch's chest.

"Mitch said a troll scared you. Did you see the troll's face?"

Keely shook her head.

Mitch tried the question another way. "What did you see, jelly bean?"

She popped her thumb out of her mouth. "I'm not a jelly bean." Eyes wide, she spread her fingers like attacking claws as if demonstrating someone had grabbed her mommy. "I see'd his voice."

"He was outside the stall," Mitch explained to G.D. He tightened his arm around Keely, not caring that her wet bathing suit was dampening his clothes. "What did the troll say, Kee?"

Keely shook her head.

"You don't remember?" The Guardian prompted her.

"Maybe you remember and you don't want to say it in a loud voice," Mitch said knowingly. "Can you whisper it in my ear?"

Mitch felt Keely's indecisiveness in the restlessness of her body—even in the straining of her tendons when she finally straightened. Her tiny hands climbed his neck as her mouth settled close to his ear. He had the most surreal feeling that he would be happy to live the rest of his life inside this magic intimate world that Stef and Keely shared. He felt a familiar emptiness inside him. He'd loved his grandfather. He and Paddy had made the best of what they had. Mitch realized he'd been alone too long. That he wanted something more.

"Come on, jelly bean," he gently coaxed her again. "Tell me what the troll said."

"Open the door," Keely confided in a frightened little voice that took Mitch hostage, made him make silent entreaties that she'd always be innocent. Always be safe.

Had this been a random attack? Or had whoever attacked Stef wanted to snatch Keely?

He kissed her damp head, amazed how natural it felt. How gratifying. He'd never kissed a child before. Never held one the way he was holding Keely. God, he was sinking deeper and deeper into the lives of this mother and daughter. How hard was it going to be to walk away when this was all over? "Good girl that you didn't listen. You should never listen to a troll."

Keely nodded sagely.

"Can I give you to Juliana, jelly bean? I'm going to go with your mommy to see the doctor."

Keely looked uncertain, her lower lip jutting out dangerously as if she were about to cry again. Or scream.

He was thrilled she no longer viewed him as the enemy.

"You'll be safe, I promise. That kiss I just gave you is a magic spell. The troll can't come back. And even if he tried, G.D. will be with you. Trolls are scared of G.D. He has an army of knights to keep you safe."

"'Kay." Keely held her arms out to Juliana, who scooped her up and kissed her pale white cheek. Mitch saw a fierce protectiveness in Juliana's eyes that was both reassuring and an unsettling reminder that she represented the Collingwood family's claim over Keely.

Mitch and the other security officers helped the

EMTs lift Stef onto the stretcher. Mitch squeezed Stef's fingers. They were so cold! Was she going into shock? "I'm here, spitfire. I'm coming with you."

Quickly and efficiently the EMTs hooked her up to an IV and put pressure on the laceration on her face. As they wheeled Stef's stretcher toward the exit Mitch promised Juliana and G.D. he'd call as soon as he had news. His gaze darted to Keely. He felt a gnawing reluctance to leave her, but he couldn't bring her to the hospital. Stef needed him, too. "You won't take your eyes off Kee, promise, G.D.?"

G.D.'s determined tone carried a promise that immediately eased Mitch's concerns. "Not for a second."

In the short time he'd been working for G.D., he'd realized that The Guardian wasn't in this business for profit. He cared about the work he did as much as Mitch cared about the children he tried to help.

Mitch followed the stretcher into the locker room. But a muffled thumping from one of the lockers stopped him in his tracks. G.D. heard the thumping, too.

Mitch reached for his weapon, silently motioning for the EMTs to remove Stef from the room. G.D. hustled Juliana and Keely safely away, as well. With two of the security officers acting as backup, Mitch opened the locker door.

A body, the head and torso hooded by a white laundry bag, tumbled out.

Mitch caught it before it hit the floor. He pulled the hood from the victim's head. It was a male Caucasian, in his mid-twenties. His chest was bare and his mouth was covered with a strip of duct tape.

His eyes were open and he appeared to be in a stupor. The type of stupor caused by a stun gun.

The security director knelt beside the injured man. "I

know this guy. He works for the hotel—in the pool area.''

Fear burned like acid in Mitch's stomach as his mouth flattened into a grim line. The attack on Stef hadn't been random. The kidnapper had been in Stef's house today, had lifted the hotel key card that would grant him access to the pool area. The kidnapper knew he had the wrong child.

THE KIDNAPPER FLED the Clairmont Hotel toward Times Square, merging into the ever-present nightly crowd that came to admire the barrage of advertisements affixed to the towering buildings—a symbol of the American way. Money.

Damn that brat. The kidnapper had been so close— mere inches from having Riana. From having everything. Ridding the towel boy of his hotel uniform had been a stroke of genius and had facilitated a successful escape.

It would be harder the next time. Riana had been well protected. Next time, there would be even more protection.

The kidnapper moved at the pace of the jostling crowd. The crowd stalled around a makeshift stall where knockoff wallets and purses were being sold. The raised voice of a woman haggling with the vendor drifted toward the kidnapper.

''Look, I bought this wallet from you last week, but it doesn't fit in my purse so I can't use it. How about I trade it for this other wallet that I want?''

The kidnapper didn't hear the rest of the conversation because the crowd started to move. But it didn't matter. The overheard conversation had given the kidnapper an idea, the perfect way to trade Emma for the real Riana.

MITCH WAITED in the Emergency Room for more than three hours. He paced. He asked the nurses for information on Stef's condition. He blatantly lied and said he was Stef's fiancé. He didn't care what he had to do to find out if Stef was going to be okay. A representative of the Clairmont Hotel, a slender woman with sky-blue eyes and dark bobbed hair, arrived at the hospital and informed the administration that the care for both victims would be covered by the hotel.

She introduced herself to Mitch as Brook Sinclair.

Mitch went into wary mode. Annette York had been arrested at Brook Sinclair's island home in the St. Lawrence River. "You're Juliana Goodhew's friend."

Ms. Sinclair gave him a circumspect smile as she shook his hand. "Yes, I own the Clairmont Hotel. I'm very concerned about what happened to Mrs. Shelton and one of my employees. So far we haven't been able to find or identify the attacker. We're checking the videotapes of the surveillance cameras in the lobby and the pool area. The Guardian would like you to call him as soon as possible."

Mitch found himself thinking that Brook Sinclair must be very tight with Juliana Goodhew to offer her the privacy of her island home as well as special accommodations in her hotel. Was she only Juliana's friend? Or had Ross and Lexi Collingwood appointed her Riana's legal guardian? Was that why she'd personally come to check on Stef?

When he had time, he was going to do some private research on Brook Sinclair. "I'll call The Guardian as soon as I know Mrs. Shelton is all right," he assured her.

Finally he was allowed in to see Stef. The doctor was finishing suturing the gash in her temple.

Stef's eyes compelled him like arms raised for a hug. Mitch wasn't in a position to refuse. He went to her side, gripped her hand, stroked the soft skin of her inner wrist with the pad of his thumb. "You okay?"

She dismissed his question with a weak smile. "I'm fine. They did a CT scan and it's okay. I was stunned apparently. No permanent damage and no broken bones—just a mild concussion. Keely's safe?" she demanded anxiously.

"She's with G.D. and Juliana. They promised not to let her out of their sight."

Stef nodded. "Good. I miss her." She winced as the doctor took another stitch. A monster of a bruise was forming on the left side of her face, but it didn't detract a bit from her delicate beauty. "I *need* to hold her." Tears welled in her eyes and Mitch was helpless to the fear that he saw reflected there. The knowledge of what could have happened to Keely.

His fingers tightened their hold on hers, sharing her fear, bolstering her courage. For the first time in his life he truly understood that his grandfather hadn't just been an honorable man doing his duty by his grandson. Paddy had gotten something priceless in exchange for the love he'd showered on a confused anger-ridden kid. He'd gotten a family. Someone to hold. Someone to care about. Someone who cared whether he lived or died.

Mitch lowered his head so Stef wouldn't see the moisture that sprang suddenly in his eyes. He had to tell Stef that the situation had escalated. That the bound staffer in the pool area indicated the attack on Stef and Keely was a planned kidnapping attempt. The kidnapper knew he had the wrong child.

How could he tell this caring, trusting woman that

there would be no ransom demand now? In all likelihood her child had been discarded, was dead.

He'd promised to tell her the truth, but Mitch would as soon cut off his arm. He cursed the bastards who'd done this to her, who'd stoop to kidnapping innocent children and heartlessly destroying two families. Mitch knew what it felt like to have someone you loved ripped from your life. To live in the emptiness of knowing you had no one left.

He had to protect her from this truth.

He felt her fingers feather through his hair. He closed his eyes, absorbing the comfort her light touch offered. "Mitch, what is it?"

He lifted his head. "It can wait until later."

Stef's hand stilled in the raw silk of Mitch's hair, words bottling in her throat. She felt immeasurably safer now that he was here. She shouldn't have insisted on taking Keely to the pool. She hadn't known how dangerous it could be. She could have lost her baby—and all because she'd insisted The Guardian's bodyguards not accompany them into the ladies' locker room. Hadn't thought it was necessary.

She swallowed hard. She wouldn't let Mitch blame himself for not being with them. He'd been with Sable, trying to trap her into revealing where she was holding Stef's baby. Stef would never be able to repay Mitch for the effort he was making. As much as she wanted to hate him for figuring out that Keely wasn't her biological child, she simply couldn't. The truth was, if Mitch hadn't shown up on her doorstep, the kidnapper might have overpowered Stef at home and snatched Keely. And the police would have had no idea why Keely had been taken.

No, she didn't hate Mitch. Keely was safe with The

Guardian. And Stef tried to hold tight to the hope in her heart for her real daughter's successful return.

"One more stitch and we're done," the doctor said. "That makes twenty-three. When's the wedding?"

Wedding? Stef wondered if she was imagining things. If it was part of the concussion.

Mitch lifted his big head, his face reddening slightly. Stef felt a molten warmth at his embarrassment. He was at his most endearing when his confidence was on shaky ground. "I told him we were engaged, sweetheart." He cleared his throat, spoke more firmly. "We're thinking Christmas, Doc. It's the season of miracles."

"Well, this will be well healed by then. You might have a faint scar."

"Scar or no scar, she's still the most beautiful woman I've ever seen."

The doctor laughed. "Spoken like a man in love."

It was Stef's turn to be embarrassed. There could never be any love between her and Mitch. No matter how much she was becoming to depend on him, she couldn't betray Keely and Brad by falling in love with Mitch.

THEY MOVED Stef to a private room to keep her overnight for observation. Mitch left her for a few minutes under Brook Sinclair's watchful eyes so he could interview the towel boy before he was discharged.

Unfortunately the towel boy had been so disoriented by the shock from the stun gun he remembered very little of the attack. He'd gone into the ladies' locker room to collect the bag of dirty towels and someone had zapped him from behind. He couldn't say whether his assailant was male or female.

Frustrated by the lack of clues, Mitch called The

Guardian from a pay phone to update him on Stef's condition.

G.D. was clearly relieved. ''Thank God she's going to be fine. I take full responsibility. She wanted to take Keely swimming and I could tell she was feeling pressured by the situation and needed some space. I struck a compromise when she insisted that having the bodyguards follow them into the change rooms was too invasive. One guard stayed in the pool area, the other out front.''

''Did they see anything?''

''Actually, no. But I've figured out what transpired, because an emergency exit door was activated. I think the original plan was to subdue Stef and Keely in the shower area, put Keely in a laundry bag and carry her out the service exit. A shower was left running, which suggests the kidnapper intended to stow Stef there to buy some time before anyone discovered her.

''But Stef and Keely went into the bathroom first and the kidnapper attacked. I'd just alerted the bodyguard that your key card was missing when Keely started screaming. The guard near the pool area entered the ladies' change room. The assailant waited until he passed and slipped back toward the pool where he left by an emergency exit. No one paid attention to him because he was wearing a hotel uniform.''

''You say *he?* Do you know for certain the suspect is a male? I just spoke to the towel boy. He doesn't know who jumped him.''

''I'm assuming it was a male because Keely told me that the troll had dark hair on his arms,'' G.D. admitted sheepishly. ''Unfortunately the surveillance camera in the pool area is angled toward the pool and the hot tub to prevent guests from becoming too indiscreet. We don't have the suspect on tape.''

Mitch massaged his forehead, trying to make all the pieces fit. ''Maybe it's this Tony. The bartender at Herman's said he hasn't seen Tony since Brad died. Unfortunately, the bartender didn't know Tony's last name, but he gave me the names of two of Brad's basketball buddies. They might know who Tony was. But my point is, maybe Tony conveniently dropped into Brad's life for a reason.'' Great, now he was searching for ways to make Brad look like a saint in Stef's eyes.

''The reason being that Tony was working with Sable?''

Mitch bemoaned the fact that the telephone cord was so short. He couldn't pace, couldn't stretch his thoughts beyond an image of Stef lying injured in a hospital bed down the corridor. ''Or someone else.'' Mitch finally realized what had been bothering him all along about the videotape. The timing! ''This Tony could have been keeping an eye on Sable and Brad. Think about it, Tony just happened to show up at Herman's just as Sable was leaving. Tony's interested in the baby and Brad's schedule. Stranger things have happened. The bartender described him as being medium height, dark hair, with a tattoo of a pair of red lips on his shoulder. Thinks he's a real ladies' man.''

''Give me the names of Brad's friends. I'll track down current home and work addresses for them.''

Mitch gave him the names.

''I could assign someone to interview them tonight if that would speed things up,'' G.D. offered.

''Thanks, G.D., but I'd prefer to conduct the interviews myself. Then I'll start interviewing the people on the list of Brad's co-workers that Sable gave me. But you could get your elves to track down a piece of property for me in the Catskills. Sable Holden told me her family has a place there—and it was worth more to her than gold.''

''Excellent, Mitch. Sable could have Stef's real daughter stashed somewhere in the vicinity.''

''It's a long shot, but it's worth pursuing.''

''Mitch, there's one more thing,'' G.D. said in a silver-spoon diplomatic tone that put Mitch's radar on high alert. ''I've moved Keely out of the hotel—to another location.''

Mitch felt an explosion of alarm in his gut, knowing how Stef would feel about that. Hell, he knew how *he* felt about Keely being moved to another location without Stef's consent. ''Was this your decision or your employer's?'' he demanded, not giving a damn that he sounded like a hard-assed jerk. For all he knew, Brook Sinclair was covertly assessing Stef's suitability as a mother right this instant.

G.D. showed no sign of taking offense. ''This decision is mine. And just for the record, when it comes to protecting an individual's life, I call the shots. My clients are made fully aware that it is a non-negotiable condition of my involvement in a situation. Please inform Mrs. Shelton of the necessity of the change. I won't give you the address over the phone for obvious reasons, but Keely's with me and Juliana. She's safe. When I explained to Keely that we were leaving she seemed relieved because she didn't want the troll to come back. I assured her that you would bring her mommy to her in the morning.''

Mitch closed his eyes and banged his head against the wall. Goddamn it. What was really messing with his brain was the fear that Keely might be meeting Brook

Sinclair or her legal guardian at this undisclosed location.

G.D. wouldn't do that, would he? No, he'd said Keely's legal guardian wasn't going to be brought into the picture until the situation was resolved. He wouldn't want to take any additional risks. They needed to focus on bringing Stef's child home safely, not be distracted by a custody battle. Mitch was still going to check out Brook Sinclair.

"G.D.?"

"Yes?"

Mitch's voice hitched. "The kidnapper knows he has the wrong child."

"I'm aware of that, yes."

"The variables have changed. There would be no reason to keep Stef's real daughter alive now."

"That's why we have to find her before that happens. You're doing a hell of a job, Halloran. If you hadn't called me when you did, the kidnapper might have succeeded in snatching Keely, too."

"I'd feel a helluva lot better if we'd nabbed the bastard."

"We will. I'll send a car for you in the morning."

Mitch smiled at G.D.'s confidence. Somehow G.D. managed to do the job and stay detached. "Tell the jelly bean that I'm taking good care of her mommy."

He hung up the phone and felt like kicking something in frustration. Time was running out. He had to find Stef's daughter. When he returned to Stef's hospital room, Brook Sinclair was flipping through the pages of a fashion magazine and Stef was sleeping, the sheets pulled up around her huddled form and her dark hair forming a pool of silk on the pillow.

Mitch kept his suspicions about Brook well under wraps as he thanked her for staying with Stef.

"Glad to be of help. Again, I'm sorry this happened in one of my hotels. I left my card on the table. If Mrs. Shelton has any concerns about her medical bills, she can contact me directly."

"Thanks."

After Brook Sinclair had left, Mitch dimmed the lights in the room and pulled a chair up to Stef's bedside. In the darkness he could hear her soft breaths, could smell her vanilla-and-home-baked-cookies scent. He touched the dark pool of her hair reverently.

He wasn't giving up hope of finding her daughter alive.

Chapter Nine

Love conquered all.

Darren Black awoke after a restless night dreaming of his lost love and finally discovered the words that he had been waiting so long to hear from Annette's lips printed in the *New York Times* for all the world to see.

> I love Darren Black. I always have. Calling off our engagement was one of the most foolish things I've ever done. I let what other people thought matter more than what I thought. But losing my sister and her husband has taught me how important love is. That it is the *only* thing. I hope and pray that when I'm acquitted, Darren and I can begin again.

She loved him. He jostled the table, spilling his corn flakes and coffee as he leaped from his chair and raised his hands in triumph to the plastered ceiling of the home he had bought to share with Annette. With their children.

The joy resonating through him vastly surpassed the egotistical glow of proving the big math theorem that had landed him his plum position at Cornell.

He'd known he was destined for a bigger and brighter future.

Annette still loved him.

He had to see her.

STEF AWOKE with a throbbing headache. But a smile curved her lips when she opened her eyes and saw Mitch had stayed the night with her, his large body cramped into a chair that was several sizes too small for him.

He was sleeping. With the bloodstains on his shirt and his hair a halo of bleached gold, he looked like Ares, the Greek god of war, in repose.

Her gaze traced the map of faint lines in his forehead and descended down the blade of his nose to the lines bracketing his mouth. Even in sleep Mitch was restless, intense. Planning his next step.

One of his hands rested on the bed not far from her own. Stef let her hand creep toward his, seeking its warmth. Its strength. She didn't know what drove Mitch, but whatever it was, she was glad he was here. He was a very special man.

Feeling safer than she'd ever felt in her life, Stef wished away the pain in her head and drifted back to sleep.

"MOMMY! MITCH!"

Her hair dancing around her shoulders, Keely raced down the hallway to welcome them to the safe-house apartment on Central Park West.

Mitch felt a powerful punch in the abdomen as he witnessed the transformation on Stef's face as she opened her arms to her daughter. Her eyes had the welcoming glow of a lighted window and her smile made the world seem right.

She'd had such a headache this morning, Mitch had glossed over his rendezvous with Sable and his subsequent interview with the bartender at Herman's. The doctor had prescribed some pain medication and told her she'd feel better after she'd eaten something and had a decent night's rest.

She hadn't uttered a word of protest when he'd informed her that The Guardian had moved Keely to a safe house. Mitch had explained that there was a chance someone had been in her home the day before and had stolen the hotel key card from his pocket.

Stef had turned ashen and suggested that Sable had sent someone to her home after their visit to her office. "You were right, Mitch. I shouldn't have spoken to her privately. She knows I'm suspicious now. I'm relieved The Guardian moved Keely to a safer location. I just hope we'll find my baby at Sable's place in the Catskills."

Mitch had nodded and said nothing.

Keely chattered happily to Stef. "I had heart pancakes for breakfast, Mommy. And Juliana read me a story. And G.D. said I was a big brave girl." Then Keely turned to Mitch and held out her hand. "This is for you!"

Lying in her grubby paw was a single black jelly bean.

Mitch recognized a token of friendship when he saw it. "For me? It's a jelly bean. Not just any jelly bean— a *black* one."

Keely gave him an impish smile. "I saved it for you."

Mitch plucked the jelly bean from her hand and popped it into his mouth. It tasted of licorice and lint.

He promptly grabbed his throat and winked at Stef. "Oh, no, it's a yucky jelly bean." He fell to his knees and clutched his stomach as Keely chortled with laughter. "The yucky jelly bean is killing me." With a final dramatic groan, Mitch flopped onto the marble floor, feigning death.

The weight of a little girl impacting his chest tore a real groan from him.

Mitch opened one eye and peered up at Keely's adorable heart-shaped face. "What is it? I'm dead."

Keely smiled a killer smile and held a second jelly bean pinched between her thumb and her index finger. "This one will save you."

As simple as that, Mitch lost his heart to her.

"DARREN!"

Darren hadn't expected to be subjugated to talking to Annette through glass, an impersonal telephone sticky with the fingers of numerous prison visitors, pressed to his ear.

He wanted to touch her delicate face, fit his fingers to hers. Fit his lips to hers and lose himself in the sensual and existential bond of their lovemaking. It enraged him to see his pixie trapped in a glass cage as if she were a dangerous animal. Her green eyes had an aggrieved sheen and there were smudges beneath them, suggesting she wasn't sleeping well in this abominable place. She deserved so much more. They both did.

He laid his hand on the glass between them. "I came as soon I read the article."

She placed her palm against his. It was daintier, but every bit his equal. "I meant every word I said. I love you, Darren.'' She moistened her lips, desperation flashing in her eyes. ''You know I'm innocent, don't you? I can't believe that anyone would think I would hurt Lexi and Ross. She was my sister. I loved her.''

Darren gazed steadily into her soul, conscious that their conversation was more than likely being recorded or monitored. He couldn't find fault with what he saw. ''I know you better than anyone, Annette. Maybe better than you know yourself. I can't stand to see you like this. I want you in my arms where you belong. In my bed.''

She melted, tears sparkling on her pale cheeks like diamonds. ''There's no evidence against me. The only thing that might be damaging is Juliana Goodhew's testimony. I don't think she's thought this through—considered the consequences of revealing Ross and Lexi's secret.''

Darren frowned. He didn't know what she was referring to. ''Secret?''

Annette mouthed silently, ''Another baby.''

Shocked, Darren mouthed the words back to her to be sure he understood so that the phone wouldn't pick up their conversation. ''A baby?''

Annette nodded. ''There was another one,'' she said in a normal tone, then reverted to speaking silently. ''A boy.''

Darren leaned back in his chair, floored by the revelation.

''Juliana knew. So did I,'' Annette said after a moment. She spelled out a four-letter name on the glass with her finger: C-o-r-t. Cort. ''You must talk to her on my behalf, Darren. Make her see reason.''

''I wouldn't know where to find her,'' he said, his brilliant mind recognizing the pitfalls of becoming involved in such an errand. Her strategy might produce an effect opposite to the one she desired.

"You can find her through a friend of hers, Brook Sinclair. She owns the Clairmont Hotels."

Darren stiffened. "And the island where you were arrested?"

Annette lowered her gaze, her lashes sweeping her cheeks. "Yes," she admitted. "Brook keeps an apartment in the Park Terrace building on Central Park West. Juliana may be staying there."

Darren made a decision. It broke his heart, but he knew in the long run it would be for the best. For both of them. "I can't do it, Annette. Talk to your lawyer. I don't think this is in your best interests. I'll be in the courtroom with you."

Anger ignited in her eyes. "Darren? Darren? Don't leave me—"

He hung up the phone, kissed his fingers and pressed them to the glass. "Trust me," he mouthed. "I love you."

He couldn't let her be executed. Not when he'd finally gotten her back.

MITCH NEEDED SPACE and exercise. After spending the night in a chair at Stef's bedside he needed to work the kinks from his body and to organize his thoughts for the interviews he planned to do today. It was already 10:00 a.m., but he could spare an hour to run three miles in Central Park, shower and dress. He needed to be on top of his game for these interviews.

And he needed to distance his emotions from Stef and Keely. He couldn't afford to lose his objectivity or his sharpness. Stef had been injured yesterday and Keely had come terrifyingly close to being abducted.

He couldn't risk screwing up. He couldn't risk Stef and Keely's safety. And there was a little girl out there who needed to be reunited with the most wonderful mommy in the world.

The most wonderful mommy in the world? Where had that thought come from? A fleeting memory of a birthday cake and flaming candles illuminating a woman who was singing to him, calling him "dear Mitchell," slammed into him, almost tripping him up. One of the few memories he had of his mother. He knew what it was like to feel abandoned. Unloved. He couldn't stand the thought of Stef's biological daughter missing out on the life Stef could give her.

Mitch pushed himself, his stride rapidly eating up ground. He'd hoped to push his emotions for Stef and Keely into the back corner of his heart sealed behind a wall of mental determination, but images of Stef's bruised face, her hand reaching out to him and the mischief in Keely's eyes as she saved him from a yucky black jelly bean kept dissolving the wall.

Out of the mouths of babes. Keely would never know that she'd saved him in more ways than one when she'd offered him that sticky piece of candy. The swift realization that he loved that irrepressible little girl had filled him with a contentment he hadn't felt since before his grandfather had died. He had a glimpse of what was missing in his life. Of how he could be the man his grandfather had wanted him to be.

And it scared the hell out of him.

Mitch ran faster, his chest burning and his thighs straining until a memory from high school besieged him. He'd been warming a washcloth and pressing it to his forehead, pretending he had a fever so he wouldn't have to go to English class because of a stupid assignment. They were supposed to make a family tree and give an oral report to the class. One half of his family tree—his father's side—was blank. His parents had never married so he couldn't even pencil in a marriage date. And his grandfather's knowledge of his mother's side of the family was pitifully sparse.

When Paddy had seen through the fever ruse, Mitch had torn up the genealogy chart he'd made and thrown the pieces on the floor.

Paddy had looked at the torn pieces and said, "Go to school, son. Do the work. There are some things you just can't run away from. These are the decisions that form you—even if they make you sweat and scare the hell out of you. Do you leave your fallen comrade to be found by the enemy or do you retrieve his body for his family? Do you steal because your friends are stealing?"

Mitch had skulked out of the room. He'd taken one picture to school with him that day instead—a picture of his grandfather in his marine uniform. His family. The teacher had given him a B.

Mitch laughed at himself, realizing he'd found what he'd been seeking. And it made him want to just keep on running. Yes, he was scared, scared of admitting that Stef and Keely were the family he desperately wanted but had no chance of having. He still had to show up and do the work. He hadn't liked the roller coaster of emotions that had come with the Carmen Lopez case, either. But he'd shown up, anyway, and somehow he'd managed to cope when Carmen Lopez's body was found and his worst fears had been realized.

He turned and headed back to the apartment. No matter what happened, he would not run away from Stef and Keely.

"I'M COMING WITH YOU," Stef insisted when Mitch was ready to head out of the apartment in a freshly pressed suit, his hair still damp from the shower.

She wore black slacks that hugged her slim hips and a black sweater with a boat neck that emphasized the beauty of her collar bone and her throat. Her coat and her purse were slung over her arm. She'd put on makeup, but it didn't disguise the shadows beneath her eyes or the nasty bruise flowering beneath the bandage on her temple.

She looked sexy and vulnerable and incredibly brave. And so kissable. Mitch felt a combination of sweat and fear, and wondered whether his grandfather would consider kissing a woman a life-defining moment. Probably.

"Sorry. You're tired. You need to rest."

"Someone attacked me yesterday and tried to take my baby. You think I'm going to be able to rest after that?"

He tried another tactic. "What about Keely? Don't you think she needs you today after what happened yesterday?"

"She seems fine. She adores Juliana. They've spent the last hour planning their day. The Guardian won't let them out of his sight. All the bases are covered."

Mitch didn't believe for a minute that she was as nonchalant about leaving Keely again today as she was pretending. "You're going to slow me down."

She tilted her chin up obstinately just like Keely did when she was determined to get her own way. "Are you afraid of being alone with me?"

Mitch recognized a trap when he saw one. He was damned either way he stepped. He glowered at her, his body hungrily acknowledging every detail of her appearance. "Let's go."

They would interview Pete O'Shay first. Marquise, the Hispanic butler who looked after the apartment along with his wife Valentina, drove them in a limousine to the engineering firm on East 42nd Street in Midtown where Pete worked.

Mitch's body thrummed with tension as he sat beside Stef in the limo. Her exposed throat was a temptation of golden satin skin he wanted to explore. He tried to keep his gaze straight ahead during the short ride and his mind on the investigation. They'd decided that they would use the same cover story they had used with Sable. Evan Mitchell was writing a biography of Brad's life and wanted anecdotes and stories to add to the book for Keely.

Obviously the basketball team's center, Pete O'Shay had a boyish face that probably only required shaving three times a week.

Pete completely fell under Stef's spell as she deflected his question about her injury with a funny story involving a wet floor and a toilet, then she gave her spiel about the book. Mitch marveled that she could look so at ease and sound so enthusiastic when he knew she'd had such a rough night. "I was hoping you'd be willing to contribute a basketball story about Brad." She beamed at Pete. "I thought if I asked you in person, you'd be less likely to say no."

Pete laughed, lapping up her attention. "Brad was an excellent defensive player. We called him the cheerleader because he was always giving us pep talks when we were losing. Sure, I'll come up with something as long as Evan here promises to fix my spelling and punctuation."

Mitch grinned. "No problem. Here's my card. You can send it via whatever media you prefer. And it would help if you could add a paragraph or two about the last time you saw Brad. We're going to visit Mike Lipetzky next. But we're having trouble tracking down Tony. Have you got his number or know his last name?"

"I had his number once, but he dropped out of sight and his number was disconnected." Pete rubbed the back of his neck. "Unfortunately, I don't remember his last name. He maybe played with us for two or three months, but he wasn't very reliable. He was tighter with Brad than the rest of us. After Brad died, he just stopped showing up."

That was the kind of coincidence that made Mitch think Tony had been hanging around Brad for the specific reason of keeping tabs on the baby. But if Tony was in on the kidnapping and the baby switch, why hadn't he snatched Keely back after Brad's death and ransomed her to her parents?

One plausible explanation came swiftly to Mitch's mind.

Was it possible Tony was dead, too? If Tony had switched the babies, it could explain why whoever sent in the second ransom demand had been unaware that they had the wrong child.

"Do you remember where he worked or anything that might help us locate him?"

"Sorry. All I know is that he worked evenings and Thursday was his night off. He might have been a door-man—I saw a uniform in a dry-cleaning bag in the back seat of his car once. But Mike may know."

Mitch rose. "Thank you."

Stef took his arm as they wove through the maze of cubicles back to the elevator, her feminine touch sending ribbons of awareness curling through him. "Do you find it odd that this Tony disappeared after Brad's death?"

Mitch looked down at her, impressed that her thoughts were echoing his own. She was not only gorgeous, she was intuitive and intelligent. Her chestnut hair framed her delicate features and the bandage on her temple. He squeezed her fingers. Touching her was too easy. "That's exactly what I was thinking. In fact, from what Pete said, I get the impression Tony showed up deliberately during the last month of your pregnancy."

Confusion rose in Stef's green-gold eyes. "I understand how Tony could have known we were having a girl, but how could he have known I'd give birth four days before my due date?"

"I don't think he knew specifically at the time that he would switch Riana with *your* daughter—that was probably an opportunity that presented itself by chance and Tony went for it because it would be easier for him to switch the babies back. My guess is Tony was picking up info about the security procedures in the hospital that you were told about on your maternity wing tour—you took a tour, right?"

"Yes."

"And he was learning personal information about you and Brad, so that he could bypass the hospital's security system. I wouldn't be surprised if he pretended to be Brad and dropped in for one of those tours. From what I saw on the videotape, Brad was a pretty proud dad, and open about sharing this experience with others."

Stef exhaled slowly. "Good, I was afraid I was grasping at straws. Despite the evidence we found at my house yesterday, Mitch, I'm not convinced Brad was directly involved in Riana's kidnapping. Maybe he was involved with some conspiracy with Sable, but I don't think for a minute that he switched our baby with the Collingwoods' baby.''

"You may be right. I have a gut feeling that Tony might be dead, too. I think he double-crossed whoever he was working for by switching the babies. And the fact that you and Keely were attacked yesterday suggests the kidnapper has just now figured that out. That's why we have to find out who Tony is. He's our link to the kidnapper.''

Stef trustingly slipped her hand into his. Mitch accepted it tenderly, for the rare treasure that it was. "I'm game,'' she said. "Let's find him.''

Mike Lipetzky worked for an insurance company in Jackson Heights. A gregarious man with silver infusing his brush-cut brown hair, his welcoming smile changed to a look of concern when he saw Stef. When she explained her accident, he commiserated with her over her clumsiness and her stitches and lightly kissed her cheek, then shook Mitch's hand warmly.

"Shall we go into my office or around the corner to the deli for a sandwich? Is this business or pleasure?''

"Pleasure, definitely,'' Mitch said. "Lunch is on us.''

They had corned beef sandwiches with dill pickles and potato salad on the side. Stef told Mike about her move to Logantown. "If I'm careful with my finances, I won't have to go back to work until Keely starts school.''

"Good. Good. I tried to talk Brad into a larger policy, but it's hard to convince healthy vital people that unforeseen accidents happen. I'm glad there was something to help you. I hope you've looked after Keely's future. Call me if you'd like to talk about estate planning.''

Mitch saw the agony reflected momentarily in Stef's features at the insurance broker's mention of Keely's future. Mitch steered the conversation toward their goal and explained the biography project.

''Ho, I could tell you a story or two about Brad,'' Mike said with a smile. ''But are you sure you want to hear about the last time I saw him?''

''Definitely,'' Mitch said. ''Sometimes we put those events into a certain perspective that tell a lot about a person's character.''

The insurance broker looked hesitant. ''I'm not so sure about this, though.''

Stef, intuiting that her presence was hindering Mike's openness, excused herself to use the ladies' room.

''I didn't mean to run you off,'' Mike protested.

Stef brushed aside his protest. ''Don't be silly. I really do have to use the rest room. So tell Mitch whatever you're thinking and let him decide whether it should be included in the book.''

Mitch wasn't alone in watching her walk across the busy deli, her body moving with vibrancy. He knew that underneath her smiles and her tigress's determination to find her biological child, it was killing her to learn so much about her husband that she didn't know. Every new piece of information they uncovered about Brad's activities inflicted a new wound.

''She's a charming young woman,'' Mike remarked. ''Brad was a lucky man.''

''Do you think he realized how lucky he was?'' Mitch asked, knowing he was personally invested in the answer. He didn't like the idea that Brad hadn't appreciated Stef.

"Yes and no. Losing his job hit him hard, made him forget sometimes how fortunate he was to have a wife and a healthy daughter. He was under a lot of pressure with a new baby to care for and no job."

"So what happened the last time you saw him?"

"It was the Thursday before Brad died. We were having drinks at Herman's after a game. The other guys had left and Brad wasn't in any hurry to go home. I asked him how the job search was going and he told me that he was in limbo, in the middle of a deal. He thought he'd had a firm offer, but now it looked like that wasn't going to happen. He was debating whether he should take the initiative and strike out on his own. He seemed anxious."

"You know any of the particulars?"

"No. He wasn't specific, which made it hard to offer any practical advice."

"Then I won't mention it," Mitch said. "Stef and I are trying to track down another old basketball buddy—someone named Tony, but I don't know his last name. Pete said he quit the team after Brad's death."

"That's right. I'm not sure Tony was the kind of person who had a last name, if you know what I mean. He didn't even bother to call and say he was bailing on us. There was something shady about that guy, but he had a decent jump shot and he could hit those three pointers. He used to live in an apartment on the corner of 39th Avenue and 100th Street in Corona. Can't miss it. The building had a wine-red awning shaped like a bat wing over the front entrance. I gave Tony a ride home once after he hurt his ankle in a tournament."

"You know where he worked?"

Mike wiped his mouth with a paper napkin. "I never got a straight answer out of him on that subject. I'm not sure how he and Brad hooked up. Take my advice, steer Stef clear of that character.''

''Point taken.''

Stef rejoined them and made excuses that they had other friends of Brad's to call on today. Mitch could see her barely contained anxiety as they returned to the limo.

''Well, what did he say?'' she demanded as Marquise held the door open for them.

Mitch quickly related the story Mike had told him about Brad's being seemingly torn over a job offer.

Stef's brows arched. ''Could it be he was torn over his arrangement with Sable?''

''I think so, especially if she was planning to blackmail Ross Collingwood with that tape. Maybe she'd promised Brad his job back if she succeeded.''

''Is it possible that Sable never intended to go through with their arrangement? Maybe the arrangement itself was a ruse so she and Tony could stay in frequent contact with Brad and keep tabs on the baby,'' Stef added passionately.

''That's an excellent point,'' Mitch acknowledged with an admiring smile, suppressing an overwhelming urge to kiss her. ''I hadn't thought of that.''

Stef was proving herself to be one hell of a woman, one who would stand by the man she loved through thick and thin. They'd found out some alarming information about Brad. No doubt she was reeling from the blows that he might have been involved in a criminal conspiracy with Sable. She might even feel that Brad had betrayed her and their family, but she was unshaken in her belief that Brad had loved their child and would never place her in a harmful position. And Mitch found he trusted Stef's instincts.

Brad had been lucky to be on the receiving end of such unwavering devotion.

Mitch saved the best news for last. "I've got Tony's address. I don't know if it's current, but it's a lead."

"You got his address?" Stef flung her arms around his neck and hugged him tightly. Her infectious warmth enveloped him and brought his body to a painful and pulsing arousal. Just for a moment he fantasized about coming home to the scented softness of Stef's arms every day—until he caught the chauffeur's eye in the rearview mirror.

He had a feeling that news of this hug would get back to The Guardian. Mitch swore silently and gruffly disentangled himself from Stef's arms. He couldn't risk being yanked off the case for fraternizing with the client.

Come hell or high water, he was going to find her baby.

Chapter Ten

They had Tony's address. Stef felt as if they were making progress when the limo pulled up outside an austere gray apartment building with a wine-red awning in Corona.

They examined the names posted over the buzzers for each apartment. There was no one obviously marked Tony. Stef held her breath as Mitch pressed the button for the super's apartment. Please God, let them find Tony here. Alive. She wanted her daughter back.

A cantankerous voice scraped over the intercom. "Yes?"

Mitch winked at Stef, planting an optimistic glow in her belly. "Sorry to bother you, but I'm trying to find my friend Tony's apartment. I'm worried he might have moved. I don't see his name posted."

"You mean Tony Conklin?"

"That's my man."

"He doesn't live here anymore. You a friend of his?"

"Yes, sir. Apparently not a close enough friend, though, he didn't bother to tell me he was moving. When did he move?"

"Hold on. I'll be down in a minute."

Stef crossed her fingers in the pockets of her coat for

good luck as the spry elderly man suddenly appeared at the front door. He wore a blue flannel shirt tucked into a pair of rugged work pants. And he carried a thin yellow sheet of paper and a pencil.

He opened the door for them, eyeing them suspiciously. "You say you're friends of Tony?"

"Yes, sir. Tony and I go way back." Mitch's hand came to rest on the small of Stef's back. "I'm in town on a business trip with my fiancée and I wanted to introduce her to him. I tried calling, but the number was listed to someone else. I figured he got a cell phone."

"Well, he just up and disappeared without paying the rent. Left all his things." The old man pointed a finger at Mitch. "You tell him I sold everything I could, applied it toward the rent. But he still owes me twelve hundred dollars." He showed Mitch some scribbling he'd done on the back of the yellow sheet, which appeared to be a rental agreement.

"Wait a minute," Mitch said. "Let me get this straight. One of your tenants disappears and leaves all his stuff and you're not the least bit concerned?"

"Of course I'm concerned. I want my rent."

"Did you call the police and report him missing?"

"Why would I do that?" the super rumbled. "Tenants run off in the middle of the night all the time. I figure he was probably arrested."

"Did you at least call his work or his family?"

"I tried his job, but they hadn't seen him, either."

Which added more fuel to the fire of possibility that Tony was dead.

Stef leaned into the solid strength of Mitch's body as if he were her fiancé. Smelled the scents of citrus and sea salt that branded him. He was as brilliant as he was gorgeous and she hoped to God that the edginess she noticed in him wasn't because of what had happened between them yesterday. He hadn't let it get out of hand. But was he worried that it might happen again?

Ever since Mitch had kissed her she'd become aware that she was starved for passion. Her cheeks burned with shame that she was thinking about making love with Mitch when her baby was missing and Keely was in danger.

She squeezed Mitch's arm. They had to find the link between Tony and the kidnapper holding her biological child. "Oh, my God, sweetheart. I hope your friend is all right."

"When was this?" Mitch pressed the super.

The old man scrutinized the contract. "July—two years ago."

Mitch pulled his wallet out of the pocket of his raincoat. "Here's six hundred dollars, that's half of what Tony owes you, in exchange for whatever contact information you have for him. I want his work number, references, whatever you got. If I find him, I'll make sure he pays you the rest of the rent. Deal? I want a receipt for the six hundred dollars."

The super waffled for a few seconds, then took the money. "Deal. I'll make a copy on the fax machine of the contract with the particulars."

Mitch was grinning from ear to ear when they walked out of the apartment building ten minutes later. Wind rattled through the bare branches of the trees lining the street and a few raindrops splotched onto the sidewalk. Stef nudged the photocopy in his hand so that she could examine it, too. "I want to see."

"Sure, sweetheart," he teased, his teeth gleaming white against his tanned face. Stef's heart skittered to a stop. His eyes held the mysteries of a blue-velvet sky.

Soft. Sensual. And unfathomable. His warm breath whispered along her cheek, stirring her hair. "You know, I just never imagined myself as someone's sweetheart."

Longing, sharp and bittersweet, tangled through her, paralyzing her tongue. She meant to say something flippant, that she was only following his lead because he'd introduced her as his fiancée. But something in his tone—a core thread of truth woven in his teasing words—egged her to respond with heartfelt honesty. "Don't underestimate yourself. Beneath that movie-star face and that bossy attitude is a big heart."

"Bossy, huh?" His gaze narrowed on her. Every nerve in her body swirled to life with awakening desire like Fourth of July sparklers.

"Yes, incredibly bossy," she said bravely as a raindrop touched her nose. They were on a busy city street and she felt an electric soul-stirring intimacy taking root with Mitch, which, if she were honest with herself, she'd never felt with Brad.

The noise of the traffic and the wind blurred behind her as she waited for Mitch to react. She took in the breadth of his shoulders and her nipples tightened to hard, aching buds. Mitch was threatening everything she held dear. Destroying her world. She couldn't betray her family like this, could she?

No, she couldn't. She was behaving like a fool and he had the decency not to take advantage of her vulnerability. And he probably didn't feel the same way.

She forced her attention back to that piece of paper. "Is there anything useful here?"

Mitch's blunt-tipped finger pointed out a handwritten address. Was it her imagination or was his voice huskier than usual? "Here's his employer—Rolston Security. Remember what Pete O'Shay said about seeing a uniform in Tony's car? Looks like Tony was a security guard.''

''Is there any other contact information? References? Next of kin?''

''No. But The Guardian has worked wonders with less. By the time we check out Rolston Security, The Guardian will have run a driver's license check, a criminal records check and a credit check.''

Stef plucked his cell phone from his belt clip. ''Start dialing, sweetheart. I want to find this jerk.''

HE SHOULDN'T HAVE BROUGHT her with him.

Mitch knew from the moment she'd waylaid him in the apartment and insisted on accompanying him that Stef would be a distraction, and she was. His pulse rate was soaring upward along with another rigid part of his anatomy. They finally had a solid lead on Tony Conklin and Mitch was being sidelined by a primitive and foolhardy urge to halt the sexual banter between them by kissing her senseless.

It was only fair. After all, she was making him senseless. So senseless he'd incorrectly dialed The Guardian's number. Mitch punched in the numbers a second time, his stomach dipping and rolling on a wave of exhilaration as the limo headed back to Manhattan to the security company's address near Union Square. Stef had called him sweetheart. And incredibly, she'd looked at him as if he were her hero.

Sweet Mother of God, it crossed every professional ethical boundary, but he'd liked it more than he would ever admit.

Mitch was sure G.D. would detect his shaky

breathing as he gave him Tony Conklin's last known address.

"Excellent, Mitch," G.D. said. "I'll do a background check on Conklin ASAP. Have you got time for an update? I've been accumulating some interesting information on my desk."

Mitch cast a sideways glance at Stef. She had her head bowed and her hands folded in her lap as if she were praying. Or was exhausted and needed a rest. "Shoot."

"I just received a fax listing the participants in the rock climbing event sponsored by Office Outfitters. Sable's name is on the top of the list. The operative who finagled the list tells me she's an experienced climber and climbs once or twice a month at the same school."

"So she had the means and the motive to make Brad's fall look like an accident?"

"Yes, although we can't place her at the scene," G.D. said with a frustrated sigh. "All we know is what she admitted to you at the jazz club last night—that she learned of Brad's death from a phone call she received while having a bath that evening. Unfortunately, the only prints my fingerprint expert lifted from the tape recorder and the pen video camera belonged to Brad."

Mitch frowned. "Maybe something more incriminating will turn up on Brad's laptop. In the meantime, I'll verify Sable's phone-call story with the store manager she claims called her. Maybe we can catch her in a lie."

"Good. And one last thing, we showed the nurse who was attacked the night of Riana's abduction a photo lineup. She couldn't identify Brad as her attacker. She told Edwards that it happened too fast. She wasn't sure about any of them. I'll call you as soon as I have the info you requested on Conklin. And you might want to look at the morning *Times* when you have a chance. Annette's still talking to anyone who'll listen.''

Mitch disconnected the call and relayed the gist of the updates to Stef.

She gave him a relieved smile that made him feel almost jealous of her loyalty to her husband. ''I told you Brad didn't abduct Riana.''

A car horn blared in the maze of traffic. Mitch felt his jaw tighten with roped-in frustration. ''I think you're misinterpreting what I said. The photo lineup was inconclusive because the nurse was too disoriented from the shock of the stun gun to get a good look at her attacker. Brad could still have been her assailant.''

Stef folded her arms across her chest. ''So you say.''

''Yes, I do. Last time I looked at my credentials I was qualified to make those kinds of conjectures. I haven't ruled him out as a suspect. He has no alibi for the night of Riana Collingwood's abduction and he was unaccounted for until approximately 1:00 p.m. the next day.''

She opened her mouth as if to say something, then closed it again. He felt her silence scorch him like a hot Santa Ana wind. She needed to stop defending Brad and to look at the cold, hard facts.

Mitch asked Marquise to stop the car so he could pick up a copy of the *New York Times* to check out the article about Annette that G.D. had mentioned. In the interests of keeping the lines of communication open between them, he showed the article to Stef. ''Look at this. Annette's having an epiphany about love from her jail cell, probably hoping it'll buy her some sympathy. Too bad she didn't decide love was the *only thing* before she blew her sister and her brother-in-law to kingdom come.''

Stef read the article and passed it back to him, stiffly. "It's kind of sad that Annette did the things she did because she was trying to earn her mother's approval. I wonder how Darren Black feels reading this, knowing she did those terrible things. I wonder if he'd defend her?"

Mitch was tempted to suggest that Darren Black was damn lucky Annette had broken off their engagement. What kind of life would that have been, constantly being compared to her sister's husband and his billions? But Mitch kept his mouth shut. He tore the article from the paper and put it in his notebook. Stef didn't say a word for the rest of the ride.

When the limo finally pulled up outside an ugly brown brick building, Mitch ground his molars together as he struggled to speak normally. Remain professional. "You still with me?"

She gave him a saccharine smile that suggested otherwise. "Sure, sweetheart."

She was pissed off at him now for again casting shadows of suspicion on her husband. Mitch rolled his shoulders, cracking the tension in the taut muscles. The three miles he'd run this morning hadn't been nearly enough. But then, he hadn't known Stef would be glued to his side all afternoon.

Do the work. Deal with the emotions, he brusquely reminded himself.

He helped Stef out of the limo, careful not to touch her any more than necessary. Though the exterior of the building was hideously ugly, the interior of Rolston Security's offices was crisply painted in shades of gray and burgundy. An artist's rendition of the company shield took pride of place on the main wall of the reception area. Mitch gave the receptionist his business card from the Find Riana Foundation and asked to speak to the manager.

A few minutes later he and Stef were ushered into a well-appointed office.

A lean man in his early fifties with caution etched in his face like cracks in a sidewalk rose from behind a handsome oak desk. He had ex-cop written all over him. Several plaques and photos on the walls testified to it. "I'm John Rolston. How do you do, Mr. Halloran?"

Mitch introduced Stef as his assistant. "I apologize for dropping by without an appointment. But it is urgent."

"About the Riana Collingwood investigation?"

"Yes."

"I was under the impression The Guardian was handling the investigation."

"He is. I was hired recently by him to investigate the tips coming into the hot line."

"Plum job. You N.Y.P.D.?"

"No, L.A.P.D."

Rolston smiled. "Lot of good detectives must have their noses out of joint. The Guardian's a legend in this town."

Mitch accepted that as a compliment. "I'm here following up on a tip we received that involves one of your employees—a Tony Conklin."

"Conklin? I'll have to check my files. It must be a serious tip if it brought you out in person."

Mitch hid a smile. Rolston was playing him, fishing for information, but he didn't have time for fun and games.

"I'm going to be straight with you, Rolston. You're a smart man—the prizes in your office tell me you're retired N.Y.P.D. I'm sure you can see the obvious advantages in assisting in the apprehension of Riana Collingwood's kidnapper. I'm sure you also understand that when I say that time is of the essence I'm not flapping my gums. Are you following me?''

''I see where you're headed.'' Ralston typed Tony's name via the keyboard on his desk and peered at the monitor. ''Mr. Conklin hasn't been employed by this company for at least a year because he's no longer in the system.'' He rose and approached a bank of blue filing cabinets that lined one wall of his office. ''I never toss the personnel files. People are a lot more careful about who they hire these days and checking previous employers.'' He thumbed through the files. ''Here it is. Conklin, Anthony James.''

He opened the manila file. ''He was one of our night patrol guards for about fifteen months, until he didn't show up for his shift and didn't call. We repeatedly tried to contact him. We even tried calling his emergency contact number, but it was out of service. A letter of dismissal and his last paycheck were mailed to his home address, but there's a note from accounting in his file that the check was never cashed.''

Mitch took notes. The chances of finding Tony alive were growing slimmer and slimmer—unless he'd gone into hiding. ''What date did he fail to show up for work?''

''July eighteenth.''

Mitch heard Stef's tiny gasp. He was sure Rolston did, too. July eighteenth was the day after Brad had died. ''Did he work a shift on the seventeenth?''

''I'll have to check another source for that.'' Rolston flipped through a box of computer diskettes. ''I employ about one hundred and twenty security officers at any given time.'' He selected a disk from the box and slid it into the computer. "Okay, here's the schedule for July seventeenth. Conklin was off that day. It was a Tuesday and he normally had Tuesdays and Thursdays off."

Mitch's stomach tightened as he caught Stef's gaze. So Tony could have gone climbing with Brad that day. "What about May ninth—the night Riana Collingwood was kidnapped?"

Rolston typed the date into the computer. He frowned at the screen, then pressed more buttons. "The ninth was a Wednesday—Conklin called in sick. In fact, he didn't report for work until the following Monday—the fourteenth."

Stef looked as if she'd swallowed a bubble. She was thinking what he was; that Conklin hadn't been sick, he'd been pulling off a kidnapping. Mitch scribbled furiously in his notebook. The pieces were fitting together and falling into place. The Collingwoods had received the first ransom demand on Saturday the twelfth, three days after the kidnapping. He drew a question mark in his notebook. What the hell had gone wrong?

And who had hired Conklin?

Sable was the obvious choice because she'd been in the bar with Brad minutes before Tony had conveniently shown up, but Mitch wasn't ruling out other suspects. G.D. had a list of people who'd wanted revenge against Ross Collingwood, and any one of them might stoop to kidnapping a baby. They had to keep digging.

He asked Rolston if he could have a look at the background check the company had done on Conklin before they'd hired him.

Rolston passed him the file. "It's all here—help yourself. I'll have the receptionist make photocopies of whatever you want."

Mitch skimmed Tony Conklin's personal information—date of birth, social security number. An F. Conklin was listed as his emergency contact person. No accompanying address was given, but the area code might be a clue to the right region. Maybe Tony had inadvertently inverted two numerals in the phone number.

He'd done a stint in the army as an infantryman. There were some gaps in his work history, but he was more likely to have been unemployed than incarcerated. If a conviction had shown up in his criminal record check he would never have been hired as a security guard.

Mitch frowned. "Any idea where he was from?"

"I can talk to his supervisor. He should be in around six tonight. I'll call you if he comes up with something."

"I'd appreciate that. Conklin might have gone back to his hood." Mitch requested copies of several pages in the file.

A light drizzle had started to fall by the time they made their way back to the limo.

"Disappointed?" Mitch asked Stef.

She gave him a fierce smile and wiped the rain from her face. Mitch hadn't lied to the doctor last night. Even bruised and scarred, Stef was incredibly beautiful. "No. Never. We're going to find him."

Mitch called The Guardian to brief him.

"I'll have to send some business Rolston's way," G.D. said after Mitch had finished. "F.Y.I., Conklin's criminal records check came back clean. We know he's not currently in prison. But he hasn't made a payment on any of his credit cards since before Riana's kidnapping—not that he made them regularly before that. And he hasn't applied for a change of address on his driver's license.''

Stef tugged on Mitch's arm. "What's he saying?"

Mitch told her, then went back to his call. "So Tony's either dead and we'll be dealing with an unknown party or Tony's hiding with the child and using an alias.'' Mitch spun out the theory that Tony was still alive. "If Tony Conklin attacked Stef and Keely yesterday, he may have someone bankrolling him—maybe someone in the Collingwood Corporation. Like Sable.''

"Or Annette.''

"Absolutely. Annette could have funded the kidnapping and it may never have been about the money. That may be why the first ransom attempt was aborted.''

"So, why the second ransom demand?" G.D. asked.

"Circumstances have changed. Annette's in prison. She needs serious money for legal fees and she wants to cast doubt on the charges against her. The only thing I can say with certainty at this point is that whoever we're dealing with now wants *money*. That's why they risked abducting Keely yesterday. They need the real Riana.''

Mitch could visualize the gears in G.D.'s brain digesting all this information.

"They won't get anywhere near Keely again," G.D. said with iron-hard resolve. "I'll assign some operatives to check out Conklin's previous addresses and the phone number you have for F. Conklin.''

"Good enough. I'm dropping Stef off at the apartment, then I'm going to squeeze in more interviews as Evan Mitchell.'' Mitch disconnected the call with a sigh, anticipating a battle.

Stef rounded on him, her eyes accusing. Mitch steeled himself, grateful he'd figured out how to raise the privacy screen in the limo so the chauffeur wouldn't be a witness to what was about to happen.

"I'm not going back to the apartment," Stef stated mulishly. "I'm staying with you."

Mitch tried to be patient. He'd spent most of the day with her, tormented and distracted by her beauty and her intelligence and the sexual tension simmering below the surface of their exchanged glances, exchanged touches. He was drawing the line. "Evan Mitchell is conducting the interviews. Not Evan Mitchell and Stephanie Shelton."

"I'll wait in the car, then." Stef folded her arms across her chest, calling Mitch's attention to the tantalizing swell of her breasts beneath the soft black knit sweater. His pulse quickened at the thought that she was probably wearing a black lace bra beneath that sweater.

"No, you're going back to the apartment to rest if I have to tuck you in bed myself." His voice charged with the reined-in frustration he'd been living under all day, matched the increasing drum of the rain on the limo's roof. Even now he could feel a driving urge to kiss her—just to grant himself a moment's release from the tension.

"Why?" she retorted.

His fingers clenched at his sides. "Because you're distracting the hell out of me, and I can't think straight. Is that a good enough reason?"

And then, to soften the harsh blow of his words, he yielded to temptation and kissed her.

Chapter Eleven

Mitch meant the kiss to be a reprieve from the tension. A gentle passionate joining because she was so determined to be brave and strong and because her poor face was bruised and sore. But hell, everything between him and Stef was explosive and reckless. Mitch felt his control ruthlessly strip away as she parted her sweet lips and greedily welcomed the thrust of his tongue.

It was a homecoming he'd never before experienced.

His ears deafened to everything around him except the soft sigh of Stef's moans. His hands skimmed over her shoulders and down her arms as he reassured himself that her firm, soft body wasn't a dream. This was a place he could stay forever. And Mitch would have stayed, drowning in desire and need for this brave vulnerable woman and throwing caution to the wind, but the limo braked abruptly for a red light, throwing them apart.

Mitch was breathing harder than a teenager caught making out with his girlfriend behind the bleachers. He caught a handful of Stef's silken hair. How could he have forgotten his purpose? He wasn't here to indulge himself in fantasies that could never come true. It was to save an abandoned child. "That's why you can't come with me," he said with self-loathing. "Right now, instead of wondering how to beat Tony Conklin out from whatever rock he's hiding under, I'm fantasizing about the color of your bra."

He shuddered as a wall of unfamiliar emotion rose in him, stronger than anything he'd ever known. His heart wrenched at the thought of what the future could hold for her. He had to bring her daughter home alive!

She put her fingers over his mouth as if to stop him from saying more, but he pulled her fingers away. "Listen to me, Stef. Really listen. The last kidnapping case I worked on a little girl died because I let myself get too involved in her family situation. She had a wonderful grandmother. Strong lady, she reminded me of my grandfather who raised me after my mother dumped me on his doorstep. I knew how much her granddaughter meant to her. And I was too late to save Carmen. I failed them."

Stef gripped his chin, her eyes softening into velvet puddles. But her voice though gentle, was feminine-coated steel. "I am so sorry, Mitch. I'm sorry that Carmen died. It breaks my heart that her grandmother lost her precious grandchild. But you listen to me, Mitch Halloran. I don't believe for one second that you failed Carmen or her grandmother. I know you. You cared about that little girl and her grandmother and I know you gave that case everything you had. From the moment I met you, you've done everything humanly possible to find my biological daughter." She gave a short, pain-filled laugh that made him reach for her. "People have failed me in my life, Mitch. But you are not one of them."

He tenderly cradled her face between his palms, wondering if what she really meant was that Brad had failed her. Failed their child. "I'm afraid, Stef." *So terribly afraid we will find a grave and that it will destroy you.*

"That's makes two of us." She swallowed hard as if she could read in his eyes the words he couldn't say. "Okay, I'll stay at the apartment. But just so you don't get any more distracted, my bra's pink. Flamingo pink. And one more thing before you go—I feel sorry for your mother. She didn't know what she was missing."

Mitch kissed her again, cursing under his breath. This was no way to conduct a kidnapping investigation.

SABLE'S PHONE had been ringing all afternoon. It was impossible to get any work done. When the phone rang yet again, she snatched the receiver from the cradle in frustration. She'd just tell Ruth to hold her calls.

A hesitant young female voice whispered over the line. "Ms. Holden? It's Phoebe—from the Rock School."

Sable pictured the personable climbing instructor. "I'm very busy, Phoebe. Why are you whispering?"

"Something weird happened today. A man was here talking to the owner about you. Asking a lot of questions."

Sable told herself not to show any sign of panic. "What kind of questions?"

"I didn't hear everything they said because they were in the back office, but they came out to the front desk and printed something off the computer. Vito also checked the log and gave the man the dates you'd been climbing. They went pretty far back."

Fear crept over Sable's body like a shadow. "Any idea what they printed?"

Sable heard a pause as if Phoebe were checking to

make sure no one was listening to her call. "I looked up the last file viewed after they'd finished. It was a list about the company party you booked here a couple years ago."

Why would somebody want that list? Sable's temper rose as the suspicion that Evan Mitchell might not be who he claimed to be seeded itself in her mind. Damn it!

"What did the man look like?"

"Old."

Sable laughed. "What are you, twenty-two? Everybody looks old. It might have been someone from my office. What color was his hair? Was he hot or a dweeb?"

"Neither. Just old—like somebody's couch potato dad. I thought he might be a cop. He wore a seriously uptight raincoat."

Or a private investigator. Sable wondered if The Guardian was nosing around in her business. Had Stef found something and gone to him? Is that why she'd suddenly dropped by asking questions about Brad's death?

Sable had gained too much since Ross Collingwood's death to lose it now. She was being granted more decision-making power and her contribution to Office Outfitter's success was finally being acknowledged. She struggled to keep her voice warm and effusive. "I appreciate the heads up, Phoebe. Next time I'm in, I'll bring you something to show my appreciation."

"That's really not necessary. You're such a nice lady. It creeped me out to hear that guy talking about you."

"Have a nice day, Phoebe." Sable slowly hung up the phone. It was time to do some damage control.

FLAMINGO PINK. The color glowed like a neon sign in Mitch's mind the rest of the afternoon as he conducted three interviews as Evan Mitchell.

His attempt to create distance between him and Stef by telling her about Carmen had backfired. To his dismay, she'd tried to make him sound like some kind of hero and it had pulled him inexorably closer to her.

His first interview was with Pasquale Pedroncelli, the manager of the midtown Office Outfitters store, who'd allegedly informed Sable about Brad's death.

Pedroncelli had a can-do attitude that Mitch warmed to immediately. He allowed Mitch to accompany him as he walked through the warehouse store. He confirmed that he had called Sable around 8:00 p.m. to notify her of Brad's death. "I knew she'd want to know," Pedroncelli explained. "Brad was part of the team for a long time."

Mitch looked up from the notes he was taking. "How'd *you* find out?"

"Stef called me. She asked me to spread the news. It was a huge shock. Everybody liked Brad. He was enthusiastic. He instigated a lot of friendly sales wars between the stores—and he set up softball tournaments to encourage team spirit. He was the regional manager and he would make a point of introducing himself to the new staff in every store he visited, asking how they liked their jobs. Did they get enough training? Could they play first base?" Pedroncelli nodded at the clerks working the checkout counters. "It's not the same now. We have one regional manager who covers three states and sales are slipping."

Mitch's second interview was with Yvette Lisgard, a tough-talking, iron-haired lady who worked as a cashier at the uptown store. Yvette had five children and thirteen grandchildren. She talked Mitch's ear off about

Brad, who'd secured one of her sons a job at another store. Mitch could understand why Brad had taken his job loss so hard. He'd earned the praise and respect of the people he worked with. He probably hadn't felt he deserved to be canned. Maybe that was why he'd gone along with whatever game Sable had been playing.

Mitch grabbed a couple slices of pizza from an Italian deli and wolfed them down as the limo crawled through rush-hour traffic to the Bronx store. The rain was still coming down. His energy was starting to flag, but he had to keep pushing it. The kidnapper might be more edgy than ever after the failed abduction attempt yesterday. Mitch hoped Stef was sleeping, gathering her strength. The days ahead would be tough.

He tracked down the shipping clerk named Al Bielac with trepidation. Al was forty pounds overweight with a sweat gland problem. He was on his dinner break in the employee lounge, eating meat loaf and mashed potatoes from a plastic container. He bought Mitch a cola and regaled him with a tale of how Brad had personally presented him and the night security guard with framed certificates and a five-hundred-dollar reward each for fingering an employee who was pilfering inventory from the stockroom during closing.

"You should have seen the wife when I brought home that reward. She wanted new curtains for the living room, but it was my reward. I bought a big TV. Bigger than my brother Harry's. He's a plumber. Always braggin' about how much money he makes." Al sighed over his mashed potatoes and gravy. "Yeah, me and Tony hit it big that day."

Mitch nearly choked on his slug of soda. "Tony?"

"Yeah, the guard. You write his name down. It was Tony Conklin, Rolston Security."

Mitch cursed silently. Al had just thrown him a curve. His assumption that Tony had been hired to strike up a chance meeting with Brad in a bar or on the street went up in flames, and a new picture emerged in the ashes. Pete O'Shay and Mike Lipetzky both described Tony as Brad's friend. Everything Mitch was learning about Brad indicated that he made a point of learning the names of the people who worked for Office Outfitters. Brad had obviously hit it off with the security guard he'd presented an award to for nabbing a thief.

Mitch jotted down Tony's name. How deep had Brad and Tony's friendship run? Had they pulled off the kidnapping together and had a falling out?

"AM I INTERRUPTING YOU?"

"Hmm?" Hunter Sinclair glanced up from the report he was reviewing of the nursery staff employed at the hospital in Queens where Stephanie Shelton had given birth to her daughter. He felt a loosening in the tension in his neck as he smiled at his beautiful wife. "Yes, but you're a most welcome interruption."

"I won't stay long, I promise," Juliana said as she slipped into the study and closed the door behind her. "I convinced Stef to take a nap, and Keely is helping Valentina in the kitchen. I thought I'd steal a few moments alone with my sexy husband."

"Continue speaking to me like that, and I'll gladly give you more than a few moments."

Smiling, Juliana circled behind him and played her hands over his shoulders, massaging the tense muscles. It was one of the hundreds of thoughtful and loving things she did that made Hunter wonder how he'd ever lived without her.

"I still can't believe we have Riana back. She's such

a darling little missy—she reminds me of Ross. I can visualize her running the Collingwood empire.''

Hunter snared one of her hands and kissed her palm. ''Your father will have his hands full teaching her everything he taught Ross.''

''He's so anxious to meet her,'' Juliana said wistfully. ''He called me three times today. And I want Keely to meet her baby brother.''

''I know, my darling. But we have to be patient.''

''That's easy for you to say,'' she said with obvious discontent. ''This is the first time I've been away from Cort this long. My arms feel empty without him. And I miss being at FairIsle. And most of all, I miss you sleeping in my bed. Are you making headway on the case?''

Amusement rumbled in Hunter's chest along with a welling of gratitude that he'd stumbled into marriage with this amazing woman. ''Thank you for the prominent placement on your list of priorities.'' He gestured at the mountain of paper on his desk that seemed to get larger every day. He had other cases he was keeping tabs on, as well. ''This Tony Conklin lead seems promising. But we're pursuing other avenues at the same time.''

''Do you think the kidnapper will make a ransom demand for Stef's daughter?''

''Mitch isn't expecting one.''

Juliana's hands stilled on his shoulders. ''Oh, Hunter. You have to find Stef's baby. We can't—'' She stopped. ''This is so hard, not telling Stef who we are. I like her. She's a wonderful mother. And she loves Keely so much. She's not going to give her up without a fight.''

''Indeed,'' Hunter said very quietly.

Juliana's arms circled Hunter's shoulders as she

pressed her cheek against his. Tears choked her voice. "Oh, my love, promise me that somehow we'll make it work for Keely's sake."

"I promise."

STEF WAS SLEEPING when Mitch returned to the apartment. And Juliana was giving Keely a bath. A bath that involved giggling and singing. Just like her mother, Keely had a way of livening up the space around her. Shaking his head at the comparison, Mitch wandered into the kitchen and took two beers from the refrigerator, one for him, one to offer G.D. He was beat. He'd have a conference with G.D. and hit the sack.

After he'd found out about the new connection between Tony and Brad, he'd called up Rolston and talked to Tony's supervisor. The supervisor confirmed that Tony had been given a special commendation by Office Outfitters. But he told Mitch that Tony had kept his personal life close to his chest. Still, he'd promised to ask around to see if any of the other guards remembered something.

Valentina, the cook, bustled into the kitchen to offer him a plate of leftovers, but Mitch assured her in Spanish that he'd already eaten.

"But the little *chica,* she make you cookies," Valentina protested. She gestured toward a plate set on the granite-topped kitchen island. It held three oatmeal-raisin cookies arranged on a white doily. Beside the plate was a homemade card addressed to him with Keely's handprint in orange paint just below it.

He felt a weird constriction in his chest as he looked inside the card. There were all kinds of black wiggly shapes colored in crayon. An adult had written "Love" just above the shapes. It took Mitch a second to figure out the shapes were jelly beans, not raisins.

Love, Jelly Bean.

Love. Amazing how one four-letter word could hold such power over a one-hundred-and-ninety-five-pound man.

Mitch blinked and told himself it meant nothing, but it did. No one had ever baked him real cookies before, much less left him a note with the word love in it. He thumbed away the moisture tearing in the corners of his eyes.

Giving Valentina a goofy grin, he carefully picked up the card and the plate of cookies with his free hand and carried them to his room. He arranged them on his bedside table where he could see them, then slid the old and faded snapshot of his grandfather from his wallet and leaned it against Keely's card.

"Look at that, Paddy. Cookies."

He ate one of the cookies, savoring every bite. It was the best damn cookie he'd ever tasted even though his stomach went through contortions at the thought that Keely would hate him one day for finding her, for taking her from her real mommy. Hell, Mitch hated himself.

He wanted to eat the remaining two cookies, but he didn't. Feeling the weight of the case on his shoulders, he took the beer to G.D.'s study to update him on the interviews.

They were discussing whether Brad and Tony had orchestrated the kidnapping when a knock sounded on the door and Keely bounced into the room, smelling like strawberry bubble bath.

"Mommy's still sleeping, so Keely needs kisses

good-night,'' Juliana explained with an apologetic smile.

''Nighty, nighty, nighty, night,'' Keely sang sweetly to G.D.

G.D. lifted her up onto his knee and gallantly accepted her puckered kiss. ''Sweet dreams, princess. Does the princess need a horsey ride to bed?''

''Yes!''

Mitch laughed as G.D. galloped her on his knee.

Giggling, Keely dismounted and skipped over to Mitch. ''Nighty, nighty, nighty, night,'' she sang.

Mitch wasn't quite sure what to do. He picked her up as G.D. had and gave her a little kiss when she lifted her adorable face up to his. Then he hugged her tiny vibrant body and whispered in her ear, ''I found the cookies, jelly bean. Thank you. You fooled me, I thought the raisins were jelly beans until I tasted them.''

Keely giggled behind her hands, her bright blue-green eyes sharing his joke.

Mitch reluctantly handed her off to Juliana. ''Sleep well, jelly bean.''

A jocund silence fell in the study after Keely left as if part of her personality had been left behind in the room like fairy dust. Mitch noticed G.D. was studying him, one brow lifted as if he were about to say something difficult in the most tactful way possible.

Here it comes, Mitch thought. Marquise had blabbed about that hug in the limo.

''That was a first time for you, wasn't it?''

''What?'' Mitch asked.

''Kissing a child good-night.''

Mitch tried to act nonchalant. ''And I thought I hid it so well.''

"So, you've never been married, never had children?"

"No. I've never dated the same woman more than a couple of months." Mitch took a sip of beer, watching G.D. keenly. If he knew his boss, and he did, G.D. already knew the answers to the questions he'd just asked. Mitch figured he'd see if G.D. was planning to be equally forthcoming. "Do you have kids?"

"Yes. A son, actually. And a new daughter."

That explained the cry of a baby Mitch had heard in the background of one of their calls.

"You must be from a big family, then," G.D. continued. "You obviously have an affinity for children."

Smooth, G.D. Mitch hid a smile. Hell, with his sources, The Guardian probably knew whether Mitch's mother was alive or dead. "Actually, I'm an only child. My mother did me the greatest favor of my life when she dumped me on my grandfather's doorstep in Los Angeles when I was twelve. Of course, I didn't feel that way when it happened. I hated my grandfather at first. Let's just say that I know what it feels like to be taken away from everything you know."

"What about your father?"

"He lost interest when I was six. What about you? You have a perfect childhood, G.D.?"

G.D. waved a dismissive hand. "Far from it. My mother had a weakness for men. A family retainer took photos of her indiscretions with my father's friends, thinking he would fund his retirement. He threatened to release the photos to the press if my father didn't fork over two hundred thousand dollars. My father was so besotted with my mother that he wouldn't even entertain the idea that she'd been unfaithful to him. He refused to pay the money and the pictures were sold to a magazine.''

Lines bracketed G.D.'s aristocratic mouth. ''When my father saw the pictures he filed for a divorce and full custody of his children. My mother took her own life when she realized that she was going to lose us.'' Grief slipped past the shield of detachment he normally wore and flickered in his eyes. ''I found her body.''

Mitch knew exactly what it felt like to unexpectedly come upon the body of a loved one. Five years had passed since he'd barged into Paddy's room teasing him that they were going to be late for his doctor's appointment only to discover that his grandfather had died peacefully in his sleep. ''Hell, that's rough, buddy.''

G.D.'s fingers tightened around the neck of his beer. ''It was a long time ago.''

But Mitch knew it would always stay with G.D. That it had been a life-defining moment that had shaped G.D. into a man who dedicated his life to helping other families deal with similar problems.

''Get some sleep, Halloran.''

Mitch recognized a direct order when he heard one. The conversation was closed.

STEF AWOKE at two o'clock in the morning. She'd laid down for a nap and slept for eleven hours. Her first thought was for Keely. Was she okay? A lump formed in her throat. Two nights in a row now a stranger had put her daughter to bed.

Stef turned on the bedside lamp, gilding the richly elegant cream-and-blue bedroom with light. If her daughter wasn't about to be taken from her to be raised in this kind of luxury, Stef might have enjoyed the pleasure of staying in this princess room. Even the bathroom taps were gold.

She slipped out from beneath the snuggly comfort of the duvet and went into the marble bathroom. She'd check on Keely first, then fix herself some tea and toast.

She carefully washed her face, careful not to wet the bandage or to press too hard on the vibrant purple-and-blue bruises that flared onto her cheek. There was swelling around her eye that she hadn't noticed earlier. Good thing her mother couldn't see her now. Stef clutched the fluffy white towel to her chest, wishing her parents weren't traveling and so out of reach. She could use one of her father's ''There, there, baby girl'' hugs. How could she possibly find the words to tell them that their granddaughter had been switched with another baby?

She was tempted to call her sister and brother-in-law in Philadelphia. Lorraine, she knew, would drop everything and come to help as she'd done when Brad had died, but Stef knew her sister, who was a paralegal, would start talking about fighting for custody and finding the best lawyers. Frankly, Stef couldn't deal with that now. Not until she had the baby she'd given birth to safely back.

At least she had Mitch to lean on. Stef trembled at the memories of the kisses they had shared this afternoon. Kisses that explored a passion beneath their fears.

Had Brad's kisses ever affected her like that?

Stef looked at herself in the mirror and knew the answer. She'd loved Brad, but there had been moments when she had wished for something more from their relationship.

Feeling guilty by that thought, Stef turned away from the mirror and slid her arms into the thick cotton bathrobe that had once been Brad's. She needed to see Keely, to reassure herself that she was safe and sound.

Stef quietly opened the door to the nursery, not wanting to disturb Juliana who was occupying the second twin bed in the room. Stef supposed she should find Juliana's attentiveness to Keely threatening, but oddly, she didn't.

A night-light had been left on in the room, allowing Stef to see Keely curled into a ball around her snuggie. Stuffed animals surrounded her in the bed like sentries. Was her biological child sleeping safely tonight, too?

Stef tiptoed into the room to kiss her baby and to adjust the covers around her. Then, smothering back a fresh spate of tears, she found her way to the kitchen.

She puttered, making tea and cinnamon toast, careful not to disturb the others by making too much noise. Her thoughts circled back to the interviews Mitch had conducted this afternoon. Had he found out anything?

Desire melted through her like spring runoff as she remembered the hot intensity of his gaze when he'd bluntly confessed that he found her distracting.

Stef trembled. She couldn't believe she'd been brazen enough to tell him her bra was flamingo pink.

Cheeks burning, she carried her dishes to the sink. She couldn't think about this anymore. Wouldn't let herself dwell on the fact that she wanted Mitch.

She headed back to her room, turning with a gasp when a door in the hallway opened as she passed.

Mitch. His chest was bare. His hair rumpled. His jaw coated with dark stubble. And naked desire radiated from his eyes. Stef gulped at the dangerous image he made.

He was wearing a pair of black running shorts with L.A.P.D. emblazoned on one leg. He was the most glorious man she'd ever seen. Hollywood eat your heart out.

"I thought that might be you," he said with a huskiness in his voice that sent a tingle up her spine. The same huskiness that had been there when he'd told her she was driving him to distraction. "How are you feeling?"

"Better. My headache's gone," she whispered. "Eleven hours of sleep has made me a new woman. How did the interviews go?"

He tilted his head and pulled the door open farther, indicating that she should come in so they could talk. Stef wondered if she was making a mistake she might regret by entering his room, but he was already turning away, opening a drawer. He found a black T-shirt and tugged it on. The cotton fabric clung like a second skin to his muscles.

"Sorry, I don't have a robe."

Stef nodded, not trusting herself to say anything as she consciously avoided the bed where the sheets were undoubtedly still warm from his body. He'd left the closet door open and Stef could see that his suits were neatly spaced one inch apart on the rod. The shirt and the tie he'd worn yesterday were haphazardly draped over the doorknob. Stef had a compelling urge to touch the tie. Not straighten it—just let the silk glide between her fingers because it was Mitch's.

Mitch cleared his throat. "Something interesting turned up in the interviews. Turns out Tony patrolled the Office Outfitters in the Bronx and helped a shipping clerk nab an employee who was stealing from the warehouse. Brad presented both men with certificates and a reward."

"I remember that," Stef said, finally daring to turn

around and lift her eyes to meet Mitch's gaze. Big mistake.

She had no doubt he was imagining her naked. Her feet rooted to the plush wool carpet and her heartbeat spiraled in a slow dizzying pound as his gaze caressed her from her painted toenails to the bandage at her temple. She should have felt self-conscious with the bruises and the swelling on her face. But she didn't. She felt beautiful.

More than that, she felt powerful. She wanted to erase the creases in Mitch's brow and to chase away the loss that haunted his gaze with slow, healing kisses.

He swallowed hard. "The thing is that it indicates they knew other. We have to consider that Brad and Tony might have been involved in the kidnapping plot together."

"No." Stef said the word on a gush of forcefulness. "So what if Brad happened to be the one presenting him with a certificate. We saw nothing on that tape to indicate there was a conspiracy going on between Brad and Tony. I still think it's more likely Tony was keeping tabs on Brad. If not for Sable, then for someone else."

Mitch's face set like stone. He didn't respond. He didn't have to. Stef knew her arguments were weak and that her strident defense of Brad was an emotional barrier to keep Mitch at arm's length. To keep her desire for him in check.

"Did The Guardian's men find Sable's family's place in the Catskills?" she asked softly.

"Not yet. But they're working on it. We've got people checking into Tony's background, too."

Stef couldn't look at him any longer without wanting to touch the smooth corded muscles that strained the sleeves of the T-shirt. Without wanting to feel his arms locked solidly around her. Reassuring her that they'd find her real baby and bring her home safe and sound. "Well, I should let you get some sleep."

She almost made it out of the room, but in her effort to leave without looking at him, her gaze fell on the plate of cookies, the homemade card and the photograph arranged like a shrine at Mitch's bedside.

Her heart gave an insistent painful tug. She paused. "What's this?" she asked.

Mitch folded his arms across his broad chest and leaned on the edge of the dresser as if he didn't trust himself to move from that spot. "A gift from Keely," he said almost defensively. "She left it for me in the kitchen."

And he'd put it by his bed along with a picture of a man in uniform who Stef was sure had to be his grandfather. Stef felt another layer of Mitch strip away.

She moved closer to examine the card and to get a glimpse of the wonderful man who had raised Mitch.

She reached her hand out to touch the photo.

"Please, don't," Mitch said in a strangled tone.

Stef stopped and looked at him, wide-eyed with concern and her heart aching for him. Why didn't he want her to touch the photo? Was he afraid of sharing even that much of his life with her?

It didn't seem fair. He knew everything about her. About her husband.

"I'm sorry, I didn't mean to intrude." She forced a brightness into her tone as she quickly stepped back from the table. "The cookies look delicious."

"They are," he said hoarsely. "I'm making them last because they're special. Nobody ever baked me cookies before."

"Nobody?" Stef's first reaction was to reply that he

must be joking, but she could see that he wasn't. Keely's gift and the photo were special to him for reasons she didn't completely comprehend. But they were a part of this complex man who was taking over her life. Who was working his way into her heart with the same dogged determination that he was searching for her baby.

Stef forgot about escaping the room. She forgot that sleeping with Mitch would be an emotional betrayal to her husband and to their daughter. She took a tentative step toward him. And another.

Mitch knew he had about two seconds to stop what was going to happen, but he couldn't. He wanted to make love to her. On a sheer gut level, no decision had ever felt more right in his life. From the moment he'd met Stef, she'd held his heart and his body spellbound. The thunderous pounding in his chest and his painful arousal were proof of both.

She took one more step toward him and Mitch went the rest of the distance. Her fingers tore at his T-shirt, peeling it off him, before she hooked her fingers around his neck and tugged his mouth down to hers.

Need, long suppressed, raced through Mitch like a raging current through newly opened floodgates. He drank Stef's kisses and demanded more, longer ones, deeper ones. His fingers fumbled with the belt of her robe. He needed to feel her skin against his.

Stef, he realized, wasn't waiting for him to catch up. She impatiently jerked his shorts from his hips, breaking a kiss as she freed his arousal and dispatched his shorts to the floor. Mitch shuddered as her fingers circled his erection in an intimate embrace. "I want you, Mitch," she murmured against his mouth. She kissed his chin, his throat. Then his collarbone. Her tongue ran a damp trail down to his sternum.

"I'm going to cut this robe off you," Mitch growled in frustration.

Stef laughed, a soft throaty, sexy sound. Her fingers nudged his aside and undid the belt. Mitch slid the cumbersome robe off her shoulders. She was wearing a pale pink nightgown with a triangle of black lace inset in the bodice. It was a lethal combination of innocence and sex appeal.

Mitch gripped the hem. "This is in the way."

Her green-gold eyes sparkled up at him. "My thoughts exactly."

She helped him lift it over her head so it wouldn't catch on her bandage.

Mitch gazed at Stef's naked body as she stood in front of him and wanted to worship at her feet. Reverently he touched her breasts, marveling in their softness and the golden hue of her skin. "You're so incredibly beautiful. I've never met anyone like you."

"Guess you've been hanging out in the wrong places," she said teasingly. Her hands skimmed over his chest.

Mitch nibbled at her ear, at her jaw, his fingers kneading and shaping her rosy-tipped nipples into sharp points. He tasted the delicate skin of her throat and finally found her breasts with his mouth.

Stef moaned and moved against him, pressing her belly against his arousal. Mitch slid his hand down over her satin skin to explore the incredible softness of her inner thighs. She was so hot.

He nudged her thighs apart and probed into the dark curls that hid the sweetest part of her. Mitch went down on his knees to taste her vanilla sweetness, parting those dark curls and seeking the honeyed pearl that would bring her the greatest pleasure. Her fingers threaded through his hair, urging him not to end her torment.

"Oh, Mitch!"

Frantically she gripped his shoulders as tremors rocked through her delicate body. Mitch savored her, with his tongue, with his fingers and finally, when he didn't think he could hold on to his control any longer, he ripped open a foil packet and covered himself. Pulling her into his embrace as they tumbled on to the bed arms and legs intertwined, he entered her.

His first thought was that she was too small, he was going to hurt her. But she wrapped her legs around his hips, accommodating him with tiny seductive wiggles and suddenly he was all the way in, and it was a perfect fit.

Mitch growled with a deep-seated pleasure he'd never experienced before. A feeling of oneness, of wholeness, exploded through him. He deliberately kept his pace slow, wanting to drag out the joy of being with Stef, but his body was hurtling him toward another destination.

He caught her face between his hands so he could see her eyes. "Stay with me, sweetheart." His thrusts became more forceful, every part of him straining to be joined with her. Perspiration beaded on his skin as they lifted and moved in a rhythm all their own. To Mitch's delight, she stayed with him, right to the spellbinding end when she called out his name.

As the sweat cooled on their bodies and they touched each other with gentle caresses, Mitch plucked the picture of his grandfather from the bedside table and placed it in her hands. He told her things he'd never told anyone else—about helping Paddy mop floors and empty wastebaskets. About some of the lessons he'd learned from that quiet-spoken old man, whom he'd gone from hating to revering. He knew that he would love Stephanie Shelton for the rest of his life. And that he could never have her.

This would have to be enough.

Chapter Twelve

"I made love with Mitch." Stef tried saying the words out loud to the bathroom mirror after her shower later that morning. The glow burning inside her at the intimacy she'd shared with Mitch was waging an all-out war with her conscience, which was fighting back with nasty jabs of guilt. How could she have made love to the man who had exposed every illusion she treasured about her husband and her daughter and traded them for heartache and danger?

Even though Brad had been dead for more than two years, Stef waffled between feeling that she'd somehow betrayed him and Keely by making love with Mitch and her mind's stubborn rebuttal that Mitch wasn't her enemy.

After the stories he'd told her about his grandfather, she knew Mitch was a noble man by nature. He'd taken on the task of reuniting a stolen child with her family and had discovered that the situation was more complex than it initially seemed. He cared about Keely—just as she knew he cared about every child he searched for. This case was tearing him apart, too.

In the bleak light of morning, her arguments seemed as transitory as the steam obscuring the bathroom mirror; a fog thinly veiling the deeper fears festering in her breast.

Fears that she'd never hold her biological child in her arms. That a judge would rip Keely from her life. And that she would be foolish to let herself believe that she could depend on Mitch forever. As soon as this case was over, another would take its place, and she would be left alone.

MITCH AND STEF had slept together last night. Marquise, the butler, discreetly informed Hunter of that fact as he entered Hunter's bedroom carrying a tray bearing black coffee, the newspapers and the stack of reports that had arrived overnight by fax.

Hunter didn't ask Marquise if he was sure. Marquise never spoke if he wasn't sure.

Two months ago Hunter would have summoned Mitch and summarily dismissed him. But this time Hunter hesitated. It had nothing to do with Mitch's considerable investigative skills or his contribution toward this case, although Hunter certainly had never met a more competent or dedicated investigator. No, it had more to do with the incongruity. Mitch Halloran had a sterling service record with the L.A.P.D. There had never been one hint of inappropriate behavior. And Mitch had told him last night that he never stayed with a woman longer than two months. Mitch wasn't the kind of man to take his pleasure with a client. Maybe Mitch's involvement with Stephanie Shelton was different. Serious.

Hunter looked longingly at the empty side of his bed, wishing Juliana was lounging beside him so he could solicit her opinion. His darling wife had a tendency to view things from a more humane perspective. She'd found the humanity in him after all. He wanted to ask Juliana if Stephanie Shelton had seen past Mitch's job to the man beneath?

He would see if Juliana noticed anything between them, then bring up the subject.

MITCH WAS SHELL-SHOCKED. His heart stammered, his hands shook and he felt nauseated. And panic was trying to push its way to the surface. Mitch was deathly afraid if that panic escaped, he might go crazy. He'd managed to avoid Stef most of the day, thank God. He was not sure how he would react to seeing her. He needed some time to let his head get control of his emotions.

In among the panic and the nausea and the fear was one other reaction. They'd made love and he wanted her again. And again. And again.

He'd found everything he'd ever wanted in Stef's arms, but he knew it couldn't possibly last. Someday she'd grow to resent him, blame him for destroying her life.

He and G.D. had been closeted in the study, going over the information that seemed to flow into the apartment on a paper river. Occasionally they heard footsteps in the hall or laughter or Keely's singing. They were compiling as much information as possible on Tony, trying to trace his life backward to his family. No record of birth could be found in New York or the nearby states. Nothing had turned up yet on the emergency contact number for an F. Conklin listed on Tony's apartment rental agreement. They were checking all the Conklins within the same area code. Two addresses had popped up on Tony's credit report, the address they knew about and an even older previous address from his days in the military. The Guardian was using his extensive contacts to pull favors, trying to get family information from Tony's military records.

One of G.D.'s operatives reported that Tony had been dishonorably discharged from Uncle Sam's army for threatening a superior officer. It was one more piece in the puzzle of Tony Conklin.

But the question remained. Had Tony met an untimely death like Brad, or was he alive and living under an alias?

Mitch plowed through The Guardian's files on the Collingwood murder investigation. Sable Holden still ranked as their main suspect because of the videotape Brad had made, but he didn't want to overlook some other connection.

In the late afternoon G.D.'s phone rang with the location of Sable Holden's family property in the Catskills. The house in Windham belonged to Sable's aunt on her mother's side of the family. Mitch and G.D. dispatched three teams of operatives posing as couples on vacation to check it out.

Mitch sought Stef out to give her the news. She, Juliana and Keely were having tea at a cloth-draped table in the living room. Keely was dressed in a pink-and-white princess dress, a tiara of glittering paste diamonds rested askew on her dark curls. Stef wore a very sexy red felt hat with a scrap of black netting that created a veil over her left eye. Juliana had a lacy shawl draped around her shoulders and ropes of pearls circling her neck. They were talking and laughing, but Mitch felt a strange sense of foreboding as he looked at the happy trio. Maybe it was the fear that this could all horribly come to an end depending on what they found in Windham.

As if sensing his presence, Stef stopped talking and her gaze found him in the doorway. Mitch tried to smile at her reassuringly, but his heart slammed down to his stomach. *He loved her.* He wanted to make her laugh for the rest of his life. Wanted to protect her from further pain.

Fear and uncertainty shaded her eyes. Mitch hoped that it was because she sensed he had important news about the case, not because she regretted what had happened between them last night.

He cleared his throat, unable to take his gaze off her, remembering how incredibly soft her skin was to his touch. "Excuse me, Princess Keely, but I need to have a word with your mommy."

Stef set down her teacup. "I'll be right back, Kee."

Mitch resisted the urge to extend his hand to her as she came toward him, her body moving with feminine grace.

With a nod of his head, he indicated they could talk privately down the hall.

He heard the quick intake of air as she dragged a breath into her lungs and rounded on him. "What is it?"

He reached for her hand then—he couldn't help it, his thumb caressing her knuckles. "We've got an address for Sable's family's place in the Catskills."

"Thank God!" Her face lit up like a candle behind a glass globe, beaming with golden light. She threw her arms around him. "She's got to be there, Mitch."

Mitch caught her to him, the contact of her sweet-scented body a poignant reminder of how seamlessly they'd melded into one just a few hours before. He tried to bring her back down to earth gently. "Don't get your hopes up too soon. This is just one of *many* leads we're pursuing. And you'll have to be patient. It could be days before we know for sure if she's there. We don't want to blow this.''

"Okay. I'll try. But it's wonderful." Mitch stilled when she kissed his cheek. He felt his face grow red with unaccustomed shyness. He wondered how many men took that simple gesture from their wives for granted.

Mitch steeled himself to let her go. He tenderly brushed a stray hair from her face. "I have to get back to work. Be strong."

So help him, God, they had to find her daughter alive.

THE WEEKEND PASSED with agonizing slowness. The operatives in Windham had secured accommodations in the area, even managing to rent a home within a half-mile walk of the property. But their surveillance efforts were hampered by the home's secluded lakeside location. It was difficult to get a glimpse inside the windows of the Victorian home because of the spruce and fir trees dotting the property. One of the couples had approached a real estate agent about the house and were told that Sable's aunt would never sell the place. The house was always overflowing with visitors and grandchildren.

Every time G.D.'s cell phone rang Mitch tensed, hoping for positive confirmation that a two-and-a-half-year-old child had been observed. Or that G.D.'s contact would come through with information on Tony Conklin's next of kin from his military records. Stef was climbing the walls. They hadn't made love again. And Mitch was relieved she was being as discreet as he was about keeping their physical relationship under wraps.

But he had a feeling G.D. might be clued in to something, though he hadn't said anything. Mitch had already figured out how he'd respond *if* G.D. called him on it. No matter what happened, he was not going to be fired from this case.

When G.D.'s phone rang Monday morning, Mitch jerked his head up from the reports he was going over to shamelessly eavesdrop. The conversation, however, was short and one-sided. G.D. hardly said a word except, "We're on our way."

"We're on our way where?" Mitch asked.

"To the office. Get Mrs. Shelton. They've found something on Brad Shelton's laptop."

STEF GRIPPED HER HANDS together as they entered the same conference room she'd been in five days ago. The dreadlocked computer tech and the ice-blond electronics specialist were waiting for them. Stef was nervous and resigned to face whatever had been found on Brad's laptop.

A hollow feeling grew inside her as the electronics expert kicked off the meeting with a simplified explanation of how a conversation taped on the recording device could be downloaded into a computer. "The conversation could then be edited, bits added or subtracted," the blonde summarized.

The computer tech cleared his throat. "We found several conversations between Sable and Ross Collingwood on Brad Shelton's laptop," he added. "Brad had been piecing them together. We believe this is the final version." He touched the Play button on the recording device.

The hollow feeling in Stef's stomach turned acidic as she listened to the tape. It was an altered version of the conversation she and Mitch had found. In this version, Ross Collingwood accepted Sable's invitation to join her in the hotel room she'd booked. The background noise changed to a quieter environment as if they'd retired to a room. Then Stef heard Ross Collingwood say, "Careful what you ask for, Sable."

"Ross, darling, I know exactly what I'm doing," Sable replied in a sultry voice. "We both knew this was inevitable." The murmurs of a kiss and the whispers of fabric being removed, played out on the tape.

The Ice Blonde stopped the tape, embarrassment touching her pale cheeks. "It goes on like that for another minute or two, then clicks off."

Stef wouldn't let herself dwell on how Brad had recorded those kissing sounds. She absolutely did not want to know. She'd reached the point where she was tired of defending him. The only thing that seemed important was getting her biological child back safely.

Beneath the table a solid thigh aligned itself beside hers, lending emotional support. She nudged Mitch's leg back slightly with her own, acknowledging the message, and leveled her gaze on The Guardian. "What do we do now?"

"Mitch and I are going to play the tape for Sable and convince her that things will go easier for her if she cooperates fully and gives us your daughter's location."

Stef realized she was trembling. And then she started to cry. She prayed Sable had taken good care of her baby.

SABLE TOOK ONE LOOK at the unflinching, uncompromising expressions on both The Guardian's and Evan Mitchell's handsome faces as they filed into her office unannounced and knew the end had come.

She mustered all the dignity she could. "Sit down, gentlemen. I've been expecting you."

Then she picked up the phone and dialed her lawyer.

STEF'S THOUGHTS gravitated between hope and fear when she was dropped off at the Park Terrace building just before 5:00 p.m. by one of The Guardian's security teams. She looked up toward the dark canopy of sky over Central Park as if searching to find a star to wish on. Maybe tonight she'd be reunited with the precious baby girl she'd only known for a few hours. It occurred to her that she didn't even know her little girl's name. It didn't matter. She loved her.

Please God, let her be healthy. Let her have been well taken care of. Give me a chance to be her mommy.

Stef beamed at the doorman as he wished her good evening. She was halfway across the lobby to the elevators when she suddenly turned on her heel. There were a lot of boutiques in the vicinity. She'd just pop over to Amsterdam Avenue to buy her daughter a gift— something special to show her how much she'd been anticipating their reunion.

The doorman asked if he could flag her a taxi. Stef told him she was going for a walk.

Stef was three blocks away, stopped at a corner waiting for the light to change, when she felt the sudden and frightening presence of a weapon pressed into the lower right side of her rib cage.

"Don't move, Mrs. Shelton. Don't scream or you'll never see your real daughter again," a man said very calmly in her right ear. "This is your one and only opportunity to negotiate her safe return."

Chapter Thirteen

Stef didn't make a sound. She didn't know whether it was a handgun or a stun gun pressed into her ribs, but she didn't care. She'd been separated from her biological daughter for two and a half long years. She was going wherever this man wanted her to go. Who was he? Tony Conklin?

He was behind her, she couldn't see his face.

Traffic moved sluggishly through the intersection. He nudged her with the weapon to cross the street. "What do you want?" she asked, trembling. Her legs were having difficulty obeying her instructions to keep moving.

"A simple exchange. Your biological daughter for the Collingwood heir."

Stef's stomach lurched. This was insane. She wasn't going to trade one child for another! "You don't need Kee—I mean, the Collingwood heir. They'll pay the ransom. They have the five million dollars. It's been ready for days."

His hot breath bathed her ear, sending chills down her spine. "Here's a news flash. I need more than just the money. You're going to bring me both."

Dear God, what was that supposed to mean? Stef's eyes searched the windows of the shops they passed, hoping to catch a reflection of the man who'd taken her hostage. But the interiors were bathed with light.

"I've timed the distance it's taken you to walk this far. Thirteen minutes." He slipped something into the pocket of her leather jacket. "Here's a cell phone. I'm going to call you in precisely twenty-one minutes. You'd better be standing at the curb outside the Park Terrace with Riana. Do anything foolish and I will slit your real daughter's throat and dump her in the Hudson. Understand?"

Twenty-one minutes! Stef knew she had to stall for time. Mitch and The Guardian weren't at the apartment. They were interrogating Sable. For all she knew Sable had confessed and both Mitch and The Guardian were speeding to her real daughter's rescue.

"How do I know you're not lying to me? How do I know my real daughter's still alive?" she said.

A photo was thrust under her nose. "Here's proof."

Stef stopped beneath a streetlight. Anguish roared through her like a tornado. She saw a solemn-faced, dark-haired little girl with a fringe of uneven bangs. She was sitting on a bed, holding the front page of the *New York Times* below her chin. Her blue eyes had a soft glow of hopefulness in them that tugged at Stef's heart. Her arms ached to hold her, to reassure her that she was loved. Wanted. Was her daughter being held somewhere in this city?

"How do I know you won't hurt Keely?"

"She's instrumental to my plans. As long as the authorities cooperate, she'll stay very much alive. She's the key that will open the doors that need to be opened. She'll be released once we're safely out of the country."

We're? Whom did he mean? He and Sable, maybe?

She peered more closely at the *Times* front-page headline and the date, distrust reverberating through her. This photo had been taken the day before Keely was attacked, probably *before* the kidnapper knew he had the wrong child.

Her throat threatened to close up with grief at the discovery. "This picture is a week old. How do I know she's alive today?"

"You'll have to take my word for it."

Stef stood her ground. "That's not good enough. Here's my counteroffer. Take me to my real daughter. Prove to me she's still alive. Then I'll do whatever I say."

MITCH'S HEART hammered like a one-hundred-pound weight against his ribs. He had to get Sable to confess her involvement in Riana Collingwood's abduction and to reveal where Stef's daughter was being held. Of secondary importance was determining to what extent Brad Shelton and Tony Conklin had been involved.

To Mitch's extreme frustration, Sable refused to talk until her four-hundred-dollar-an-hour lawyer arrived in his well-earned Italian suit. Then when they played her the videotape Brad had taken of their meeting in Herman's, Sable stuck to the same answers like a parrot, her face the color of wood putty.

"Yes, I paid Brad to splice together several conversations that Ross and I had," she freely acknowledged. "Brad needed the money and I needed someone I could trust. Ross had relegated me to an empty title on the Collingwood Corporation's board of directors while he squeezed every dime of profit—and every ounce of humanity—from my company. I thought it was time to squeeze Ross into giving me more control."

Her blood-red nails fanned over her elegant desktop. "Ross was in a vulnerable position and there was a good chance the tape would upset his oh-so-perfect marriage."

Mitch wasn't buying her explanation. "Be honest, Sable. You'd already had his baby daughter abducted. You wanted to completely destroy Ross's life by ruining his marriage, too."

Sable's silvery eyes widened. "Oh, no, wait a minute. I had nothing to do with Riana Collingwood's abduction. I may come across as the Wicked Witch of the West sometimes, but I would never hurt an innocent baby. Planning to bring Ross to his knees gave me an outlet for my rage over the takeover, but I couldn't bring myself to pick up the tape from Brad. I knew I couldn't resort to underhanded ploys to get back operating control of my company. Not when I was at fault for taking my family's company public. Ross was just a shark in the larger pool I'd placed myself in."

Her gaze shifted from Mitch to G.D. "I called Brad and told him our deal was off, and that I'd help him get a new job."

"How did Brad react?" Mitch asked, tamping down on his impatience to catch her in a lie. Every guilty person wanted to tell their story in their own way.

"He was angry. I'd let him down and he'd been counting on me. Ironically, now that Ross is gone, I've been handed more leadership of the company because sales figures have been falling. I could have given Brad a job."

"What day did you tell Brad you'd changed your mind?"

Sable didn't hesitate in answering. "Two or three days after I met him in Herman's."

Mitch flipped through his notebook to the notes he'd taken of his interview with Mike Lipetzky. Sure enough, Sable's answer meshed with what Brad had told Mike about a job offer that had fallen through and he was trying to decide whether he should take the initiative and strike out on his own.

Strike out on his own. Mitch blinked as he reread those five words. How desperate had Brad been to get his beloved job back? Desperate enough that he'd captured Sable's duplicity on tape? Mitch read his notes to Sable. "What do you think Brad meant when he told his friend he was striking out on his own?"

She sent him a look of exasperation. "Obviously that he was going to find a job on his own."

Mitch propped an elbow on the edge of her desk. "Come on, Sable, you're smarter than that. I wonder if Ross Collingwood would have given Brad his job back if he showed him this video footage of the two of you? Is that why you killed Brad, because you didn't trust him to keep quiet?"

Sable's voice caught with horror. "You think I killed Brad? Oh, my God. That's sick! All we did was tape a few conversations, I swear!"

Mitch wasn't letting up. Stef was at the apartment, counting on him to bring her news of her daughter. "We'd like to believe you, Sable, but there are a couple of facts that suggest you're involved in the kidnapping. The kidnapper exited the hospital with Riana by rappelling to the ground from a window in the maternity wing. That's the kind of escape route a climber would dream up. You're a climber. So was Brad."

"What of it? That evidence would hardly convict me." Sable glanced at her lawyer.

Was she looking for help?

Mitch stayed cool and applied more pressure. "Brad fits the kidnapper's description."

Sable lost her temper. "Brad did *not* abduct Riana Collingwood. That's ridiculous."

"Why? You just told us he was the type of man who'd be involved in an extortion conspiracy. Why not kidnapping?"

"Because just like me, Brad was a decent person."

"So decent he switched his own daughter with the Collingwood's daughter."

Mitch would have liked a snapshot of Sable's face at the instant he dropped that neat little bomb. Her mouth formed an O large enough to swallow a small state. The news obviously came as a complete shock to her lawyer, too.

"What?" she whispered faintly.

"You must have been angry when you realized he'd double-crossed you and switched the babies. Or was it Tony Conklin who pulled that off?"

Sable covered her mouth with her hands and stifled a sob. Tears stained with her mascara trickled slowly over her fingers. "Are you saying that Keely isn't really Stef and Brad's daughter? Oh, my God. Does Stef know?"

Mitch stared at her. Sable was either an incredible actress or she wasn't behind Riana's kidnapping. She hadn't reacted at all to his mention of Tony Conklin's name. He exchanged a worried glance with G.D.

The four-hundred-dollar-an-hour lawyer rubbed Sable's shoulder. "Gentleman, I believe my client has answered all your questions truthfully and without hesitation. This discussion is over."

The hell it was. Mitch couldn't stand the thought of Stef being separated one more night from her real

daughter. He walked around the table and squatted beside Sable who was sobbing into her hands. He lightly
touched her elbow.

"Sable, I know this is painful—maybe you got yourself in deeper than you ever imagined. I know you've
taken good care of Stef's little girl. Tell me where she
is."

Sable lifted her head and Mitch knew the instant he
gazed into her smudged, tear-filled eyes that this lead
was rapidly fizzling toward an unexpected dead end.

"I told you—I don't know what you're talking about,
and I'll take a lie detector test right now to prove it! I
would never take a baby away from its mother."

Mitch rubbed his face. God help him, he believed her.
She hadn't hired Tony to keep tabs on Brad. Mitch's
jaw locked as he stared grimly at The Guardian. They
wouldn't be bringing Stef's daughter back to her tonight.

Tony Conklin had been working for someone else.

STEF WAS TERRIFIED and disoriented. The kidnapper had
given her a choice of traveling to her daughter via the
trunk of the sedan or lying on the floor of the back seat
with a blanket covering her. She'd chosen the back seat
and the blanket option as the lesser of two evils, but
what the bearded man who'd taken her hostage didn't
tell her was that the back seat included a shock from
the stun gun if she so much as moved an inch. She tried
to remain very still even though her body was cramped.
Let him think she was still in a stupor.

He'd taken back the cell phone. She had no idea how
long they'd been driving or in which direction they were
headed, but she assumed her captor was Tony Conklin
and that he was taking her to the Catskills. She'd tried

to ease the blanket away from her eyes in hopes of glimpsing an overhead exit sign on the thruway, but her angle was all wrong.

Even though Stef knew she was asking for the impossible, she prayed that Mitch would find her, that he wouldn't let her down when she needed him most. Not like Brad. As she lay drenched in the sweat of cold fear, she finally accepted what she had been fighting ever since Mitch had bulldozed his way into her life. She loved Mitch Halloran. The same bluntness and unflagging determination that had once irritated her, now seemed his most endearing qualities. Most women might worship his Hollywood good looks, but she loved the hurt little boy inside that facade who was the gate-keeper to his heart.

When she saw him again, she might just tell him she loved him—just to scare the hell out of him.

Stef felt a sharp pat on her back.

"Wake up!" her abductor said. "We're almost there."

Stef debated what she should do. Stay silent? Or respond? The kidnapper gave her another slap.

"I know you're awake," he said in a condescending tone. "Each shock only lasts fifteen to twenty minutes."

If he weren't her only link to her real baby, Stef would have thrown the blanket over his head and caused an accident. Her mouth tasted like chalk. "I was waiting for you to say please."

Her abductor laughed. "Very funny. Listen up. This is what's going to happen if you want to stay alive. In about ten minutes we're going to drop by my aunt Helen and uncle Fred's house. They've been looking after Emma."

Her daughter's name was Emma. Tears stung Stef's

eyes as she greedily absorbed this unexpected revelation.

Her mind scrambled to catch up to what the kidnapper was saying. "I convinced them that their good-for-nothing son had knocked up a woman, who'd then turned around and abandoned the baby on my doorstep when Tony cut out on her."

Tony? Stef absolutely froze. Was he talking about Tony Conklin? She was afraid to ask, afraid to let him know that she knew anything. But if this man wasn't Tony, then who was he?

"Are you listening?"

Sarcasm shot through her tone. "I'm taking notes."

"When I sent the ransom demand to the Find Riana Foundation," the kidnapper continued, "I told my aunt and uncle that I had heard from Emma's mother's sister, and that she might be willing to take care of Emma. My aunt was relieved. She's sixty-three and too old to be caring for a toddler. So you're going to be Emma's aunt Stef from Seattle, who flew to New York on an unexpected business trip and wants to collect her younger sister Lori's child."

The kidnapper took on the tone of a teacher issuing orders to an unruly class. "You are going to be pleasant and reassure them that Emma will be fine with you. You will not do or say anything to alert them that this visit is not what it seems. They're old. I've already had to dispose of their worthless son. I would hate to have to kill them, too, because you did something stupid."

Stef was repulsed. Whoever this arrogant jerk was, he'd just admitted to killing someone, probably Tony!

She swallowed hard, dredging up the courage to ask what had really happened to Brad. How had he been involved in this? She didn't know if she'd get another chance to ask. "Did your cousin kill my husband?"

The car swerved on the road. "Your husband is dead?"

"Yes, two years ago July seventeenth. He went climbing with someone named Tony at the Giant's Kneecaps. He fell and Tony disappeared."

"That explains a lot," the kidnapper replied. "So Tony knew your husband. Tony came to see me later that night in a panic, insisting we had to attempt another ransom demand. He said someone he knew was growing suspicious and might connect him with the kidnapping. I didn't know at the time he'd double-crossed me and switched the babies. He was a loose cannon and he was going to ruin everything. If it makes you feel any better, he died July seventeenth, too."

No, that didn't make Stef feel better, but at least she knew now that her husband had not heartlessly involved their baby in a kidnapping.

The car slowed. "Climb up onto the back seat and make yourself presentable," the kidnapper ordered.

Stef struggled to obey his instructions. The muscles in her arms and legs were cramped and she felt dizzy. She smoothed her hair as she looked out the window at their surroundings. Night-cloaked fields stretched off in all directions. They were in the middle of nowhere at the foot of a lane that led to a small, neatly kept, white farmhouse. A light burned on the front porch.

Stef's heart clenched. This was the house where her daughter had said her first words and taken her first steps. *Oh, God, just let her be healthy. I can make the rest better,* she told herself. It was all she could do not to charge out of the car calling for Emma.

She licked her dry lips, flexing her fingers and her

toes, trying to bring feeling into the traumatized muscles. There wasn't another house visible in any direction. She knew the kidnapper had both a gun and the stun gun. She couldn't blow this. "What's my younger sister Lori's last name supposed to be?" she asked.

"Rogers. I told Aunt Helen that she bums around from bar to bar, dancing topless."

Great. "It shouldn't be too hard to invent a life for myself as Emma's aunt that will beat that. What am I supposed to call you? I don't even know who you are."

"My name's Darren," he said. "Darren Black."

In a blinding flash of recognition, Stef remembered the newspaper article Mitch had shown. Annette York had publicly admitted that she still loved Darren Black, the college mathematician she couldn't bring herself to marry because he didn't measure up to her sister Lexi's husband.

So Darren had stolen the one thing Ross Collingwood had valued more than money—his baby daughter.

"Darren," Stef said very softly. "Why didn't you ransom Emma back sooner?"

"Because Annette was enjoying Lexi's misery."

That was sick. Stef tried to stop the quaking in her limbs. Darren still loved Annette. He'd do anything for her. Even kill Keely if it would make Annette happy. Oh, God, she needed Mitch now.

"THEY'RE BA-ACK!"

Mitch's stomach fisted into a knot as Keely raced down the long hallway of the apartment to the front door to greet them with Juliana in hot pursuit. Stef would be devastated when he told her they'd hit a dead end.

Keely launched herself toward Mitch's knees in a running tackle. "Hiya, Mitch! Hi, G.D.!"

"Hey, jelly bean!" Mitch caught her giggling, squirming body and pumped her up and down a few times as if he were doing bicep rolls. He'd have thought Stef would be on top of him, asking for news, the moment they came in. "Where's your mommy, kiddo?"

"She's not with you?" Juliana asked.

Mitch felt the world drop out beneath him. He checked his watch and exchanged a worried look with G.D., careful not to say anything that might upset Keely. "We sent her back in a car three hours ago."

Where the hell was she?

G.D. was already pressing his cell phone to his ear. "I'll check with the team who dropped her off."

"I'll take Keely to the kitchen," Juliana said meaningfully, her face pale with concern.

Mitch paced as G.D. contacted the team leader. His heart shrunk to the size of a pebble when G.D. verified that Stef had been dropped off at four forty-five.

He and G.D. headed for the lobby in unison, where the doorman informed them that Mrs. Shelton had entered the building briefly, then turned around and announced she was going for a walk.

Something was wrong. Mitch could feel it.

Damn it, Stef. Where are you? He palmed the back of his neck. "What do you think, G.D.?"

The Guardian frowned. "Do you think she went to check out Sable's family's place in the Catskills on her own?"

"Possibly. She'd do anything to get her daughter back. I can see her talking her way into Sable's aunt's house."

"I'll call the chopper."

Mitch hoped they were right.

HER LITTLE GIRL was adorable. Stef felt a lump of joy melt in her throat at the shy little girl who approached her with big solemn eyes as she clung to her grandmother's gnarled hand.

Stef smiled, even though her heart was shuddering with terror. Darren scrutinized her every movement. She brushed away real tears. She didn't have to pretend to be excited to meet Emma.

"Hello, Emma. I'm Stef. I'm so happy to meet you! You're such a big girl." She turned to Helen Conklin, who moved with the slowness of arthritic limbs. "She's about the same age as my daughter, Keely. I'm sorry I showed up on the spur of the moment. But once I saw Emma's picture I knew I had to come and bring her home." Stef perched on the edge of the sofa so she was eye to eye with Emma, aware her bruises and her bandage must be a scary sight. "Do you like stories, Emma?"

Emma nodded, the traces of a smile touching her lips. "What happened to your head?"

Stef resisted the urge to hug her as tightly as she wanted. She told herself there would be time for all that once they were safe. She told Emma a silly story about how she'd fallen and bumped her head. "I also know stories about your mommy when she was a little girl like you. And you have other grandparents, too."

"Really?" Helen Conklin asked, smoothing the bangs from Emma's bright eyes with a loving hand. "Listen to that, Emma. You have another grandma and grandpa."

"Yes, and they like to be called Nana and Pops. They have a big trailer that they go camping in, and we toast marshmallows and drink hot chocolate. And Nana knows the stories the birds tell when they sing.''

Emma's eyes shone with curiosity. ''I like birds.''

''So do I, love. Nana and Pops are looking forward to meeting you.''

''And what about your sister?'' Helen asked. ''Do you hear from her?''

Stef shook her head. ''Lori doesn't stay in touch.''

Helen exchanged a look with her husband, Fred, a skinny man with stooped shoulders and a shock of snowy hair. ''We know how that can be.''

Stef felt Darren's unblinking hazel eyes on her. Nausea stirred in her stomach knowing that Fred and Helen's son Tony would never come home. What would Darren do to her and Emma once they left the house?

Helen offered Stef a cup of tea. Stef coaxed Emma into joining them at the table in the kitchen. Emma munched on a cookie and played with an animal puzzle at the table, stealing curious peeks up at Stef while Helen plied Stef with questions. ''What does your husband do?''

''He's a pilot, which means we'll be able to arrange frequent visits. I know you don't want to lose touch.''

Stef answered Helen's other questions while Darren and Fred hunted for a suitcase to pack Emma's belongings. Darren had told the Conklins that Stef had a flight from Newark to Seattle early the next morning.

After their tea, Stef helped Helen check Emma's bag, listening to her instructions regarding Emma's favorite foods and her bedtime. Stef's heart filled with gratitude that Emma had been raised by this kind, gentle woman. ''She's a good girl, but you've got to keep a close eye on her. She's either quacking like a duck and climbing on something or quiet as a mouse getting into some type of mischief. I'm going to miss her terribly.''

Stef hugged the frail elderly woman. ''Thank you for taking her in. I promise I'll treat her like my own child.''

Emma let Stef take her hand as they walked out of the farmhouse toward Darren's car, but Stef saw the uncertainty in her daughter's eyes as she looked back over her shoulder at the elderly couple stifling tears and waving goodbye from the porch. Emma didn't cry or fuss, but she kept a tight hold on her brown stuffed rabbit.

Stef experienced a glimpse of how stoic Mitch must have been when his mother had left him with his grandfather all those years ago. She held her baby's hand and promised herself that Emma would spend a happy life with her.

''Where are we going now?'' she asked Darren once they were driving down the lane.

''You'll see.''

Stef wasn't reassured. She stroked Emma's hair, talking to her softly, learning that she liked animals and had a real bunny named Snowflake at Gamma and Pappy's. They passed through two towns called Mahopac and Croton Falls.

Then Emma fell asleep in her carrier seat and Darren ordered Stef to cover herself with the blanket so that she couldn't see the last leg of their journey.

She reluctantly complied. When the sedan slowed and began to bounce over an uneven road, Stef was petrified that she and Emma were about to be shot and their bodies dumped in a ditch. But when Darren told her she could remove the blanket, she saw they'd arrived at a cottage.

Stef nearly drowned in panic. Mitch was never going to find them here! She kissed Emma's head as Darren got out of the car, the gun in one hand.

Stef expected Darren to break into the cottage, but he crouched beside the screened porch and removed a key hidden underneath the skirt board. He opened the door and came back to the car, taking a flashlight from the glove compartment. "Bring Emma inside."

She carefully removed her sleeping daughter from the carrier. Even in her terror, her body took comfort from the miracle of having Emma's warm weight snug in her arms.

The cottage was tiny and smelled of disuse. In the sweeping narrow beam of the flashlight she saw a galley kitchen that opened onto a main room and two doors that led into dark caves. There was a thick coat of dust on the floor and the evidence of mouse droppings on the furnishings.

Darren led her toward one of the doors. "You can sleep on the bed in here." The flashlight beam played over a double bed and a dresser crammed into a narrow room. "The window's boarded up from the outside, so don't even think about escaping." He gave her just long enough to lay Emma on the bed, then he closed the door, leaving Stef standing in the dark. She let her eyes grow accustomed to the dark, wondering if she should try to jump Darren when he entered the room next. No, he had a gun and the stun gun, both of which could render her unable to protect Emma.

She could hear Darren doing something to the door, probably tying it closed. She squeezed into the passage between the bed and the window and lifted the heavy musty-smelling curtains. Darren hadn't lied, she could see the horizontal strips of boards covering the window.

Stef eased onto the bed and curled her body protectively around Emma. There was no escape.

Chapter Fourteen

Mitch was frantic. The words "too late, too late," screeching in his mind. It was 3:00 a.m. and Stef had been missing for eight and a half hours without a word. The woman he'd made love to, whom he'd let inside his heart, was missing and he was helpless to find her. He'd flown to Windham and back in the chopper, hoping to find Stef camped out in the shrubbery. He'd spoken to Sable's aunt, who'd allowed him to search the house, but Stef wasn't there.

Stef had literally walked out the door of the apartment building and disappeared. The fear that Tony Conklin had abducted her was eating away at him. Making him crazy. It also occurred to him that Riana's legal guardian would be saved the trouble of a custody fight if Stef suddenly turned up dead, so he surfed the Internet for information about Brook Sinclair while G.D. made phone calls trying to find out what the hold up was on Tony Conklin's military records.

Mitch was so intent on reading about Brook Sinclair's third marriage and divorce that he wasn't aware G.D. had come up behind him.

"What are you doing?"

Mitch swiveled around in the chair to face him. "I'm

investigating the possibility that someone other than Tony snatched Stef—someone like Riana's legal guardian, who'd benefit if Stef turned up dead. It's interesting that Brook and Juliana are so tight. Why is that?''

Anger banked in G.D.'s eyes. ''You're way off base, Mitch. And very close to finding your way out of a job.''

Mitch's jaw hardened. ''Am I? Then tell me who Keely's guardian is and let me judge for myself.''

''I'm afraid I can't do that.''

''Are you willing to stake Stef's life on that answer?''

G.D. was saved from saying anything further by the ringing of his cell phone. ''What?'' He reached for a pen and started writing on a notepad. ''Thank you!''

He thrust the pad at Mitch. ''There's Tony Conklin's parents' address. Take the chopper. We'll continue this conversation *after* we find Stef.''

Mitch's arrival at their farmhouse by helicopter roused Fred and Helen Conklin from their beds. Fred Conklin held a rifle on Mitch and threatened to call the police until Mitch explained he wanted to talk to them about their son.

Helen Conklin invited Mitch and the pilot in for tea. As she put the kettle on, Helen told Mitch that she hadn't seen her son in two and a half years.

A part of Mitch curled up and died. He'd reached another dead end.

DARREN WOKE UP Stef and Emma just before 4:00 a.m. He made them use the bathroom. While Stef was in the bathroom, he told Emma he had a surprise for her and he slipped the snug-fitting brightly colored vest he'd made for Riana over Emma's shoulders. He smiled at

Stef's cry of horror when she came out of the bathroom and spotted the stick of dynamite attached to the back of the yellow vest.

He pointed to the daisies he'd painted on the vest around the word *bomb*. ''Isn't it pretty, Emma?''

Emma, in her innocence, patted the pretty flowers.

Stef Shelton's eyes pleaded with him. ''Please, you can't be serious...she's just a baby.''

''Oh, I am deadly serious. Tomorrow morning Annette will be making an appearance at the Essex County Courthouse for a motion for further discovery by the defense. She'll be leaving the courtroom with me, and Keely, who will have this lovely vest strapped around her shoulders. I rather doubt the police are going to prevent our escape and risk having the lost Collingwood heir be blown to bits in front of the network news cameras. Now, if you don't want Emma to go boom, you are going to tell me which Park Terrace apartment Keely is in, who else is staying in the apartment and the security measures in force.''

He removed a small remote control from the pocket of his polar fleece coat and held it so Stef could see it in the glow of the oil lamp he'd lit on the table. ''Before you consider misleading me, be aware that this red button activates the bomb. If I'm stopped, I simply push this button and Emma goes boom.''

''Boom!'' Emma repeated with a giggle.

From the whiteness of her face, Darren could see that Stef had gotten the message. She told him everything he needed to know.

He locked them in the bedroom, leaving them the child's potty, the box of cereal and containers of juice that he'd bought in readiness for holding Keely here.

''By the way, Mrs. Shelton,'' he called through the

door. "I wouldn't try to remove the vest or let Emma exert herself too strenuously. The vest is fitted with a pressure sensor. Try to remove it and Emma goes boom."

Stef clutched Emma's hand in the darkened room, her body taut with nausea and terror. Darren had put a bomb on her baby! Stef needed Mitch more than she'd ever needed anyone in her life. She had to save both her daughters. Somehow she had to get help before Darren reached the apartment in New York City.

MITCH WAS LEARNING a lot about Tony Conklin from the man's parents, but nothing that would help him find Stef—until he realized that the shiny yellow object hanging from the hook by the back door was a tiny child's raincoat.

"Do you have grandchildren?" he asked the Conklins.

"Only the one—Tony's daughter, Emma," Helen said. "She's a lamb. She's been living with us until recently."

Stef's daughter? Mitch felt dread scrape the pit of his stomach. Was he too late again? "How recently?"

Worry creased Helen's worn face. "Just last night. Darren, our nephew, finally located Emma's aunt and brought her by to pick up Emma. She's taking her back to Seattle."

Darren? Mitch finally saw the big picture. "Is your nephew Darren Black?"

"Yes."

"Did Emma's aunt have a bandage on her face?"

Helen nodded, her gnarled hand pressed to her heart. "I think perhaps you'd better tell us what you're really doing here, Mr. Halloran, or I will call the police."

Mitch reached for his cell phone. "Don't bother. I'm calling the police. Then I'll tell you what I know."

STEF TRIED EVERYTHING to get out of that room. She yanked on the door, hoping the rope would fray. She searched fruitlessly through the dresser drawers in the predawn darkness for something she could use to pop the pins out of the door hinges, all the while telling Emma a wild story about this being a game. Poor Emma huddled on the bed hugging her bunny, watching her with solemn eyes.

Stef ripped the curtains from the wooden rod. "Okay, baby, Mommy's scrapping the door plan. We're going out the window." She fumbled with the clasp on the double-hung windows, but it wouldn't budge. Warning Emma to cover her ears, she broke the glass with the curtain rod. Cold fresh air flooded through the window.

"Yea, Mommy," Emma said, bouncing on the mattress.

Fear lanced Stef's heart that she might accidentally set off the bomb. "No, Emma, sweetie. You stay nice and quiet on the bed with your bunny. When Mommy has the boards off the window we'll climb out."

Stef pushed her hair out of her face and tried using the curtain rod as a hammer, but the darn rod was too long to wield with the force necessary.

She checked her watch, calculating the time it would take Darren to drive to New York City. It was almost six o'clock. He could be there soon. She didn't have much time. "Okay, Emma, don't try this at home." She grabbed a drawer from the dresser and used it as a battering ram against the boards. She actually felt something give!

Twenty minutes and several additional bruises later,

one of the boards actually fell off. Light was just beginning to streak the sky. Stef's hands and arms were screaming with pain and Emma was whimpering, her tiny hands covering her ears, but Stef couldn't give up.

She was battering away at the boards when she became aware of a buzzing sound. It grew louder and louder until she realized it was overhead. It was a helicopter!

And it was setting down somewhere nearby.

Mitch! Stef knew, as surely as she knew that the sun would come up, that Mitch was in that helicopter. Relief flooded her heart on a wave of love.

"Mitch!" Stef started screaming and banged at the last boards with the drawer. She had to get his attention. The bomb could go off at any time. "We're here! Help!"

Miraculously she heard the splintering of wood as the door to the cottage was kicked open and Mitch was calling her name. "Stef! I'm coming!"

And then Mitch was standing in the bedroom doorway, blond and ferocious. And Stef loved him more than she ever thought she could love a man.

Panic and fear streaked her voice. "Mitch! He put a bomb on Emma! It could go off at any second!"

A BOMB! Mitch swore under his breath as he took charge. He made swift sense of Stef's incoherent story that Darren was headed for the apartment to kidnap Keely and would set the bomb off at any second if he was challenged.

Trying to calm both Emma and Stef, Mitch simultaneously called G.D. to alert him to what was happening. G.D. told him he'd be waiting for Darren and he'd get a bomb tech on the line with Mitch stat.

"Stef, leave the room," Mitch ordered her.

Stef didn't budge from Emma's side. "No, she's my baby. I'm not leaving her."

"Keely needs you, too," he reminded her.

Stef kissed Emma's hair. "It's okay, Em, Mommy's here. Everything's going to be fine. Mitch will help us."

Mitch couldn't find the words to tell her he'd just as soon she not get blown to bits. "You are so stubborn—"

His cell phone rang. "Halloran, here."

"New York State Police. Let's get a look at the bomb, Halloran. Tell me what you see."

Mitch described the vest and the battery and detonator attached to the stick of dynamite. "The witness was told it's rigged with a pressure sensor."

"That's what we've got to find first. Look at the dynamite. There will be a wire that leads from the dynamite to the pressure sensor. Can you find it?"

Mitch's heart swelled with fear as he bent over the child to examine the bomb. Emma's solemn eyes were stamped with fear. "I'm not going to hurt you, Emma," he told her as he searched for the wire. "Okay, found it."

"Follow that wire to see where it ends. Look for a very small bump. That will be the sensor."

Mitch traced the wire to a small bump located just below the armhole of the vest. "Got it."

"Now slide something between the little girl's body and the bump and apply steady pressure to the bump while you remove the vest. Once you apply pressure you can't let go."

Sweat dampened Mitch's body as he folded a business card in two. He gave Stef a quick, searching glance, committing her beautiful face to memory. "Just in case I don't get a chance to say this again, I love you.''

A tear slipped onto her cheek. "I love you, too."

He flashed her a cocky grin that belied the shaking of his fingers. "Those are the sexiest words I've ever heard. We're going to make it through this, babe. You, me and Emma. Failure is not an option." Holding his breath, Mitch slid the card into place, squeezing the bump between his thumb and index finger. "Okay, let's get it off her."

Slowly they removed the garment, both of them trying to calm Emma as she whimpered and squirmed. An incredible wave of relief rolled through his limbs as Stef pulled Emma into her arms. Emma was safe. Sometimes the good guys won a few rounds. "Get her out of here. Now."

"Mitch?" Stef protested.

"Go! Run!"

A bead of sweat rolled down Mitch's back. "What now?" he asked the bomb tech.

"We're going to pull the wire between the power source and the detonator."

Mitch found the wire and pulled it.

Stef heard the explosion as she carried Emma toward the helicopter. Oh, my god. Mitch!

DARREN BLACK didn't even make it into the building. Weapons drawn, Hunter and four members of his security team surrounded the courier van that Darren had hijacked a few minutes earlier. Darren was caught in the act of changing into the courier's mud-colored uniform.

"It's over," Hunter barked. "Drop your weapons."

"I don't think so." The mathematician held up a remote-control device. ''Bring me Riana Collingwood or Stephanie Shelton's daughter goes up in smoke. Now.''

Hunter pointed the gun at Darren's forehead. ''You can't have her. Go ahead, push the button.''

With an evil smile, Darren called The Guardian's bluff and pushed the button. '''Bye, 'bye, baby.''

Chapter Fifteen

Six hours later Stef was still shaking. She wasn't sure she'd ever stop shaking. She'd endured the state police's interrogation. She'd answered all their questions about her abduction. But her mind wasn't on her ordeal.

Mitch had been taken to the emergency room, and they hadn't allowed her to go with him. Tiny pieces of metal were buried in his skin from the detonator exploding when he'd pulled that wire. He called them scratches.

Once the police had finished with her, The Guardian had whisked her and Emma back to New York City.

Juliana and Keely had greeted them with hugs and kisses and Stef had introduced Keely to her sister Emma. While the little imps fed lettuce and carrots to Emma's stuffed bunny, Stef and Juliana had cried and had tea and cried again.

Stef was listening for Mitch's return. She needed to see that he was okay. To thank him for taking such a foolish chance by dismantling the bomb.

When the door opened and she heard a pair of deep male voices, she flew out of the living room and down the hall.

And there was Mitch filling up the hallway. Filling

up her heart. Every handsome inch of him. There were small bandages on his face and his hand. His shirt and suit jacket were tattered in places. Heat lit his cobalt eyes as he welcomed her into his arms.

Stef barely heard Juliana tell The Guardian that she thought they ought to be given some privacy.

Mitch pulled back and framed Stef's beautiful face with his hands. He kissed the tip of her nose. "I meant what I said earlier. I love you."

She gripped the lapels of his jacket not wanting to let go. "I love you, too."

"I think I'm out of a job now, so I'm not breaking any ethical rules by telling you that I have plans for us. You, me, Keely and Emma." His voice grew husky. "Plans that include you wearing a wedding gown and me learning how to be a dad and a husband—and the best lover you've ever had."

"Are you *asking* me to marry you?"

Mitch shuddered and pressed his forehead to hers. Stef loved him. He loved her. They *had* to find a way to make this work. Had to find a way to keep Keely or they would never have a future. "No, I'm *telling* you we have a future together. The Guardian paid me an obscene amount of money to take this case. We'll use it to hire a lawyer." He stroked her hair. "Keely belongs with you. You're inseparable."

Anguish laced through her tone. "Did The Guardian tell you what happens now with Keely?"

His arms tightened around her, sheltering her. "He's going to arrange a meeting with Keely's legal guardian in forty-eight hours. There's going to be a media storm when it's announced that Riana Collingwood has been returned."

Stef started to cry. "Oh, Mitch, I can't lose her."

Mitch closed his eyes and imagined a future that didn't include his jelly bean. A future where Stef eventually grew to resent him and the love between them died. "I know. I can't lose her, either."

THE MEDIA erupted into a feeding frenzy over Darren Black's arrest and the details of the kidnapping and the baby switch. Annette York and Darren Black were making declarations of love to each other via the papers. The state police had found human skeletal remains on the Conklin property near Waccabuc Lake where Stef and Emma had been held hostage.

Mitch was being hailed as a hero and inundated with job offers from police departments across the country.

And The Guardian had given Stef the DNA lab results confirming that Emma was her and Brad's biological child. Stef had almost forgotten the tests had been ordered.

She'd spent the past two days mentally preparing to be introduced to the person Ross and Lexi Collingwood had appointed to raise their daughter. Juliana still refused to give Stef any hints about her employer and Stef had stopped asking. Now, as the helicopter swooped down like a dragonfly and landed next to a fairy-tale castle set on an island in the sparkling blue waters of the St. Lawrence Seaway, Stef was assailed by insecurities. She couldn't compete with this kind of grandeur!

Mitch squeezed her hand reassuringly, and Stef caught a strained look that passed between The Guardian and Juliana. The tension in the helicopter was palpable. Only the girls were oblivious to it.

An elderly, dignified butler with an imposing face awaited them at the entrance to the house. He held a cooing blond infant in his arms.

Juliana embraced the old man, taking the baby into her arms. He immediately curled his chubby fists in her hair. Smiling, she turned to Stef and Mitch. "I'd like you to meet my father, Nigel Goodhew. He was the Collingwoods' butler for many years. And this delightful young man is Cort." Juliana's voice wavered with emotion. "He's Ross and Lexi's son. The Collingwoods kept his birth a secret."

Stef stared at the beautiful little baby, her heart clenching. Keely had a brother! This was more complicated than she could even contemplate. She felt the steady presence of Mitch's hand at the small of her back.

Juliana laid a hand on Keely's shoulder. "Papa, this is Keely."

Stef saw tears form in the elderly butler's eyes. It was a very strange feeling to acknowledge that these people genuinely loved the little girl she considered her own.

"I am very pleased to meet you, Miss Keely. And you, Miss Emma. And the very courageous, Mrs. Shelton. You are all most welcome. Ladies and young ladies, you are to adjourn to the drawing room. Mr. Halloran and The Guardian, your presence is requested in the study for a few moments."

Mitch kissed Stef's temple and breathed in the scent of her hair to give himself courage. They'd have an uphill battle to retain custody of Keely. "I'll be back."

Mitch took in the jewel-toned rays of light that filtered through the stained-glass ceiling as they mounted the staircase to the third floor. The butler punched a code into a keypad and opened the heavy wood door. The study reminded Mitch of the one in the apartment overlooking Central Park. It was sleek and high-tech only on a larger, grander scale. He expected to see Brook Sinclair ensconced in the chair behind the desk, but no one was waiting to greet them.

"I'll take it from here, Goodhew," G.D. said.

And suddenly Mitch knew. This castle was The Guardian's home and he was Riana and Cort's legal guardian. Suddenly Mitch's dreams of making a family with Stef seemed only that—dreams.

G.D. held out his hand to Mitch. "Allow me to introduce myself. I'm Hunter Sinclair and Juliana Goodhew is my wife. We married suddenly after Ross and Lexi were killed and told people Cort was our son to protect him. Ross was my best friend. We went to Harvard together."

"And you're Riana's and Cort's legal guardian," Mitch finished for him.

Compassion rose in G.D.'s eyes. "Yes. I married Juliana because she'd been caring for Cort since his birth. I didn't expect to fall in love with her—that took me by surprise. That's why I didn't say anything when I noticed what was happening between you and Stef."

The story was starting to make sense. It explained the looks between Juliana and G.D. And yet it filled Mitch with dread. He couldn't deny that G.D. and Juliana would be great parents to Keely. Except that Keely already had a great mommy.

Mitch nodded. "And Brook Sinclair is…?

"My sister. She runs the family hotel business and I run this—"

"The family-saving business."

G.D. lifted a brow. "You're very astute."

Not astute enough. Mitch shrugged. "It comes and goes."

"You've done an excellent job, Mitch. I'd like to know your plans."

Mitch's jaw set. "Since you asked, I'm going to do everything in my power to convince Stef to marry me and we're going to fight you for custody of Keely. I don't understand how you can justify taking Keely away from the only mother she's ever known when I know you wouldn't dream of separating Cort from Juliana. Didn't you just tell me Juliana's the only mother *Cort's* ever known?"

G.D. sank onto the leather couch and pinched the bridge of his nose. "It's more complicated than that."

"I find it hard to believe that *you* can't solve a complicated problem."

Hunter stared at Mitch for a few moments, struggling to make a decision that would affect all of their lives. Mitch had made a blunt point. And yet, Hunter could not lightly disregard the responsibility that Ross had entrusted him with. He thought, too, of Juliana who'd brought such love into his life. The idea of Keely joining their family made him feel richer. Blessed. He'd been looking forward to having Keely in his life.

And he thought of Keely and what was best for her. She'd not only captured Hunter's heart, she'd captured Mitch's, as well. And Hunter saw in Mitch a dedicated, caring man who understood that a family is the greatest treasure a man could ever have.

Hunter drummed his fingers on his thigh. Mitch was right. There was a solution to this problem. He cleared his throat. "I would be willing to let Keely remain with Stef on two conditions. One, you marry Stef and set up your own residence here on FairIsle where Keely can be protected and grow up with her brother. And two, you agree to join me as my partner in my security business. Now that I have a family, there's more work than I can comfortably handle. It's not always abductions, but you would be helping people protect their families.''

Mitch laughed in his face. "You have a sick sense of humor, G.D., dangling a big carrot like that in front of me. First of all, I'm a grown man and nobody tells me who I should marry. But fortunately for you, I'm so in love with Stef I wouldn't mind living on this puny rock for the privilege of being Keely's and Emma's daddy. And since I'm here, I may as well make myself useful and give you a hand now and then.''

Hunter grinned and held out his hand, relieved that Mitch had his priorities in order. "You're hired, partner.''

Six weeks later, on the day after Christmas, Stef Shelton descended the grand staircase at FairIsle on her father's arm. Bands of colored light shot through the stairwell as if by magic. Two smiling girls in matching red-satin dresses sprinkled rose petals through the foyer and into the drawing room.

Stef and Mitch stood in front of drawing room windows that gave a dazzling wintry view of the St. Lawrence River and exchanged their vows in front of the minister and their guests. Hunter and Juliana Sinclair witnessed their union as best man and matron of honor.

"I didn't know what love was until I met you,'' Mitch whispered huskily in Stef's ear after he'd officially kissed the bride at the ceremony's end.

The guests gathered around, offering congratulations. And then Hunter asked for everyone's attention. Even Keely and Emma stopped tossing their rose petals.

"On behalf of the Find Riana Foundation, I'm honored to present Stef with this reward for her assistance leading to an arrest in Riana Collingwood's kidnapping.''

Stef blushed as Hunter handed her a thick white envelope. He winked at her. ''Consider it a nest egg so you can build that house in the spring.'' Stef peeked inside the envelope and her mouth went slack. It contained a check made out for two million dollars!

She showed it to Mitch, dazed. ''Do you see how many zeroes there are on that check?''

Mitch laughed and tucked Stef securely in the crook of his arm. ''It's only money, sweetheart. We've already got everything we need.''

Stef looked from Mitch's handsome face to the people who were sharing in this special day with them. Her family. Hunter and Juliana and Cort. Brook Sinclair and her two rambunctious sons. Goodhew. Keely. And Emma.

Emma who had been lost and was now found, who added her voice to the melody of Stef's life. Mitch was right. They had everything they needed. With love, compromise and great faith, they could make this extended family work.

HARLEQUIN®
INTRIGUE®

Our unique brand of high-caliber romantic suspense just cannot be contained. And to meet our readers' demands, Harlequin Intrigue is expanding its publishing schedule to include **SIX** breathtaking titles every month!

Check out the new lineup in October!

MORE variety.
MORE pulse-pounding excitement.
MORE of your favorite authors and series.

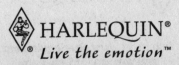

HARLEQUIN®
Live the emotion™

Visit us at www.tryIntrigue.com

HI4T06T

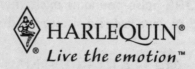

Is your man too good to be true?

Hot, gorgeous AND romantic?
If so, he could be a Harlequin® Blaze™ series cover model!

Our grand-prize winners will receive a trip for two to New York City to shoot the cover of a Blaze novel, and will stay at the luxurious Plaza Hotel. Plus, they'll receive $500 U.S. spending money!
The runner-up winners will receive $200 U.S.
to spend on a romantic dinner for two.

It's easy to enter!

In 100 words or less, tell us what makes your boyfriend or spouse a true romantic and the perfect candidate for the cover of a Blaze novel, and include in your submission two photos of this potential cover model.

All entries must include the written submission of the contest entrant, two photographs of the model candidate and the Official Entry Form and Publicity Release forms completed in full and signed by both the model candidate and the contest entrant. Harlequin, along with the experts at Elite Model Management, will select a winner.

For photo and complete Contest details, please refer to the Official Rules on the next page. All entries will become the property of Harlequin Enterprises Ltd. and are not returnable.

Please visit www.blazecovermodel.com to download a copy of the Official Entry Form and Publicity Release Form or send a request to one of the addresses below.

Please mail your entry to: **Harlequin Blaze Cover Model Search**

In U.S.A.	In Canada
P.O. Box 9069	P.O. Box 637
Buffalo, NY	Fort Erie, ON
14269-9069	L2A 5X3

No purchase necessary. Contest open to Canadian and U.S. residents who are 18 and over.
Void where prohibited. Contest closes September 30, 2003.

HBCVRMODEL1

HARLEQUIN BLAZE COVER MODEL SEARCH CONTEST 3569 OFFICIAL RULES
NO PURCHASE NECESSARY TO ENTER

1. To enter, submit two (2) 4" x 6" photographs of a boyfriend or spouse (who must be 18 years of age or older) taken no later than three (3) months from the time of entry: a close-up, waist up, shirtless photograph; and a fully clothed full-length photograph, then, tell us, in 100 words or fewer, why he should be a Harlequin Blaze cover model and how he is romantic. Your complete "entry" must include: (i) your essay, (ii) the Official Entry Form and Publicity Release Form printed below completed and signed by you (as "Entrant"), (iii) the photographs (with your hand-written name, address and phone number, and your model's name, address and phone number on the back of each photograph), and (iv) the Publicity Release Form and Photograph Representation Form printed below completed and signed by your model (as "Model"), and should be sent via first-class mail to either: Harlequin Blaze Cover Model Search Contest 3569, P.O. Box 9069, Buffalo, NY, 14269-9069, or Harlequin Blaze Cover Model Search Contest 3569, P.O. Box 637, Fort Erie, Ontario L2A 5X3. All submissions must be in English and be received no later than September 30, 2003. Limit: one entry per person, household or organization. **Purchase or acceptance of a product offer does not improve your chances of winning.** All entry requirements must be strictly adhered to for eligibility and to ensure fairness among entries.

2. Ten (10) Finalist submissions (photographs and essays) will be selected by a panel of judges consisting of members of the Harlequin editorial, marketing and public relations staff, as well as a representative from Elite Model Management (Toronto) Inc., based on the following criteria:

Aptness/Appropriateness of submitted photographs for a Harlequin Blaze cover—70%
Originality of Essay—20%
Sincerity of Essay—10%

In the event of a tie, duplicate finalists will be selected. The photographs submitted by finalists will be posted on the Harlequin website no later than November 15, 2003 (at www.blazecovermodel.com), and viewers may vote, in rank order, on their favorite(s) to assist in the panel of judges' final determination of the Grand Prize and Runner-up winning entries based on the above judging criteria. All decisions of the judges are final.

3. All entries become the property of Harlequin Enterprises Ltd. and none will be returned. Any entry may be used for future promotional purposes. Elite Model Management (Toronto) Inc. and/or its partners, subsidiaries and affiliates operating as "Elite Model Management" will have access to all entries including all personal information, and may contact any Entrant and/or Model in its sole discretion for their own business purposes. Harlequin and Elite Model Management (Toronto) Inc. are separate entities with no legal association or partnership whatsoever having no power to bind or obligate the other or create any expressed or implied obligation or responsibility on behalf of the other, such that Harlequin shall not be responsible in any way for any acts or omissions of Elite Model Management (Toronto) Inc. or its partners, subsidiaries and affiliates in connection with the Contest or otherwise and Elite Model Management shall not be responsible in any way for any acts or omissions of Harlequin or its partners, subsidiaries and affiliates in connection with the contest or otherwise.

4. All Entrants and Models must be residents of the U.S. or Canada, be 18 years of age or older, and have no prior criminal convictions. The contest is not open to any Model that is a professional model and/or actor in any capacity at the time of the entry. Contest void wherever prohibited by law; all applicable laws and regulations apply. Any litigation within the Province of Quebec regarding the conduct or organization of a publicity contest may be submitted to the Régie des alcools, des courses et des jeux for a ruling, and any litigation regarding the awarding of a prize may be submitted to the Régie only for the purpose of helping the parties reach a settlement. Employees and immediate family members of Harlequin Enterprises Ltd., D.L. Blair, Inc., Elite Model Management (Toronto) Inc. and their parents, affiliates, subsidiaries and all other agencies, entities and persons connected with the use, marketing or conduct of this Contest are not eligible to enter. Acceptance of any prize offered constitutes permission to use Entrants' and Models' names, essay submissions, photographs or other likenesses for the purposes of advertising, trade, publication and promotion on behalf of Harlequin Enterprises Ltd., its parent, affiliates, subsidiaries, assigns and other authorized entities involved in the judging and promotion of the contest without further compensation to any Entrant or Model, unless prohibited by law.

5. Finalists will be determined no later than October 30, 2003. Prize Winners will be determined no later than January 31, 2004. Grand Prize Winners (consisting of winning Entrant and Model) will be required to sign and return Affidavit of Eligibility/Release of Liability and Model Release forms within thirty (30) days of notification. Non-compliance with this requirement and within the specified time period will result in disqualification and an alternate will be selected. Any prize notification returned as undeliverable will result in the awarding of the prize to an alternate set of winners. All travelers (or parent/legal guardian of a minor) must execute the Affidavit of Eligibility/Release of Liability prior to ticketing and must possess required travel documents (e.g. valid photo ID) where applicable. Travel dates specified by Sponsor but no later than May 30, 2004.

6. Prizes: One (1) Grand Prize—the opportunity for the Model to appear on the cover of a paperback book from the Harlequin Blaze series, and a 3 day/2 night trip for two (Entrant and Model) to New York, NY for the photo shoot of Model which includes round-trip coach air transportation from the commercial airport nearest the winning Entrant's home to New York, NY, (or, in lieu of air transportation, $100 cash payable to Entrant and Model, if the winning Entrant's home is within 250 miles of New York, NY), hotel accommodations (double occupancy) at the Plaza Hotel and $500 cash spending money payable to Entrant and Model, (approximate prize value: $8,000), and one (1) Runner-up Prize of $200 cash payable to Entrant and Model for a romantic dinner for two (approximate prize value: $200). Prizes are valued in U.S. currency. Prizes consist of only those items listed as part of the prize. No substitution of prize(s) permitted by winners. All prizes are awarded jointly to the Entrant and Model of the winning entries, and are not severable - prizes and obligations may not be assigned or transferred. Any change to the Entrant and/or Model of the winning entries will result in disqualification and an alternate will be selected. Taxes on prize are the sole responsibility of winners. Any and all expenses and/or items not specifically described as part of the prize are the sole responsibility of winners. Harlequin Enterprises Ltd. and D.L. Blair, Inc., their parents, affiliates, and subsidiaries are not responsible for errors in printing of Contest entries and/or game pieces. No responsibility is assumed for lost, stolen, late, illegible, incomplete, inaccurate, non-delivered, postage due or misdirected mail or entries. In the event of printing or other errors which may result in unintended prize values or duplication of prizes, all affected game pieces or entries shall be null and void.

7. Winners will be notified by mail. For winners' list (available after March 31, 2004), send a self-addressed, stamped envelope to: Harlequin Blaze Cover Model Search Contest 3569 Winners, P.O. Box 4200, Blair, NE 68009-4200, or refer to the Harlequin website (at www.blazecovermodel.com).

Contest sponsored by Harlequin Enterprises Ltd., P.O. Box 9042, Buffalo, NY 14269-9042.

If you enjoyed what you just read,
then we've got an offer you can't resist!

Take 2 bestselling
love stories FREE!

Plus get a FREE surprise gift!

Clip this page and mail it to Harlequin Reader Service

YES! Please send me 2 free Harlequin Intrigue® novels and my free surprise gift. After receiving them, if I don't wish to receive anymore, I can return the shipping statement marked cancel. If I don't cancel, I will receive 6 brand-new novels each month, before they're available in stores! In the U.S.A., bill me at the bargain price of $3.99 plus 25¢ shipping and handling per book and applicable sales tax, if any*. In Canada, bill me at the bargain price of $4.74 plus 25¢ shipping and handling per book and applicable taxes**. That's the complete price and a savings of at least 10% off the cover prices—what a great deal! I understand that accepting the 2 free books and gift places me under no obligation ever to buy any books. I can always return a shipment and cancel at any time. Even if I never buy another book from Harlequin, the 2 free books and gift are mine to keep forever.

182 HDN DU9K
382 HDN DU9L

Name	(PLEASE PRINT)	
Address	Apt.#	
City	State/Prov.	Zip/Postal Code

* Terms and prices subject to change without notice. Sales tax applicable in N.Y.
** Canadian residents will be charged applicable provincial taxes and GST.
  All orders subject to approval. Offer limited to one per household and not valid to
  current Harlequin Intrigue® subscribers.
® are registered trademarks of Harlequin Enterprises Limited.

INT03

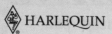

HARLEQUIN
INTRIGUE®
COMING NEXT MONTH

#729 FAMILIAR DOUBLE by Caroline Burnes
Fear Familiar

When Familiar, the famous cat detective, signed on as a stunt double for a movie, he soon found himself up to his whiskers in another mystery! Nicole Paul had been framed and arrested for a theft she didn't commit. After her sexy boss, Jax McClure, bailed her out of jail, the two were swept into discovering who really stole the cursed diamond twenty years ago…*and* the secrets of their hearts.

#730 THE FIRSTBORN by Dani Sinclair
Heartskeep

When Hayley Thomas returned home to claim her inheritance, she found strange things happening around her—doors locked by themselves and objects disappeared before her eyes. The only thing she wasn't confused about was her powerful attraction to blacksmith Bram Myers…but did the brooding stranger have secrets of his own?

#731 RANDALL RENEGADE by Judy Christenberry
Brides for Brothers

Rancher Jim Randall never expected to hear from his college sweetheart again. So when Patience Anderson called him to help find her kidnapped nephew, Jim knew he had to help her…even if it meant facing the woman he'd never stopped loving. This Randall had encountered danger before, but the battle at hand could cost him more than his renegade status.

#732 KEEPING BABY SAFE by Debra Webb
Colby Agency

After Colby Agency investigator Pierce Maxwell and P.I. Olivia Jackson were exposed to a deadly biological weapon that they were sure would kill them, they gave in to their growing passion. But when they miraculously lived, they were left with a mystery to solve…and a little surprise on the way!

#733 UNDER HIS PROTECTION by Amy J. Fetzer
Bachelors at Large

When a wealthy businessman was murdered, detective Nash Couviyon's main suspect was Lisa Winfield, the man's wife and the woman Nash had once loved. Would he be able to put aside past feelings—and growing new ones—to prove Lisa was being framed?

#734 DR. BODYGUARD by Jessica Andersen

Someone wanted Dr. Eugenie "Genius" Watson dead, so her adversary, the very sexy Dr. Nick Wellington, designated himself her protector. But when painful memories of the night she was attacked began to resurface, Genie discovered some shocking clues regarding the culprit…and an undeniable attraction to her very own bodyguard.

Visit us at www.eHarlequin.com

HICNM0903